Life and Death at St Luke's Maternity Hospital

Robert Ray-Gregson

Contents

About the Author

Robert Ray-Gregson has been working as an Obstetrician and Gynecologist in various maternity hospitals in the United Kingdom for over thirty years, progressing from a young aspiring trainee doctor to a senior consultant.

He draws on this extensive experience to write realistically and interestingly about life and work in maternity units, where the lives of the staff and those of the pregnant women and their families are inexplicably intertwined.

He describes in plain and clear language how clinical events in pregnancy and labour can have a tremendous impact on all those involved. The complicated love story in the novel develops hand-in-hand with clinical situations as they ebb and flow.

Chapter 1

A stranger arrives

A young midwife rushed into the labour ward's office at St. Luke's Maternity Hospital in London, where a group of midwives were waiting for the 'morning handover', which was when the night shift's team would tell the morning team about the women who were on the labour ward overnight. The young midwife sat down on one of the chairs around the desk, obviously out of breath and very excited. She said in a loud and very serious tone of voice, 'You wouldn't believe what I have just seen'.

Sister Melanie Smith, the senior midwife who was in charge of the labour ward that morning, was the one sitting at the desk looking at a list of the women currently on the labour ward and a list of the midwives available for the morning shift. Sister Melanie Smith was 30 years old, blonde, with green eyes and a very pretty round face. Her tight uniform showed all her feminine curvatures, of which she was very proud. She had a domineering personality and always made sure that all those who worked in the labour ward knew that she was the one in charge.

You could hear a pin drop as the other midwives sitting around Sister Smith waited with abated breath to see how sister Smith would react to this midwife who not only arrived late for the handover but also dared to interrupt the sister's train of thought when she was trying, with great difficulty, to decide what job to allocate to each of her midwives. This was always a complicated problem because the number of women in active labour often exceeded the number of available midwives in most shifts, and this morning's shift was no exception. There were just not enough midwives for the tasks at hand, which always put sister Smith in a bad mood.

Sister Smith lifted her eyes from the sheets of paper in her hands, stared angrily at the hapless midwife and shouted at her, 'Well then, what exactly did you see? What is this earth-shattering event that you are going to be regaling us with?'

The terrified midwife sank in her chair as she mumbled in a very low and shaky voice, 'Sorry, sister. I didn't mean to interrupt. It was nothing, really.'

Sister Smith's face was getting bright red with anger, and her eyes widened as she was about to explode even more, but the panicky midwife rushed to say, in an attempt to stop the sister from screaming at her, 'I saw Mr Stewart, the consultant, putting his arm around his senior house officer, Alison Richardson, while she was showing him some results. He was almost cuddling her in his office.'

Curiosity immediately replaced anger as sister Smith paused for a moment before saying inquisitively, 'Really?'

The midwife breathed a sigh of relief as she saw that what she had said was of some interest to sister Smith. She hastened to add, 'Oh, yes, sister. They were standing very close to each other with his arm around her waist. His hand was almost touching her bottom.'

Sister Smith was obviously keen to hear more details as she asked, 'And that is it? This is all you have seen?'

The midwife nodded and remained silent. Sister Smith shrugged her shoulders and said as she went back to the lists she was looking at, 'Well, it is none of our business anyway.'

Moments later, Dr Alison Richardson, the senior house officer, entered the office. She was a junior trainee doctor who had graduated from the medical school the year before. She looked more like a fashion model or a movie star than a doctor. Her black shoulder-length hair and blue eyes complemented perfectly the beauty of her delicate facial features. She wore an elegant bright green above-the-knee dress, which highlighted her tall and perfectly proportioned figure. All the midwives in the office stared at her with a mixture of admiration and envy. As she sat down, she said with a warm smile, 'Good morning, sister Smith. Good morning, all.'

Some of the midwives responded to her greeting, but the majority just giggled. Sister Smith looked at Alison with a sarcastic smile and said, 'Good morning, Alison. How are you this morning?'

Alison looked puzzled at the midwives' reaction to her morning greeting and the way sister Smith asked about how she was. Before she could respond, the sister added, 'Have you seen Mr Stewart today? I wanted to ask him about one of his patients.'

Sister Smith's smile broadened as she waited for Alison's answer, and the midwives' giggling started again.

Alison's puzzlement increased as she replied, 'I had just seen him in his office a little while ago.'

Sister Smith and the rest of the midwives looked at Alison intently, waiting for her to expand on her statement. Alison stared back at sister Smith and said, 'Are you waiting for me to say something else?'

Sister Smith shook her head with her smile remaining wide as she replied, 'I was just wondering whether you were talking to him about the same patient I have in mind on the labour ward, Mrs Guy.'

'No, I didn't talk to him about this one. I showed him the notes of Miss Anderson, who is an inpatient on the antenatal ward'.

'Did you show him anything else?' Sister Smith asked.

The inquisition was stopped abruptly as Mr John Stewart entered the labour ward's office. He was one of the two Consultant Obstetricians in the department, a tall man in his early fifties, starting to go bald and slightly overweight. He was totally infatuated with this young junior doctor in his team, Alison Richardson, and everyone in the department knew that because whenever Alison was anywhere near him, he always behaved like a dizzy teenager who was unable to control his urges.

Everyone in the room stood up as he entered, except Alison, who remained seated. He said loudly, 'Good morning' while his eyes zoomed straight away on Alison's crossed legs.

'I just wanted to let you all know that a new Registrar is starting today. He has qualified and trained in Egypt. This is only his second job in the UK. He worked as a locum registrar in Manchester for three months and came highly recommended by the consultants there. So, hopefully, he should be able to cope with the workload here.'

He then looked at sister Smith and said, 'I trust you will show him the ropes, Melanie, and you too, Alison. I shall leave him in your capable hands, the lucky devil.'

He then winked at Alison and left the office. Sister Smith looked annoyed as she never liked being called by her first name in front of the other midwives by anyone, not even by the consultants.

Sister Smith asked as she sat down again. 'I wonder what he is like.'

Alison frowned and said, 'I hope we can understand his accent more than his predecessor, Dr Dimalulu, whose accent was just dreadful. I often had to keep asking him to repeat what he said two or three times before I could work out what he was saying.'

Once Alison said that she was startled to hear a voice from behind her saying, 'I will certainly work very hard on my accent to make myself understood.'

This was the voice of the new registrar, who obviously spoke perfect English with only the slightest trace of a Mediterranean accent.

Alison turned round to see a handsome young man, tall, naturally tanned with an obviously athletic body and curly dark hair. The most striking feature about him was his haunting, large brown eyes. From the moment he entered the labour ward office, he seemed to have a dramatic effect on all the women in the room. Sister Smith nervously adjusted her hair, as she had always done when she was anxious or surprised. All the midwives stared at him with a sense of delight and excitement at the prospects of working with such an exotically attractive doctor.

The new registrar continued while walking towards sister Smith, 'You must be the big chief, sister Smith. I heard a lot about you.'

He stretched his hand towards her and shook her hand firmly. He then introduced himself while smiling at her warmly. 'I am Samy Samir, the new registrar. Please call me Samy.'

He then turned towards Alison with a bigger smile and shook her hand as he said, 'Very nice to meet you, Dr Richardson. I saw your name on the rota, and that is how I knew your name.'

Alison blushed, and she said, 'I am sorry for what I have just said about foreign accents. This was really rude'.

Samy laughed and said, 'Not at all. I think it was rather funny. I fully understand how some foreign accents can be awfully hard to understand. Mine certainly is at times.'

Sister Smith then proceeded to introduce him to each of the midwives in the room, and to their delight, he shook hands with each of them.

After the night team handed over the cases who were on the labour ward overnight, Samy turned round to sister Smith and said, 'When you are ready, sister, shall we go round to see what you would like me to do today?'

Obviously, Samy knew where the real power was in the labour ward, and for this reason, he wanted to stay on the right side of sister Smith from the start by acknowledging her status and authority as the head midwife.

Sister Smith smiled and led the way, followed by Alison and Samy. The rest of the midwives went to their different labour ward rooms in accordance with the allocation list that Sister Smith had already worked out earlier.

****

They all stopped in front of one of the delivery rooms, and sister Smith said, 'The first lady you need to see is Mrs Green. She is 25 years old and is having her first baby. She has been making slow progress in labour, and the baby's heartbeat is starting to slow down at times.'

They all went in, and sister Smith introduced Samy and Alison to Mrs. Green and her husband. Samy looked at the CTG machine that was recording the baby's heartbeat and said to Mrs Green in a calm, reassuring voice, 'I hear that you are doing very well, Mrs Green, although the little one is taking his or her time to come out, as first babies often do.'

He then looked at the chart that documented the progress of labour and said, 'We will need to examine you again, and if the neck of the womb has not opened up any further, we will need to ….'

Suddenly, a loud siren sounded from Samy's and Allison's bleeps, followed by a clear voice saying, 'Room 6 on the labour ward. Severe fetal bradycardia.'

The message was repeated three times as sister Smith, Samy, and Alison ran out as fast as they could towards room 6 to attend to the woman whose baby's heartbeat was getting very slow, indicating that the baby was severely distressed. The midwife in charge of Mrs Green's labour explained to her that there was obviously a serious emergency in room 6, and for this reason, they all had to rush out in this very sudden way.

There was no time for formal introductions in room 6. The midwife who was looking after the woman said to Samy as soon as she saw him, 'The baby's heartbeat dropped suddenly to 40 beats per minute. I have just examined her, and she is only 5 cm dilated, with the baby's head still high in the pelvis. There was a gush of fresh bleeding when I examined her. This is her second pregnancy, having been delivered by Caesarean section the first time.'

Samy had one look at the baby's heart trace, which was very slow and said to Alison, 'Please call a category one Caesarean section immediately.'

He then turned to the terrified woman and said, 'We have to do a Caesarean section straight away because the baby is not happy in there, but do not worry, you and the baby will be fine. We just have to hurry.'

The woman's partner asked while shaking like a leaf, 'Can I come in with her during the section'?

Samy replied while helping the midwife push the patient's bed out of the room towards the operating theatre, 'I am sorry, but you cannot come into the operating theatre because the operation is very urgent and will have to be done under general anaesthesia, so, your wife will be asleep. You would have been able to come to attend the operation if it was not that urgent and there was time for your wife to have an epidural or spinal anaesthetic instead of a general anaesthetic. Alas, this is not the case, and for this reason, we will ask you to stay in this room, and we will let you know as soon as the baby is safely delivered. The operation should not take long, and you will see them both very soon after we finish.'

The husband looked more relieved than disappointed because he did not really want to watch his wife being operated on in such dramatic and frightening circumstances. He quickly kissed his wife and remained in room 6 to wait for news.

As soon as the patient entered the Caesarean section theatre in the labour ward, she was transferred from her bed to the operating table, where the anaesthetist and his assistant were already waiting with all the required drugs drawn up into several syringes and the anaesthetic machine fully primed. As Samy and Alison scrubbed and gowned up, the patient was anaesthetised and cleaned, and the scrub nurse covered her in sterile green drapes.

The scrub nurse handed Samy the knife to start the operation. Samy looked at the anaesthetist, who nodded to him, indicating that the patient's anaesthetic was fully working and the operation could be started straight away. Samy swiftly made a large incision across the woman's lower part of the tummy and got to the womb within seconds. He then carefully opened the womb, and with one hand, he lifted the baby's head out of the womb, followed by the baby's body. The umbilical cord was double-clamped and cut. The lifeless, limp baby was handed over to the waiting neonatologist, the baby's specialist, who was standing behind Samy, ready to take the baby to the resuscitation station in the corner of the operating theatre. Two assistants from the neonatal department were standing by the resuscitation station to help the consultant neonatologist in trying to revive the baby girl, who looked to be in a very poor condition, barely alive. The baby was delivered in less than three minutes from the time Samy started the operation.

Alison and the scrub nurse looked breathless and dazed because of the speed and great skill with which Samy got the baby out in such a short time. They could hardly keep up with his instructions to hand him certain instruments or to pull the retractor one way or another. Having handed the baby to the neonatologist, Samy then gently delivered the placenta, the afterbirth, and closed the opening in the womb in two layers of stitches. He then said to Alison, 'Have you noticed, Alison, that the placenta was partially separated from the wall of the womb, and this would have caused the bleeding, which the midwife noticed when she examined the patient? Of course, this separation would have also caused severe fetal distress as the blood flow from the mother to the baby was being drastically reduced.'

Samy closed the abdomen with the same efficient speed. As he was closing the skin, a faint cry from the baby in the corner of the operating theatre brought a smile to everyone in the operating theatre. A few minutes later, the baby's cry got louder and more vigorous, and Samy said, 'That is it, little one. Welcome to our world.'

Samy then said loudly, 'Could someone please let the husband know that all is well with mother and baby?'

One of the attending midwives left the operating theatre to talk to the husband. Once Samy had finished the operation, he warmly thanked the anaesthetist and his assistant. He then said to the scrub nurse and Alison, 'Thank you both very much for your help. You have both been absolutely wonderful.'

As he was taking his gown and his gloves off, he said loudly to everyone in the theatre, 'Well done, team. Great job. Thank you all very much.'

Samy walked to the far corner of the operating theatre, where the baby was still being monitored and assessed by the neonatal team. He was reassured that the baby was in perfect condition and that there was no obvious evidence that the distress the baby suffered in labour had left any lasting effect, but it was certainly a very close call.

The neonatologist said to Samy, 'Well done you. This baby certainly needed to come out in a hurry if brain damage was to be avoided.'

Samy just smiled and said, 'Thank you very much for your expert help with the resuscitation.'

The scrub nurse and Alison were covering the woman's skin incision with a dressing when the scrub nurse whispered to Alison, 'Who is this guy? A Caesarean section from start to finish in less than twenty minutes? Amazing.'

Alison smiled, looked in the direction of Samy, who was still talking to the neonatal team in the far corner of the operating theatre and replied, 'He has just started at St Luke's this morning. He is obviously very clever and very experienced.'

She then mumbled to herself, '… and incredibly good-looking too.'

As soon as Samy and Alison left the operating theatre, they went to talk to the woman's husband in room 6 and reassured him that the operation was straightforward and both mother and baby were fine. Sister Smith then took the husband to see his wife and the baby in the recovery area next to the operating theatre.

****

When sister Smith returned, she accompanied Samy and Alison back to Mrs. Green's room so that they could continue talking to her about the management plan for her slow labour.

Samy apologised to Mrs and Mr Green for having to rush out of the room so abruptly. He then explained to them the plan of management of their prolonged slow labour.

'Because the progress of your labour has been slow, we need to give you something to make the womb contract more efficiently and speed things up. This is a drug called syntocinon, which is similar to the hormone you produce naturally to make your womb contract in normal labour. This will be given to you in a drip, and hopefully, with stronger and more regular contractions, you will deliver very well.'

The woman, who looked exhausted, asked, 'For how long do I have to carry on with this drip? I am extremely tired and have no more energy left.'

The husband added in an equally exhausted and fed-up voice, 'So am I.'

The woman then added, 'Can't I just have a Caesarean section now? I have not slept for four days, having been having contractions on and off all this time. I have been in active labour on the labour ward for over twelve hours. I have just had enough.'

The husband mumbled in the same quiet voice, 'So Have I.'

Samy smiled sympathetically and said, 'Of course, it is up to you, and I will do whatever you want. But you are already five centimetres dilated, which is half the job. Your observations are fine, and the baby's heartbeat is normal now, so we still have a chance for a normal delivery if we just give you a bit more time with the syntocinon drip. In a first delivery, we must try our hardest to avoid putting you through a Caesarean section as long as you and the baby can tolerate labour for a bit longer. You may wish to consider having an epidural inserted into your back to take the labour pains away completely and enable you to have some rest and even have some sleep while the drug works on the womb. I promise you that if there is any sign of trouble with the baby or yourself while we are doing this, we will do a Caesarean section straightaway. I really believe that you still have a very good chance for a normal delivery, and for this reason, it is worth carrying on for just a bit longer.'

The woman agreed reluctantly to have the epidural inserted into her back for pain relief and try syntocinon infusion into her arm. Once the epidural relieved her labour pains completely, she managed to fall asleep for a couple of hours while the syntocinon drip worked on her womb.

When the midwife examined her three hours later as planned, she was found to be fully dilated, and shortly after that, she delivered normally a healthy boy weighing eight pounds.

****

After they finished seeing all the other women on the labour ward, sister Smith said to Samy and Alison, 'As there is nothing imminent at present, it must be time for Coffee and biscuits.'

Samy replied, 'What a good idea. I will go and get coffee and cakes for the whole team from Costa's coffee shop downstairs. My treat, as this is my inaugural labour ward shift.'

Alison went with him to help him carry all these coffees and cakes from Costa's coffee shop on the ground floor, but more importantly, to have the opportunity to talk to him on his own.

As they walked down the stairs, she said, 'This was one really fantastic Caesarean section. I have never seen it done so fast.'

Samy smiled, shrugged his shoulders dismissively and said, 'It was nothing special really, but thank you for saying that.'

He obviously felt uncomfortable about being complimented, and for this reason, he changed the subject quickly. 'This is such a lovely hospital. To be so close to the famous Hampstead Heath is a huge bonus for me. All the hospitals I have worked in before have always been in the middle of crowded, noisy cities, far away from any parks or gardens.'

'How long are you with us for?' Alison asked.

'Well, Mr Stewart told me that I am on probation for three months and if I am good enough, I will be employed for two years.'

Alison smiled and said, 'Judging by the operation you have just performed, I don't think that there will be any need for a probation period. You are obviously very experienced for someone who is so young.'

Samy laughed and said, 'I am not really that young. I will be thirty in a few weeks' time.'

'Where are you staying? Do you live in the hospital, or have you rented a place in town with your wife or girlfriend?'

This was Alison's not-so-subtle way of discovering if he was single or not.

'I have a single room in the doctors' residence here as I have no wife or girlfriend. More to the point, I certainly cannot afford the rental rates in London, so it is hospital accommodation for me.'

This was the answer Alison had hoped for. To her relief, Samy was free and available.

While Samy and Alison were queuing for drinks at Costa's Coffee shop on the ground floor of the hospital, sister Smith and some of the midwives were talking in the labour ward office about Samy's performance in the operating theatre, not only about his amazing speed and his obviously fantastic surgical skills but more importantly, about his calm and confident way with which he handled such an urgent critical case.

The senior registrar, Jeremy Bell, entered the office. He was the most senior trainee doctor in the Maternity hospital, not far off finishing his training and becoming a consultant. He was six foot tall, attractive, with blond hair and blue eyes. He had a sexy, muscular body, which he flaunted as much as he could. He said to Sister Smith and the other midwives with a cheeky smile, 'You are all obviously engaged in a very deep and meaningful conversation. So, who are you slagging off now?'

Jeremy Bell was known in the department as a 'lovable rascal' because he had a naughty sense of humour, liked to play practical jokes on anyone and everyone, but more importantly, he had an insatiable appetite for women. His behaviour, both verbal and tactile, was often inappropriate around pretty nurses and midwives, but he always got away with it because of his good looks, irresistible sense of humour and his influential position as the most senior trainee in the hospital. He was certainly the most eligible bachelor in the team, which made him potentially a very good catch for any single member of the staff. So many of them fell for him with the aim to tame him and get him to tie the knot, but in vain.

Sister Smith replied, 'We were not slagging off anyone. Far from it, we were being very complimentary about the new registrar, Samy Samir.'

'Oh, yes. I heard he is starting today. What is he like?'

'He is obviously excellent. He delivered a case of severe fetal distress by CS in less than twenty minutes from start to finish, with hardly any blood loss.'

Jeremy frowned and said, 'This is not a good start. I must watch him closely because I do not like a registrar who gets admired by my gorgeous midwives from day one on the job. I do not like competition.'

'Don't worry, Jeremy. There will be no competition because he is much better looking than you are and obviously far more clever.' replied sister Smith with a teasing smile.

Jeremy frowned and said, 'I hate him already.'

When Samy and Alison returned with the coffee and cakes, he was introduced to Jeremy Bell, and they shook hands warmly. Jeremy said to Samy, 'I have just been told about your heroics in the operating theatre this morning.'

Samy again looked uncomfortable with this compliment as he said, 'It was an excellent team performance. I was delighted to see that everyone and everything worked so perfectly. Obviously, the staff here are very special.'

Samy then quickly changed the subject. 'I am not clear about how the on-call rota works, so I will be grateful if you can explain it to me when you have the time.'

'Of course. This is important, especially as you are on-call this weekend.'

As Samy and Alison distributed the coffees and the cakes to the midwives, Jeremy asked, 'All these Costa coffees and cakes, what are we celebrating?'

Sister Smith replied, 'This is Samy's treat for us all. Something you have never done, Scrooge!'

One of the midwives came in and asked Samy to come and look at the baby's heart trace in room 11. Samy politely excused himself and left the office with Alison following.

Jeremy Bell said to sister Smith, 'I will have to teach this boy some proper manners. He is obviously too nice and too polite for my liking.'

Melanie shook her head, looked at him disapprovingly and said, 'Just leave him alone. If you watch him closely, you may learn some good manners yourself.'

The other midwives in the office left to go back to their delivery rooms, leaving sister Smith and Jeremy on their own. Sister Smith stood up to go and see what was happening with that baby's heart trace, but as she walked past Jeremy, he put his arm around her waist and whispered into her ear, 'When are you going to ease my heartache, Mel? I just want one little kiss.'

Melanie pushed his arm angrily. 'If you do not stop touching me every time I come near you, I will not only break off both your arms, but I will also cut off all your dangly bits which seem to rule your life. I really mean it. What would the midwives say if they saw you holding me like this?'

'They will say that I love you. My heart is aching for you.'

Melanie pushed him in his chest as she left the room, saying, 'The problem is not your heart, if you have one, that is. The problem is mainly your overflowing hormones.'

Chapter 2

The beginning of a bitter rivalry

Samy and Alison went with the midwife into room 11 to see Miss Hatfield because of her prolonged labour and abnormal baby's heartbeat. He greeted her cheerfully and introduced himself and Alison. The patient and her partner responded coldly. They both looked tired and fed up. Samy looked at the CTG monitor to check the baby's heartbeat and then looked at the chart that documented the progress of the labour. He asked the midwife a couple of questions about her last examination's findings and then turned round to speak to the couple.

Before Samy could say anything, the woman said with an angry tone of voice, 'I will not have a Caesarean section, whatever you say. I thought you ought to know that before you start.'

Samy smiled calmly and said in a very quiet voice, 'I fully understand that. Caesarean section is always the very last thing we would want for anyone in labour. What I wanted to say is that you were last examined two hours ago, so do you mind if I examine you myself and see if things have changed? Your neck of the womb has been stuck at 4 centimetres dilatation for over eight hours now, and the baby's heartbeat is starting to drop, so we really must find out whether there is any progress or not. Is that OK with you?

I know that you must be getting very uncomfortable from all these internal examinations, but I will be very gentle and very quick. It will only take a minute.'

Miss Hatfield looked at her partner, who just shook his head in despair. She sighed and said, 'If you have to, then get on with it. I've had enough of all this.'

After Samy had finished the examination, he said to the woman, 'I am afraid that there is no progress at all. If anything, the cervix is going backwards because it is now markedly swollen, so the dilation is reduced from four to three centimetres. Moreover, the baby's head is showing a swelling in the scalp, which we call 'caput' and overlapping of the bones of the skull. These are nothing sinister, but they both indicate that the head is really jammed in the pelvis.'

Miss Hatfield started to cry, and her partner just stared at Samy angrily without saying anything. Samy did not wait for a response as he carried on in a clear, authoritative voice. 'Of course, it is up to you to decide what should happen next. I fully appreciate your desire to have a normal delivery, but you have been in labour for a long time and have been having syntocinon infusion for the last six hours to try and get the cervix to dilate further. All the signs indicate that the labour is obstructed, and there is no prospect of a vaginal delivery any time soon. You have been very patient and very brave, but if you choose to continue with labour, you will be taking a significant risk of serious damage not just to the baby but also to yourself. The pattern of the baby's heartbeat is not alarming yet, but it is not reassuring either.'

In that critical situation, Samy did not mince his words as he had to be clear and decisive for the sake of the mother and the baby. He made sure that both the woman and her partner appreciated the potential for very serious risks if labour was allowed to continue for much longer. He left the room for a few minutes to give them the chance to discuss the situation on their own. When he returned, he found that the couple's angry and hostile attitude was replaced by a look of resignation. They agreed to have the Caesarean section after all.

Samy explained to the couple in detail the procedure and answered their questions about the aftercare. The woman was relieved to know that she would have the operation under spinal anaesthetic, which meant that she would be fully awake throughout the operation and would see the baby as soon as it was born. Also, her partner would be with her from start to finish, which was very important to both of them. This was the closest they could get to a normal delivery.

After this discussion, the couple's tone of voice changed to a more friendly and understanding one. As Samy was about to leave the room, Miss Hatfield asked, sounding anxious, 'Will you be doing the operation?'

Before Samy could reply, the midwife said, 'Mr Samir's shift finished half an hour ago, so it will be the evening on-call team who will do the operation for you.'

Miss Hatfield looked very disappointed, but Samy quickly said, 'I will be delighted to do the operation for you, Miss Hatfield, whether my shift has finished or not. I will see you in the operating theatre shortly.'

Miss Hatfield breathed a sigh of relief and smiled, which was the first time the midwife who had been with her all day saw her smiling.

Samy left the room, and Alison stayed behind to complete the consent form and the rest of the paperwork for Miss Hatfield's Caesarean section, following which she re-joined Samy in the labour ward's office. She was annoyed to see sister Smith having a cosy conversation with him. Obviously, Alison was not the only one who had fallen for the charms and good looks of this Egyptian.

As Alison sat down next to Samy, he turned round to her and said, 'Please feel free to go home, Alison. The shift is over, and my promise to this lady to do her operation does not oblige you to stay on. You have worked really hard today, and you have been a great help to me. I am very grateful.'

Alison smiled back and replied, 'I would like to stay on if that is OK with you.'

Samy's smile broadened as he said, 'That will be wonderful. I think we make a very good team.'

On hearing this friendly conversation, it was sister Smith's turn to feel jealous and annoyed with Alison because she sensed that she had her eyes on Samy as much as she herself did. Sister Smith knew that the competition with Alison for Samy's attention would be tough, but she certainly thought that he was worth fighting for.

****

At the beginning of the evening shift, Samy got to meet the other registrar in the department, Mohammad Khan and the other senior house officer, Alison's opposite number, Maria Nichos. Both Mohammad and Maria were going to be the overnight team who would take over from Samy and Alison.

Mohammad Khan was short and slim. He was obviously Asian in origin, with a beard and a moustache. He wore thick glasses because he was very short-sighted, and this made him look much older than he really was. His Pakistani parents emigrated to England before he was born. As he was born and bred in England, he spoke perfect English but with a heavy cockney accent, which indicated which part of London he was brought up in.

Maria Nichos was a Greek girl who had qualified from the medical school in Athens and then came to England for her postgraduate training in obstetrics and gynaecology. She was rather overweight but had a pretty and very expressive face. Her short black hair was always a mess as she never bothered to style it. She always dressed for comfort rather than for elegance. Baggy trousers and simple T-shirts were her usual attire most days. She spoke English reasonably well but with a heavy Greek accent. She had a volatile temper but was kind, reliable and very keen to learn her trade.

Sister Smith did the introductions. 'Come in, Samy. Meet Mohammad Khan, the registrar on-call this evening and Maria Nichos, the senior house officer. In keeping with the international nature of our team, Mohammad is from Pakistan, and Maria is Greek.'

They all burst out laughing as Mohammad and Samy shook hands, following which Maria shook Samy's hand so hard he felt that she was going to crush every bone in it. She was a big, strong girl who did not always appreciate her own strength.

Samy briefly discussed with Mohammad and Maria what had been happening in the labour ward all day and what was left for them to sort out. He then asked politely for Mohammad's permission to be allowed to do Miss

Hatfield's Caesarean section, and of course, Mohammad readily agreed.

Mohammad said to Samy in a sarcastic tone of voice, 'Such dedication. Only a new registrar would volunteer to stay on after his shift has ended to do an operation. Wait until the novelty wears off, and you will be running out of the door as fast as you can once your shift is over.'

Sister Smith intervened sharply. 'Speak for yourself, Mohammad. I think that Samy is not the kind to rush to leave at the end of his shift, unlike you.'

Mohammad winked at Samy and said with a cheeky smile, 'You lucky devil! This is your first day here, and you have already captured sister Smith's affection, something I failed to do in a whole year. She never came to my defence like this.'

Sister Smith blushed, and Samy quickly tried to put an end to Mohammad's irritating sense of humour by saying, 'She was just being kind as I am the new kid on the block who is still trying to settle in. Anyway, I need to go to the operating theatre to get on with this section and get out of your way. Have a nice shift.'

****

The operation went smoothly and quickly. A beautiful baby girl was delivered and was screaming the place down from the moment her head was delivered out of the womb. Miss Hatfield and her partner were over the moon, especially as they were able to see the baby being delivered out of her tummy. After the baby's umbilical cord was cut, the midwife wrapped the baby in a warm towel and passed her on to the excited parents.

The midwife asked Miss Hatfield, 'Would you like to have 'skin-to-skin' contact with your baby?'

The couple seemed surprised, and Miss Hatfield asked, 'Is that possible while the operation is going on?'

Samy replied, 'Of course it is. We will put up the screen that separates our side of the table from you and your partner, and you can then do whatever you want with the baby.'

Once the screen was up again over Miss Hatfield's chest, the midwife lowered Miss Hatfield's gown to expose her chest and put the baby directly on her bare chest after the towel that was covering the baby's body was removed to get the 'skin-to-skin' contact. As soon as the baby's mouth came close to Miss Hatfield's nipple, she latched on to it and started suckling straight away.

The amazed partner said, 'Wow. When did she learn how to breastfeed? She has just been born.'

Everyone in the theatre burst out laughing.

When the operation was over, Samy thanked everyone before leaving the operating theatre to go to the changing room. The couple were too absorbed in their baby to notice that the operation was over and Samy was leaving, which meant that they never thanked him for all that he had done for them.

Samy came out of the changing room to find Alison already changed and waiting for him in the corridor. He looked surprised as he thought that she would have gone home by then. He said to her, 'Alison, why haven't you gone home? Haven't I delayed you enough today?'

Before Alison could reply, sister Smith came running down the corridor and said to Samy with a pleading look on her face, 'I am very sorry, Samy. I know that you should have gone home long ago, but Mohammad is about to do a ventouse delivery in room four, and he would like a second opinion before he goes ahead. He is rather inexperienced, especially in instrumental deliveries. You are the only experienced obstetrician in the hospital at present, and your input will be very much appreciated. Please, please, please.'

Samy smiled and said, 'For you, sister, anything.'

Alison frowned and stared angrily at sister Smith, who had spoiled her plan to talk to Samy on his own at the end of such a busy day. Samy turned to her and said, 'Well, Alison, I will say good night then. Thanks again for all your help and support today. You really made my initiation at St. Luke's as pleasant and as smooth as it could have ever been.'

Alison was not going to give up that easily, so she said, 'I have a lot of results of investigations on the antenatal ward that need actioning urgently, so I will do that while you sort out this ventouse delivery. So, come and get me from the antenatal ward after you finish because I want to talk to you about something.'

'That is fine. I will come to you on the antenatal ward as soon as I finish.'

Sister Smith took Samy into delivery room four and introduced him to the woman and her partner. The woman already had her legs suspended in stirrups and was covered with sterile green drapes. Mohammad and Maria were gowned up in readiness for delivering the baby with the suction instrument similar to the forceps called 'ventouse', which is a cup connected to a suction machine. The cup sticks firmly to the top of the baby's head because of the vacuum effect produced by the suction machine, and then the head can be pulled out.

Mohammad whispered into Samy's ear with the ventouse in his hand, 'Samy, this lady is too tired to push this baby out herself, having been fully dilated for a long time. The head is low in the pelvis, but I am not absolutely sure which part of the head is coming first. It feels rather irregular and knobbly. Could you please just check for me before I apply the ventouse?'

After taking the woman's permission, Samy examined her gently and then said to her, 'My colleague was absolutely right to ask for a second opinion because the baby is coming as what we call a face presentation, which is very rare.'

Mohammad's face dropped, and he quickly put the ventouse back on the trolley next to him.

He felt that the head was 'irregular and knobbly' because he was not actually feeling the smooth top of the head, which is normally the part of the head that comes down first into the pelvis in most labours. He was actually feeling the face with its nose, eye sockets, mouth and cheekbones. If Mohammad went ahead and used the ventouse, the suction could have caused very serious facial injuries to the baby's face, eyes and nose. Samy continued to explain to the woman what face presentation meant as he and the midwife put her legs down from the stirrups so that she could lie more comfortably flat on the bed.

'We will take you to the operating theatre, and we will need to deliver you by Caesarean section because this particular type of face presentation is impossible to be delivered vaginally. Fortunately, you have an epidural anaesthetic already on board, so we will have this topped up now, and we can start the operation straight away. You and the baby will be perfectly alright.'

The woman replied with a big sigh of relief, 'That is fine. I never wanted this horrible suction instrument shoved up my vagina anyway. I prefer the section.'

Mohammad and Maria were standing behind Samy, looking at each other in horror at what they were about to do. As Samy left the room, Mohammad got out of his gown very quickly and ran after him while Maria started completing the consent form for the operation and then got the patient to sign it.

As soon as Mohammad caught up with Samy in the corridor, he hugged him and said, 'Samy, you are my hero.'

Sister Smith was coming towards them from the other side of the corridor, and when she saw the hug, she laughed and said, 'Hey, you two lovebirds. Control yourselves.'

Samy looked embarrassed and did not respond to her, but Mohammad did. 'It was a bloody face presentation, and I was about to suck the baby's eyes out with the ventouse if it wasn't for this man. What a near miss!'

Samy tried to make Mohammad feel better. 'Don't exaggerate, Mohammad. If you applied the ventouse cup to the face, the chances are it would not have stuck to it because the irregularity of the surface of the face would not have allowed for a proper seal to be achieved, so you may have never been able to get any suction at all with the ventouse.'

Mohammad said, 'Seal or no seal, I do not care. I still say you have averted a potential disaster. You saved the baby from serious injuries and saved my career from utter ruin.'

Sister Smith smiled and said, 'So you see, Mohammad, I was right to tell you that if you were not happy with your examination, you should get a second opinion from an expert.'

Samy's embarrassment increased as sister Smith called him 'an expert', and he said, 'Anyone can miss a face presentation because it is so rare. The important thing was that you suspected that there was something that was not quite right, and this is what saved the day.'

Samy then quickly tried to divert the discussion towards the Caesarean section. He said to Mohammad, 'Do you want me to scrub with you to give you a hand with the section?' Mohammad quickly said, 'No, no, no. You have done enough. I am perfectly happy to do the section with Maria assisting. You go home. I am eternally grateful.'

'I will hang around in the labour ward's office until the baby is out, just in case.'

This pleased sister Smith to no end because it meant that she would have some time with Samy on his own, away from Alison. Mohammad was also delighted because although he was competent at doing Caesarean sections, he had never done any sections for a face presentation, so having Samy in the background gave him more confidence.

'Would you like a cup of coffee, Samy?' asked sister Smith as they both approached the empty labour ward's office.

Samy gratefully accepted, and the sister went to the kitchen and made the coffee as quickly as she could. Before she returned to the office, she unbuttoned the top button of her uniform. She wanted to attract Samy's attention to the best two of her many physical assets. Undoing the top button of her uniform would expose just enough of her cleavage and the edge of her black bras, which should get him thinking, or so she thought!

Sister Smith handed Samy the mug of coffee and then presented him with a plate of chocolate biscuits while leaning forward as he was choosing which biscuit to have. This would have given him a bird's eye view of her ample breasts. However, to her utter disappointment, his eyes never strayed from the plate of biscuits. He picked up the biscuit he wanted and took a bite while staring down his mug of coffee. Sister Smith had to straighten out and go around to the other side of the desk, quickly buttoning up her uniform before anyone else saw her in that semi-exposed state.

Samy let out a tired sigh and said, 'Thank you very much, sister. This is just what I needed at the end of a busy shift. You are very kind.'

'Not at all. You have really worked very hard today, and we are all very impressed with your skill. How come you are so experienced and clever?'

He replied while trying to avoid prolonging the conversation about his skills, 'There is nothing clever about any of this, but thank you for saying that. I went into training in obstetrics and gynaecology straight from medical school, so I have been at it for a good few years now. In addition, in England, a maternity unit is considered to be a large one if the number of babies delivered in it is five or six thousand every year. In Egypt, my hospital delivered twenty-five thousand babies a year. Also, unlike in England, where trainees can only work fifty hours a week, there is no set limit for the number of hours trainees can work in Egypt and on many occasions, I worked over a hundred hours a week. This meant that I saw a lot and did a lot before coming to England.'

Sister Smith gasped, 'Wow, twenty-five thousand deliveries a year in one hospital? This is amazing.'

Samy laughed and said, 'Making babies seems to be the favourite national pastime in Egypt, as is the case in many third-world countries.'

'Do you come from a medical family? Over the years, we had several registrars from the Middle East, and most of them seemed to come from medical families.'

'Not in my case, though. My father was a schoolteacher, and my mother was a housewife. As far as I know, there are no doctors at all in my extended family.'

'They must be very proud of you.'

Samy had a sad expression on his face as he nodded and said, 'Unfortunately, they both died in a car accident when I was four years old, and I was brought up by my uncle, my father's brother.'

Sister Smith said with a mixture of admiration and sympathy, 'I am very sorry to hear this. I am sure your uncle is very proud of you.'

Samy laughed sarcastically and said, 'Completely the opposite. He did not want me to go to university at all, let alone to the medical school with its long and expensive courses. He did not have any sons of his own, only three daughters, so he wanted me to help him in running his convenience store. He believed that I owed him that after all that he had done for me over the years, bringing me up following my parents' death. When I insisted on going to medical school, he threw me out and never allowed me to have any contact with him or with his three daughters, who were like sisters to me.'

Sister Smith frowned angrily and said, 'How cruel! How did you manage financially on your own?'

'Fortunately, in Egypt, if you are a high achiever in your GCSE exams, you get a fairly generous monthly grant throughout your university years, provided that you continue to achieve high scores in your yearly exams. I was lucky enough to achieve that for six years in medical school, and that was how I survived. Without that grant money, I would have never made it. I also earned a bit of extra money on the side from doing odd jobs here and there in the evenings and at weekends whenever I could.'

This brief interlude with Samy made sister Smith utterly determined to grab him for herself. It was no longer just a matter of physical attraction or admiration of his professional skills; there was a lot more to admire and like about his personality and his background. She thought to herself that there was no wonder he behaved in such a mature and reassured manner after coming through these traumatic and very difficult circumstances.

＊＊＊＊＊＊＊＊＊＊＊＊＊＊＊＊

The Caesarean section was uneventful, and Samy was able to leave the labour ward to go to see Alison on the antenatal ward as they had arranged previously. As soon as Alison saw Samy, her face lit up with a beaming smile.

She asked. 'This seemed to have taken a long time. I thought sister Smith just wanted you to give Mohammad a quick second opinion about a ventouse delivery. Is everything alright?'

'I am sorry for being so late, but second opinions in obstetrics are never quick.'

Alison frowned and mumbled to herself, 'I might have known that this cow would endeavour to keep you on the labour ward for as long as she could.'

Samy sighed and said, sounding tired, 'Anyway, I am ready to leave now if that is OK with you.'

'Absolutely. I have managed to sort out a lot of the results and the paperwork that have been hanging over me for so long, so I am ready to leave, too.'

As they walked out of the maternity unit, Alison said, 'It is a lovely summer's evening, and there is still a fair bit of daylight. Shall we get some sandwiches and go for a walk on Hampstead Heath? If you are not too tired, that is.'

Samy smiled and replied, 'What a brilliant idea! This will be such a relaxing thing to do after a busy, eventful day. I have never been on the Heath before, but I heard a lot about it, so it will be great to have you as my tour guide on my first visit.'

'I will be delighted to be your tour guide, kind sir, but I must let you know that I will expect a generous tip.'

Samy laughed and said, 'I am only a poor Egyptian immigrant. Would a ham sandwich do for a tip?'

'You drive a hard bargain. Alright then, but you have to add a can of Pepsi to the ham sandwich.'

The two went to the Hospital's cantine, where they bought the sandwiches and the drinks, following which they walked slowly the short distance to Hampstead Heath. As they walked around the various parts of this famous park, Alison made sure that she showed Samy all the areas which she considered to be the most beautiful. They went up and down the various hills, sat down for a while in the rose garden and fed the ducks in the large lake at the centre of the Heath.

The conversation was more of an interrogation than a chat. Alison wanted to know everything about Samy, his family, his background, and his goals. Samy never liked talking about himself, but Alison's persistence was not to be denied. Every time he tried to take the conversation away from himself, she quickly brought him back to the story of his life with more searching questions. By the time it became dark, Alison knew everything she wanted to know about Samy. The thing she admired most about his life story was the fact that he did not seem bothered in any way about his poor background and the difficult and deprived life he had. He did not make any attempt to hide his miserable circumstances and responded honestly and readily to any questions that came his way, however sensitive or personal they were.

As they walked back towards the exit of the Heath, Samy said, 'I have never talked so much about myself as I have done today, first with sister Smith and then you.'

Alarm bells sounded in Alison's head as soon as she heard sister Smith's name. She frowned and asked, 'What did this woman want from you?'

'Nothing. She was just being friendly and interested in a stranger from a faraway land.'

'She is only friendly when she is after something. Be careful.'

Samy laughed and said innocently, 'What would she want from me? You are not being fair to her.'

'I just know her too well. You will soon find out what she is really like.'

Samy walked with Alison to her car in the staff car park at the back of the hospital. He was very impressed with her bright red sports car. 'Wow, Alison. What a car! I have never seen anything like it. What is it? I don't even know what make it is.'

Alison blushed and looked embarrassed. Knowing how Samy had struggled to make ends meet all his life, she did not want to be flashing her new car in front of him. 'It is a Mercedes AMG. It has not been released into the open market yet.'

'It certainly suits you very perfectly.'

'You mean it is like me loud and pretentious.'

'Not at all. Like you, it is elegant, classy and beautiful.'

Alison smiled happily as Samy opened the car door for her, but before she got in, she asked, 'What sort of car do you have?'

Samy laughed and pointed to an old yellow car on the other side of the car park. 'Do you see this yellow rust bucket over there? This is my chariot, a Triumph Toledo with a hundred thousand miles on the clock. I bought it in

Manchester for six hundred pounds. I bet you have never even heard of a Triumph Toledo before.'

Alison smiled uncomfortably and said, 'No, I cannot say that I have. What does it matter anyway? A car is a car is a car is a car!'

The obviously vast difference between their financial situations did not seem to bother Samy in the slightest, but it certainly worried Alison, who thought that this might make him feel that she was too inaccessible, which is the last thing she wanted.

This was the first of many walks in Hampstead Heath the two of them took together over the following few weeks. They obviously enjoyed each other's company right from the word go.

Chapter 3

The ward round from hell

Early the next morning, Alison went to the labour ward office to get a set of notes in preparation for Mr Stewart's weekly ward round, which always started at exactly 8 am. Sister Smith was the only one in the office. They exchanged the morning greetings coldly, and Alison started to look through a pile of notes on one of the shelves.

Mr Stewart came into the office and said, 'Good morning, ladies. I am glad that I got you both on your own to get your assessment of our new registrar. How did he do yesterday on the labour ward?'

Sister Smith rushed to answer enthusiastically. 'He was absolutely wonderful. I think he will turn out to be the best registrar we have ever had.'

Alison joined in, sounding even more enthusiastic. 'I second that. His clinical judgement and management plans are spot on. His operating skills are amazing, so precise and very fast.'

Mr Stewart did not like to hear Alison being so complimentary about another man, especially if that man was much younger and much better looking than him. He paused for a few moments, and then, through gritted teeth, he said, 'I do not like trainees who are described as 'very fast' because this suggests that they are over-confident, which always spells disaster sooner or later.'

Alison realised immediately that her contribution was a mistake because she knew full well that Mr Stewart was obsessed with her, and he always got jealous if he felt that Alison admired or was nice to any man under any circumstances. She did not want to provoke Mr Stewart's hostility towards Samy, and for this reason, she tried to remedy the situation by saying, 'Of course, I am just a senior house officer, and I have only assisted in a limited number of Caesarean sections with a couple of other registrars, so, he seemed very fast to me in comparison with what I have seen before. But with the speed aspect of his surgery aside, the operations he performed looked very neat throughout, and there was hardly any blood loss. The scrub nurses in theatre noticed that too.'

Mr Stewart stared at her with an angry frown as he said menacingly, 'I am not going to be judging him as quickly as you two seem to have obviously done. I shall keep an eye on him, and I hope that your opinion of him is correct.'

He then turned round to leave and said, 'Alright then, Alison, I will see you shortly on the antenatal ward for the round.'

****

Mr Stewart turned up on the antenatal ward to do his ward round, looking rather grim and in a bad mood. Waiting for him on the ward were Samy, Alison, sister Sheila Morrison, who was in charge of the ward and two very frightened final-year medical students, Jack and Rachel. Mr Stewart was feared by all medical students because he always treated them aggressively and disrespectfully. Rather than looking at medical students as doctors of the future, he always felt that they were stupid, incompetent and useless. If he had a choice, he would have never allowed any medical students on his ward rounds, in his clinics or on operating lists, but teaching them was a contractual obligation which he could not wriggle out of, especially as the hospital received annually a substantial amount of money from the medical school in return for having their students getting practical experience from spending time in the various departments of the hospital.

'Good morning. What do you have for me today, sister?' said Mr Stewart with a serious look on his face as he scanned his waiting audience until his gaze fell on Alison, and a wide smile replaced the serious look.

Sister Morrison replied, 'There are three antenatal patients for you to see, and you may also wish to review a woman who had a Caesarean section three days ago and has been having significant problems since then.'

Mr Stewart usually never used to see women who had already delivered unless he absolutely had to. Once a woman had had her baby and 'finished the job', so to speak, whatever problem she might have then was rarely worthy of his time and expertise. The midwives and trainee doctors should be able to sort out any postnatal problems as he always had more important things to do.

To everyone's surprise, Mr Stewart suddenly exploded in sister Morrison's face. 'This is not a good start. I have not got time today for any nonsense. Do I really need to see this postnatal patient? What is she doing on the antenatal ward anyway? Shouldn't she be on the postnatal ward?' asked Mr Stewart in a voice that clearly expressed a mixture of anger and frustration.

Samy was even more surprised to hear the sister responding to Mr Stewart in an angry and disrespectful tone of voice, 'You do whatever the hell you want to do, but in my professional opinion, this patient needs to see her consultant because she has been getting worse since her delivery and although she had already had the baby, she is still your responsibility because she has been admitted under your care. She is on the antenatal ward because the postnatal ward was completely full.'

Mr Stewart stared at her with his face getting redder by the second, and his lips twitched, but he did not say anything. The sister returned his furious gaze with a defiant and equally furious gaze of her own. She then turned round to go to the first antenatal patient that needed reviewing, and the rest followed her in silence.

Alison touched Samy's arm to attract his attention as they walked behind Mr Stewart and out of his sight. She whispered in his ear, 'Sister Morrison is his ex-wife!'

Samy's eyes widened in disbelief, but this statement enabled him to understand the way the sister and Mr Stewart interacted with each other in this little episode. This was promising to be a very long morning for all concerned.

They all went into a four-bedded ward and stopped in front of the second bed. The curtains were pulled around the bed so that they had some privacy with the patient, as there were three other patients in that ward. Of course, the curtains were not terribly useful in this regard because everyone on the ward could clearly hear what was being said behind the curtains.

The sister smiled at the patient, then turned round towards Mr Stewart and handed him the patient's notes. As she looked at him, her smile was quickly replaced with the same angry expression that she had earlier. 'This is Mrs McDonald, who was admitted yesterday with pre-eclampsia …'

Mr Stewart interrupted, 'Good morning, Mrs McDonald. Let us get one of the medical students to tell us your history if that is alright with you.'

The patient nodded in agreement. Mr Stewart turned towards the two medical students, who looked like two terrified rabbits caught in the headlights of a truck that was about to run them over.

'Come on then, Jack. What is the story here? I trust you had time to take a full history and examine Mrs McDonald yesterday or earlier today,' said Mr Stewart while flicking through the patient's notes.

With a trembling voice, Jack replied, 'Yes, sir, I did. Mrs McDonald is a twenty-eight-year-old lady having her first baby. She is 34 weeks pregnant and was sent in by her community midwife because her blood pressure was high…'

Mr Stewart interrupted, 'What does 'her blood pressure was high' mean? Give me an exact figure, man, be specific.'

'It was 150/100 when the community midwife measured it.'

'And what was it on admission? Speak up. We haven't got all day.'

The trembling of Jack's voice increased as he said, 'It was the same. She also had a lot of protein in her urine. She herself was feeling well and did not have any symptoms.'

'Does she have any risk factors in her background to indicate that she may have blood pressure problems in pregnancy?' asked Mr Stewart impatiently.

'Not that I know of, sir.'

Mr Stewart made a dismissive gesture with his hand as he said, 'The answer should be a 'yes' or 'no'. In managing this patient, if we relied on what you may or may not know, we would all be in big trouble. She is having her first baby, and her mother had pre-eclampsia when she was pregnant. Both are risk factors for pre-eclampsia in this pregnancy.'

He then turned to the patient and, in a completely different tone of voice that was kind and respectful, 'Would you mind Mrs McDonald if I get the other student to examine your tummy to check the baby?'

Mrs McDonald again nodded in agreement and gave the second student, Rachel, an encouraging smile as she exposed her tummy in readiness for the examination.

Rachel went to the patient's right side of the bed and proceeded to put her hand on the patient's abdomen. She almost jumped out of her skin when Mr Stewart shouted at her, 'You silly girly! How many times have I told you never to touch a patient before you personally, politely, and respectfully ask for her permission to allow you to examine her? The fact that I have already asked her does not excuse you from asking her again for her permission because you are the one doing the examination.'

A very nervous Rachel asked for Mrs McDonald's permission, who granted it, and she then started to examine her. When she finished examining the patient, Mr Stewart, still in the same condescending and aggressive tone of voice, said, 'Very poor examination technique. You have done several antenatal clinics with me, and still, you look like someone who has never seen a pregnant woman before.'

He then proceeded to examine the patient himself while explaining to the students how it should have been done.

To the students' great relief, it was now the turn of the registrar and the senior house officer to suffer Mr Stewart's inquisition. If Samy was worried about what was to come his way from Mr Stewart, he did not show it. As for Alison, she could not care less as she knew that Mr Stewart had always treated her differently.

Mr Stewart looked in the direction of Samy and Alison and asked, 'What investigations do we need to do for Mrs McDonald?'

Samy started to answer, 'Full blood count, liver functions tests and ....' but he was abruptly interrupted by Mr Stewart, who gave him a penetrating angry look. 'The question was not for you. As a registrar, if you do not know by now the investigations for high blood pressure in pregnancy, then there is a very serious problem with your training in obstetrics, and you should find something else to do. The question was for young Alison.'

Alison did not wait for him to ask the question again, and with a blank look on her face, she proceeded to answer in a rather robotic and indifferent way: 'Full blood count, Liver and kidney function tests, urine tests, scan to check the baby's growth and a baby's heart trace.'

Mr Stewart looked at Alison with a beaming smile and eyes full of admiration as if she had just discovered a cure for cancer and said, 'Absolutely right, as usual. How clever you are!'

Alison continued to have the same indifferent expression on her face; the sister looked disgusted, and the patient looked bemused by the sudden change in Mr Stewart's attitude. Samy just looked expressionlessly at Mr Stewart and remained silent. Mr Stewart asked Samy about the possible causes of this high blood pressure during pregnancy and the options for treatment, which Samy answered clearly and decisively in a cool and controlled way.

Mr Stewart seemed annoyed that Samy's answer was perfect, which deprived him of the chance to belittle him in front of Alison and everyone else. However, he did not give up, and for the rest of the morning, he continued to fire at Samy one question after another in the hope of detecting a defect in his knowledge, but in vain. Samy obviously knew his subject very well, and Mr Stewart failed to trap him.

Everyone noticed that while Mr Stewart complimented Alison for answering a simple question, he did not have a single word of encouragement for Samy, who had been answering perfectly one question after another. The two medical students did not care about any of this as long as Mr Stewart's attention was directed away from themselves.

At the end of these discussions and questions, Mr Stewart turned to Mrs McDonald and, with a warm smile, said, 'Thank you very much for allowing us to discuss your case with the students and trainees. This was very kind and very helpful. High blood pressure in pregnancy is very common, and, in most cases, it comes to no harm at all and is easily controlled. So, you and the baby will be fine.'

He then proceeded to explain to her that she would be kept in hospital for a few days for further investigations and monitoring. She would have some tablets to lower the blood pressure, and when it was settled, she could go home and continue to be monitored closely as an outpatient. Worst case scenario, if the blood pressure did not settle or there was any problem with the baby, labour would be started early.

****

The next patient to be seen on the ward round was a twenty-five-year-old patient who was pregnant with twins and was admitted with abdominal pain at twenty-eight weeks gestation. Mr Stewart asked Rachel to present the history, which she did hesitantly in a very shaky voice, pausing at the end of each sentence as if she was expecting to be interrupted by Mr Stewart, but he was listening silently for once. Could it be that her history was good enough for the forever critical and dissatisfied Mr Stewart? Could it be that he was unable to find anything to criticise?

When she finished, Mr Stewart stared at her with a disapproving look and said, 'This could have been a fairly reasonable history for once, but true to character, you just had to spoil it at the end; otherwise, it would not have you, would it?'

He then turned to the other medical student, Jack and asked him, 'What is missing here, Jack? There is a whole section missing from this history.'

Jack froze, and although his lips moved nervously, he did not utter any words. Mr Stewart shook his head in despair and then asked Samy, with a wicked look on his face, as if he was finally going to catch Samy and embarrass him in front of everyone, especially Alison, 'Come on then, Samy. You better tell these two students what was missing from the history.'

Samy calmly replied without any change in his indifferent facial expression, 'The history of the patient's previous pregnancies.'

This was the correct answer, but again, no compliments were coming Samy's way as Mr Stewart turned to Rachel and shouted, 'Yes, the details of her previous pregnancies, which is always very important in any case but is particularly interesting in this case.'

He then turned to the patient and said, 'You tell them, Miss Carter, about your other two pregnancies.'

The patient blushed and said in a very quiet and embarrassed voice, 'This is my third pregnancy in the last five years. The other two were also twins. This is my third twin pregnancy.'

Both students couldn't help but give a spontaneous loud gasp of amazement.

Mr Stewart Smiled at Miss Carter and said, 'Well, Miss Carter, I hope that you have a big enough house.'

She shook her head and replied, 'We live on the tenth floor in a two-bedroom flat in a high-rise block. We have been waiting for over two years for the council to sort out a house for us.'

She then sighed and added, 'But this is not my main problem at present. My biggest worry at the moment is my partner. He is almost suicidal at the thought of having six children under the age of five to bring up. It is not just a question of the financial cost, but also the social and personal burdens.'

Mr Stewart replied, 'I can fully understand how he might feel. However, we can certainly help with this situation. Sister Morrison will get the hospital's social worker to review your circumstances and liaise with the council about your housing situation. We can also make arrangements for some home help to support you and your family after you deliver this lot, at least for the first few weeks.'

He then looked at her intently and said, 'We will have to have a very serious talk about family planning and contraception after you deliver this time. You have a very strong family history of twins, and after having three sets of twins yourself, you will need to think very carefully about the future and how many more children you can really cope with.'

Miss Carter quickly said, 'Oh, no more. I want to be sterilised after this delivery.'

Mr Stewart replied emphatically, 'You are too young for that, and in ten or twelve years' time, after the children have grown up, you may feel you want another pregnancy, or your circumstances may change to make you want to have another pregnancy with a different partner. However, if sterilisation is what you choose after a cooling-off period, we can get this organised for you.'

'Trust me, I will never ever under any circumstances would want to get pregnant again, a different partner or not.'

The rest of the ward round continued in the same pattern, with dismissive humiliation of the medical students, discourteous exchanges between Mr Stewart and the sister and unwarranted compliments to Alison. Samy held his own very well, answering all the questions thrown at him without ever receiving a word of encouragement or appreciation, but this did not seem to bother him in any way.

****

Having finished seeing the pregnant women on the antenatal ward, it was then time to see the woman who had been having problems after her Caesarean section. Mr Stewart expected this to be a quick and simple review, but it turned out to be anything but.

Mr Stewart and the rest of his entourage followed the sister to a single room in the antenatal ward to see the patient who had been having problems after her Caesarean section.

The sister outlined the situation briefly before they went into the patient's room 'Mrs Olumati is an asylum seeker from Somalia whose baby's weight was estimated by scan at the thirty eighth week of her pregnancy to be over ten pounds. As this was her first baby, she was very concerned about obstructed labour and possible damage to her or to the baby, so she requested a planned Caesarean section. She declined to wait to see how spontaneous labour would go or to have labour induced early to avoid the baby putting on more weight. The operation was done three days ago, and she lost two pints of blood during the surgery. Following the operation, her temperature kept going up and down, and she has been getting a lot of abdominal pains intermittently. Her abdominal wound looks inflamed and is discharging blood-stained fluid. She was started on antibiotics yesterday, but there has been no improvement. Her temperature today is 40 degrees centigrade.'

As they entered the room, sister Morrison introduced Mr Stewart to the patient. He smiled at her and made some admiring comments about her beautiful baby, who was lying quietly in the cot next to her bed. The patient did not respond or react in any way. Mr Stewart proceeded to examine her abdomen. She was obviously a very large lady who weighed at least twenty stones. She seemed very tense and unhappy. Her bad mood worsened even more when Mr Stewart gently squeezed the Caesarean section incision, and a lot of pus and blood poured out. The patient screamed in pain and stared very angrily at him.

'I am very sorry, but I had to see if there is a collection of fluid under the skin, which is obviously the case. I think that you had significant bleeding in your tummy, and this had collected under the skin. On top of that, infection had set in, and this accumulation of blood has now turned into an abscess. This is why you have been having a fever and have been feeling so unwell.'

The patient responded to him angrily, 'You could have been gentler. This was very sore.'

Mr Stewart apologised once more and continued, 'This is one of the most common complications of Caesarean sections, and you will be fine in no time at all. We just need to add some more antibiotics to what you are already on, and we will get you scanned to check the wound area and the deeper layers of your tummy to have a clearer idea about the size of this collection of fluid and pus.'

He then turned to Alison and said, 'Please write her up for cefuroxime and metronidazole to be given into the vein for eight hours and arrange an urgent CT scan to assess the abdomen and pelvis. Also, contact the microbiology department to see if they have managed to identify from the wound swabs that they received two days ago the type of bacteria that had caused the infection and get their advice about any additional antibiotics we need to add.'

The patient asked through gritted teeth, 'What caused this blood and pus collection? Why did I have this abscess?'

'We do not always find a clear reason for this sort of problem, but the tummy becomes full of large blood vessels as a result of the pregnancy, and when a Caesarean section is done, one has to cut through these blood vessels to get to the womb which sometimes causes excessive bleeding. The infection is also common because the area we are working in is by nature not clean, and the little bits of membranes and placenta that are inevitably left behind in the womb also increase the risk of infection.'

The patient was clearly sceptical about the response she got from Mr Stewart, so she continued to quiz him in a loud and aggressive tone of voice. 'So you don't think the problem was caused by the negligent surgeon who did the operation. He looked very young, and I think he must have been very inexperienced.'

Mr Stewart glanced at the patient's notes to confirm who the surgeon was and responded in the same calm tone of voice, 'The surgeon was Mr Jeremy Bell, who is a very experienced obstetrician and he is thirty-five years old although he may look much younger. He is a senior registrar, the most senior trainee in the department and will become a consultant in the very near future. We never allow trainees to perform Caesarean sections or anything else unsupervised until we are certain that they are very competent and safe, so you were in very good hands. This sort of complication can happen to any surgeon irrespective of how old or how experienced he is.'

The patient shook her head disapprovingly as she said, 'You would say that, wouldn't you? You doctors always stick together.'

She then continued to express her dissatisfaction with the care she received 'The reason I had the section was that I was told the baby's weight was going to be over ten pounds according to the scan at thirty-eight weeks, but as you can see, the baby turned out to be under eight pounds in weight, so, I could have had a normal delivery and avoided all these complications.'

Mr Stewart again flicked through the notes to look at the scan reports and then said, 'The scan's estimation of weight is not always accurate, especially if the tummy of the woman is rather increased in thickness and this possibility of inaccurate estimation is documented in the scan report in your notes which states that the views of the baby were rather limited. The midwives and the doctors you saw during the pregnancy have also discussed with you the other option of just waiting for natural labour to start, whenever that was going to be and see what happens. You were also offered early induction of labour if you were concerned about the baby's weight. Your decision to have a section was not unreasonable, and the other two options could have also resulted in an emergency section for one reason or another, which could have been even more complicated than a planned Caesarean section.'

The patient's facial expressions clearly indicated that her anger and frustration were escalating at an alarming rate, especially after Mr Stewart referred to her as overweight, although he used a polite and indirect term to describe her obvious obesity, which could have been the major cause for the scan's inaccuracy and the complications of the operation.

Mr Stewart paused for a moment and said, 'Is there anything else on your mind that you would like to discuss?'

The patient shook her head and looked away without saying anything else, obviously still very dissatisfied.

Mr Stewart said as he was leaving the room, 'Have a good day, and I hope you feel better soon.'

Sister Morrison had a faint, wicked smile on her face as they left the room. She obviously enjoyed seeing her ex-husband treated with such aggression and disrespect by the patient. On the other hand, Samy was full of admiration for Mr Stewart's cool handling of such an angry patient. The medical students were absolutely amazed to see this powerful senior consultant mauled by the patient publicly in this way. Inwardly, they were very pleased that the patient talked to him in this aggressive way in front of everyone so that he could have a taste of his own medicine. Alison looked indifferent as she had seen Mr Stewart in action under different circumstances many times before, and she knew that he was perfectly capable of handling any difficult or aggressive patient. His professionalism and skills as a consultant were never in question; it was only his personal behaviour around her that was the problem.

As they left the postnatal ward to return to the sister's office, Mr Stewart said to Samy, 'Make sure that the CT scan is done right away to see if we need to take her back to the operating theatre to drain the abscess in her tummy under general anaesthetic. I can see this patient submitting a formal complaint or even suing the hospital for compensation, so be very careful.'

As they all walked down the corridor, Rachel, the medical student, whispered to her fellow student, 'I am surprised that Mr Stewart let her talk to him in this rude and disrespectful way.'

Jack whispered back, 'I know, it is very surprising. If it was me, I would have told her that all her problems were because she is such an obese fat lump!'

Alison, who was just ahead of the two, turned round and whispered to both of them, 'That would have been very unprofessional, Jack. You never make the patient feel guilty or blame her for the problems she has. There will be a suitable time later on to talk to her about her obesity and the risks this will pose in future pregnancies, but the time for this is certainly not now. She has enough problems on her plate at present.'

****

After the ward round had finished, they all sat down on the antenatal ward in the sister's office, where a tray with mugs of coffee and tea, as well as a selection of cakes, was waiting for them. Sister Morrison collected her mug of coffee and a piece of cake and left immediately as she obviously did not want to sit with her ex-husband. Before she could leave the room, Mr Stewart said to her, 'Sister Morrison, please get the Postnatal Depression Councillor to come and see Mrs. Olumati. Her behaviour in this aggressive and rather detached way indicates to me that she must have postnatal depression.'

Sister Morrison stopped to listen to what Mr Stewart said but did not turn to face him or acknowledge his request. She just left the office without saying anything. Mr Stewart shook his head and murmured to himself, 'Good riddance!'

He then looked at the two medical students, who chose to sit as far away from him as possible. 'Well, boys and girls, the lesson of this morning is that you should never react to angry patients, irrespective of how unreasonable they are. Maintain your cool, respond to their comments politely and professionally and never lose your temper. Most patients are in a lot of pain and distress, which may cloud their judgement and the way they see things, hence their erratic and sometimes aggressive behaviour.'

Mr Stewart then changed the subject and asked the students, 'Now that you are in the final year and will qualify in a few months, although you are nowhere near ready, what do you intend to specialise in after you qualify?'

The two students looked at each other, with each of them hoping that the other would be the one to answer first. As Mr Stewart was about to shout at both of them for the delay in answering his question, Jack rushed to say, 'I think I would like to train in psychiatry, sir. There are a lot of mental health problems nowadays, and I feel that I …'

He was interrupted by Mr Stewart shouting in an angry, dismissive voice, 'That figures. This is exactly what I would have expected from you. Psychiatry? Most of the so-called psychiatric conditions are fictitious, diagnosed in most unscientific ways, with no specific investigations or definitive treatments. All a psychiatrist does is talk, talk, talk and then prescribe some sedatives or antidepressants. They do not cure anybody, and their job can be done just as well by any good listener without any need for medical training. It will be a waste of your medical degree if you ever manage to get one.'

He then turned to Rachel and asked her in a cynical tone of voice, obviously not expecting a satisfactory answer, 'What about you, Rachel? What would you like to specialise in?'

With a shaky voice, Rachel said, 'I hope to train in obstetrics and gynaecology. This has been the speciality I enjoyed most in my training rotation, and I hope to make a career of it.'

If Rachel was hoping that this would endear her to Mr Stewart, she was very much mistaken. Mr Stewart laughed loudly and said, 'You? Having a career in obstetrics and gynaecology? Don't be ridiculous. You have not exactly shined in the time you have been with us. You should find something less demanding that suits your very limited abilities.'

Samy sat silently, feeling helpless and unable to interfere on behalf of these two poor students who had been mercilessly attacked by Mr Stewart all morning. He started to think about what he should say if Mr Stewart asked him about his plans for the future. He needn't have worried because Mr Stewart did not have any interest in him or his plans.

Alison, however, had heard enough abuse for one morning, although none of it came her way. She said sharply, 'I don't think that medical students can really decide on the speciality they will be doing for the rest of their lives until they have qualified and started working in the pre-registration year that follows because they can see by then how they got on with the various specialities in real practical terms.'

Mr Stewart was listening attentively to every word Alison was saying as she continued, 'And I must say, sir, that Rachel and Jack have been outstanding students during their attachment in our department. Not only have they been very helpful around the wards, clinics and operating theatres, but also during the out-of-hours shifts, which they attended frequently although they did not have to. Their standard of knowledge and clinical sense are way above most of their peers. Both of them are certainly far better medical students than I have ever been when I was at their stage.'

Samy and the students stared at Alison in horror at the way she talked back to Mr Stewart, but she obviously knew in advance that she would get away with it, and she was right.

Mr Stewart smiled warmly at Alison and replied softly, 'That is good to hear. I may be too tough with the medical students at times, but this is really for their benefit. I want them to develop a thick skin and learn to cope with criticism and pressure. You should have seen the way my generation was treated when we were medical students.'

The rest of the break was spent in general chats about the weather, planned holidays and sport, with Mr Stewart doing most of the talking and Alison contributing reluctantly every now and then. Samy and the two students remained completely silent throughout. All three of them were grateful for being ignored by this bully and hoped that this break would come to an end as soon as possible.

At exactly 10.00 am, Mr Stewart stood up, which indicated that the break was over. He told them that he needed to go and see his secretary before joining them again in the antenatal outpatient clinic as planned.

Chapter 4

A disaster that could have been prevented?

Once Mr Stewart left the antenatal ward, everyone in the team breathed a sigh of relief. This was a very stressful ward round for those who were at the receiving end of his abuse and bullying, as well as those who watched from afar. Alison was the first one to start the conversation, 'What a nasty piece of work he is. I think he was particularly cross today because of his encounter with his ex-wife, sister Morrison, and also because of the way Mrs Olumati, the postnatal patient, talked to him in front of us. Although he never shows it, he hates being criticized or disrespected publicly by anyone, least of all by a patient or by his ex-wife.'

The medical student Jack said, 'I think he is always like this. We have been attached to his team for four weeks now, and he never had a good word to say to us.'

Samy noticed that the other medical student, Rachel, had tears in her eyes. He tried to give her some support and stop her from bursting into tears, 'I really liked the way you tried to pacify him, Rachel, by telling him that you want to train in obstetrics and gynaecology. Clever girl!'

'It didn't work though, did it?' said Rachel while wiping her tears. She then put her arm around Alison's shoulder warmly and added, 'But Alison, the heroine, stood up for us. What a brave girl!'

Jack said quietly, 'I thought it was more suicidal than brave.'

Samy laughed loudly while Alison said nothing. She did not offer any explanation for the very different way she was being treated by Mr Stewart because everyone, except for Samy, knew about Mr Stewart's feelings for her.

Samy then said to the students, 'I know that Mr Stewart has been pretty tough on both of you today, but this is probably because he sets very high standards for his students. When I was a medical student, most of my teachers treated me in a way similar to Mr Stewart's. I actually found that their abuse did not hamper my ability to learn from them. Moreover, learning to cope with such teachers made me a stronger and more resilient person. Coping with aggression, abuse, and unjustified criticism is an integral part of a doctor's life, I think. However, this is more than counterbalanced by the very large number of compliments, thank you cards, and boxes of chocolate that one gets from grateful and appreciative patients.'

Alison added, 'Also, remember that you enjoy the support and encouragement of everyone else in this department, so just ignore him. He is an arrogant pig who is not worth bothering about.'

The two students laughed, but Samy looked displeased to hear Alison talking about a senior consultant in this way. He was not yet familiar with Alison's frank and rather blunt way of talking. She certainly had no problems saying it as she saw it, irrespective of who was on the receiving end of her opinions.

****

Samy and Alison left the antenatal ward to go and join Mr Stewart in the antenatal clinic, where they spent the rest of the morning. This was a very busy clinic with a lot more women to be seen than the time slots available, but the staff just got on with the tasks in hand as quickly as they possibly could. Many of the patients complained about the long delays in being seen, and all the staff could do was keep apologizing while the delays got longer and longer.

At the end of the clinic, Alison came to Samy's consulting room to accompany him back to the antenatal ward, as they were scheduled to join Mr Stout, the other consultant in the department, on his afternoon ward round. As they hurried to the antenatal ward, Alison laughed and said, 'You wouldn't believe what happened in the clinic today.'

'It must have been something really funny if you are laughing so much before you even talk about it.'

Alison's laughter escalated as she struggled to talk, laugh, and breathe all at the same time, 'I saw at the beginning of the clinic a Miss Waterman who is 39 weeks pregnant with her partner Paul Ferguson. Then, two hours later, near the end of the clinic, Mr Paul Ferguson turned up with another pregnant woman called Miss Butterworth, who was also 39 weeks pregnant. He was horrified to see me for the second time because, obviously, neither woman knew that he was two-timing her, so he was worried that I would expose him.'

Samy frowned and said, 'That is a real pickle for that man. What would he do if the two of them went into labour at the same time? And what will these poor women do when they find out about this situation?'

'He deserves to be in a pickle. I hope the two of them will castrate him when they find out. I really enjoyed toying with him. I prolonged the consultation as much as I could and kept giving him stern looks while his face got paler and paler. As soon as I finished, he rushed out of the room like a bullet without waiting for his partner.'

'For someone who looks so sweet and innocent, you obviously have a very large naughty streak.'

'You better believe it.'

Because the antenatal clinic finished late, there was no time for a lunch break for Alison, Samy or the two medical students. Mr Anthony Stout's ward round was scheduled to start as usual at 2 O'clock, and it was almost time. Fortunately, Mr Stout was late, so they all had time to gobble up some of the left-over cakes from the morning's break with Mr Stewart. The kind sister Morrison also got them some cold drinks from the ward's fridge. Sister Morrison looked a different woman from the one who went around the ward in the morning with Mr Stewart, her ex-husband. She looked happy, friendly and relaxed. She joked and chatted with Alison and the medical students. With Samy, though, she was rather reserved but with no obvious hostility or disrespect.

Mr Stout was fifteen minutes late, and as soon he entered the office, he apologized for that. He explained that his morning operating list finished late because there were too many cases on it, which was not uncommon. The sister offered him a cup of tea and some sandwiches as he had not had time for lunch. He thanked her but declined. Mr Stout was markedly overweight and of a short stature. He was approaching his mid-sixties but looked much older than that with his grey hair and very wrinkled, tired face.

Mr Stout made a point of welcoming Samy warmly as this was the first time they met, 'I hope you will be very happy with us, Samy. I know from your CV and your references that you're an experienced registrar, and hopefully, you will be able to build up on that with us here. You should have ample opportunity to train in the more complicated procedures and operations. You will also find that we are a closely knit and happy team, which is what enables us to cope with our massive workload.'

Alison let a sarcastic laugh and said, 'Yes, indeed. He had just had a ward round with Mr Stewart, which showed him how happy and closely knit team we are.'

The two students chuckled. Mr Stout gave Alison a stern look and said to Samy, 'Ah, that. Well, Mr Stewart's bark is much worse than his bite, and there is a lot you can learn from his clinical and surgical skills. You just have to get used to his way of conducting things.'

Samy said, 'I will do my best, sir, and thank you very much for your welcome. I am sure that I will learn a lot from two such eminent consultants.'

Obviously, Mr Stout was the complete opposite of Mr Stewart. He was kind, friendly and respectful of everyone. He treated the medical students as if they were colleagues rather than students, and they loved it. He was always encouraging and supportive, even when they gave the wrong answer to a question. The atmosphere around him was relaxed and friendly, which meant that all those who worked with him always looked forward to his sessions.

Sister Morrison led the group around the antenatal ward to review the patients who were admitted under Mr Stout's care. The two students were competing with each other to present the histories of the patients to Mr Stout. He discussed the cases with them in a stimulating and pleasant way, never criticizing or insulting them. From time to time, he would involve Alison and Samy in the discussion, asking their opinions and encouraging them to think outside the box and consider the unexpected. He also made sure that he asked sister Morrison for her opinion, what she thought about his management plan for each patient and whether there was anything else she would like to add. It was very important for him to make sure that the midwives were treated as equal partners to doctors, and he certainly always showed that in all his dealings with them.

It took them two hours to go around all the patients they needed to see, and no one in Mr Stout's entourage bothered about the time or was in a hurry to finish. They all then retired to the sister's office, where a fresh tray of tea, coffee and cakes was waiting for them. On the tray, there was also a plate of sandwiches, which was ordered by sister Morrison for Mr Stout, as he had missed his lunch.

'Thank you very much, sister Morrison. You are a lifesaver. Nowadays, I don't cope terribly well without lunch. I think I am getting too old for that.' said Mr Stout, and they all laughed.

He then asked Samy about his training and his future plans. Samy replied, 'I am not sure about the long-term plan, sir, as my circumstances are rather complicated. However, the priority in the next two years is sitting the final part of the examination for the membership of the Royal College of Obstetricians and Gynaecologists in London while gaining as much clinical and surgical experience in the field as I can.'

Mr Stout said as he turned his attention to the two medical students, 'I am sure you two budding doctors will do very well, whatever you decide to do after you qualify. Have you had any thoughts about which speciality you would like to train in after you qualify?'

The two students looked at each other, and then Rachel said with a sad expression on her face, 'According to Mr Stewart this morning, we should both look for a different profession altogether.'

Mr Stout cringed, paused for a moment and then said, 'I am sure he didn't mean that. You have both done very well, and the feedback about you from everyone is excellent. Mr Stewart can sometimes sound very harsh with the students because he believes that this will motivate them further.'

He took a deep breath and looked as if he was trying to convince himself that what he was saying about Mr Stewart was true, 'Remember that in every type of medical practice, doctors are not infrequently subjected to complaints, criticism, insults and even physical aggression. So, if you manage to survive Mr Stewart's sessions, you will be able to cope with anything that comes your way in your future medical career.'

The students smiled, and Alison winked at them encouragingly. They all felt that Mr Stout had managed to repair the damage to their morale that was inflicted on them by Mr Stewart.

✳✳✳✳✳✳✳✳✳✳✳✳✳✳✳✳✳✳✳✳✳✳✳✳

Mr Stout left to go to the private hospital in central London to see a patient he had operated on the previous day, while Samy and Alison remained in the antenatal ward to look for the result of the CT scan that they had arranged for Mrs Olumati, whom they saw with Mr Stewart in the morning with an abdominal abscess after her Caesarean section. They were both pleased to see that the scan showed that there was no evidence of a deep abscess or internal bleeding inside the pelvis. There was only a small amount of fluid and pus collecting superficially under the skin. They went to see Mrs Olumati to tell her about the result while wondering what sort of reception they would get from her, having seen how angry and aggressive she was with Mr Stewart.

Samy introduced himself and Alison again to Mrs Olumati and said, 'I am very pleased to tell you that the CT scan showed that there is nothing to worry about. There is only a small, insignificant collection of fluid under the skin, which is obviously draining freely and should hopefully settle down completely with the antibiotics over the next few days. There is no sign of any problems deep in the tummy or the pelvis, which means that there will be no need for any surgical intervention or going back to the operating theatre.'

The patient looked at them blankly and then looked away without saying anything. Samy waited for a reaction of any kind from her, but nothing was forthcoming. He looked at Alison, who was starting to get angry with the patient and was unable to offer any suggestion that would help get the patient out of this black mood.

Samy asked 'Is there anything that you want to ask? Is there anything you need?'

The patient continued to stare into space with her head turned away from Samy and remained silent.

'We will leave you to rest, Mrs Olumati, and we will come to see you again tomorrow, but meanwhile, if you have any problem or need anything at all, let your midwife know straight away, and we will come back to see you.'

Samy went to the sister's office on the ward and asked if he could speak to the midwife looking after Olumati, and when she came, he said to her, 'You need to keep a very close watch on Mrs Olumati. As Mr Stewart said earlier this morning, she may be brewing severe postnatal depression.'

The midwife nodded in agreement and said, 'I thought she might. I think she has a lot on her plate, over and above the Caesarean section and its complications. Since she came in, she had no visitors at all, which suggests that there is no husband or family of any kind to support her. Also, she seems to have a serious problem with the Home Office about her immigration status. Apparently, she is here illegally, and thus, she does not have the right to free NHS treatment. For this reason, the hospital administrators came to see her yesterday to inform her that she would be charged for her antenatal care and delivery. I believe the figure they mentioned to her was seven thousand pounds.'

Samy raised his eyebrows in amazement at the sum of money demanded from this woman while Alison became more understanding and sympathetic to her.

Alison said, 'No wonder that she thinks that we're all just a bunch of heartless bastards. Her operation is messed up, and we then demand from her seven thousand pounds, following which we plan to throw her out of the country.'

Samy paused for a moment and then said, 'The main thing now is her well-being and recovery. I will inform Mr Stewart about all these circumstances to seek his advice, but meanwhile, please check that the sister has contacted the Postnatal Depression Councillor to see her as a matter of urgency. We must all watch her very carefully because the risk of her harming herself or the baby is very high. As you know, suicide as a result of postnatal depression is the commonest reason for death of women after having a baby.'

The midwife replied with a despondent expression on her face, 'The one and only postnatal depression counsellor will not be able to see her till next week. She has too many cases on her list, and she is the only counsellor available. The other councillor is on long-term sick leave with stress and depression.'

Samy frowned, but Alison couldn't help but laugh at the irony of the midwife's last statement. The depression councillor is off sick with depression.

Samy phoned Mr Stewart with the information about Mrs Olumati's circumstances and was surprised at his reaction. He was obviously angry with sister Morrison for not warning him about all these issues that the patient had over and above her Caesarean section problems. His anger was also partly directed at the patient for taking her difficulties out on him and for being so discourteous and impolite. Finally, he was angry with Samy for disturbing him with this information when there was nothing he could do about it.

'I am very sorry about disturbing you, sir, but I thought you might be able to put in a word on her behalf with the hospital's administrators and the Home Office to give her a breathing space until she gets better and…'

Mr Stewart's anger escalated as he shouted down the phone, 'I have no influence whatsoever in these matters. It is a government policy, and I happen to support it. People like her should not have been here in the first place. The NHS and the country as a whole cannot cope with this influx of illegal immigrants, but they just keep coming expecting to have the same rights to everything the British citizens have. She was not even grateful or appreciative of all that we provided for her and her baby.'

He then slammed the phone down without waiting for a response.

****

Mr Stewart, sister Morrison, Samy, Alison and the rest of the staff of the maternity team spent the next morning giving statements to the police who descended on St Luke's hospital in large numbers because, in the early hours of the morning, Mrs Olumati jumped off the roof of the hospital, holding her baby in her arms. They both died instantly.

The death of Mrs Olumati and her baby had a huge impact on all the staff of St Luke's Hospital, even those who had nothing to do with the maternity department. It was hardest, though, for the midwives and doctors who were directly involved with her care. Their deep sadness was mixed with feelings of guilt and helplessness. The one exception to this was Mr Stewart, the consultant, who was in overall charge of Mrs Olumati's care, although he met her only once on the day before she committed suicide. If he was upset about what had happened to her, he did not show it. He certainly felt sorry for the baby, but as far as Mrs Olumati herself, he thought that she had only got herself to blame.

This tragedy and its aftermath hung over St Luke's Hospital for several weeks because the incident had to be thoroughly investigated by so many agencies. There was the police investigation, the coroner's, the hospital's own internal investigation and the confidential enquiry of the Health Quality Improvement Partnership (HQPIP). They all asked the staff the same questions time and again, which increased their stress and wasted a lot of everyone's time. It would have been far better and more efficient to have just one agency investigating all the issues thoroughly from the legal, medical, social and administrative points of view, but in the NHS, any process must be burdened with complex and mostly unnecessary bureaucracy, form filling, repetitive reports, and very long meetings.

The media, in general, as was the case almost always, lost interest in Mrs. Olumati's death very quickly, especially as the victims were illegal immigrants. Some commentators blamed the hospital's administration for staff shortages and lack of mental health support, some blamed the politicians who allowed illegal immigration to get out of control and for overseeing an inadequate health service, and some blamed the patient herself, who should not have been in England illegally and should not have got herself pregnant in her difficult circumstances.

As usual in these situations, the hospital's managers expressed deep sorrow and promised to learn lessons from this tragedy, but very quickly, they forgot all about it and went about their business as if nothing had happened. No lessons were learnt, and no changes of any kind were made.

****

At the beginning of the week, all the trainees and the two medical students managed for once to get to lunch together in the hospital's canteen. The atmosphere was rather subdued because of Mrs Olumati's death, with Samy and Alison being the most upset as they were the ones who were most closely involved with her just before she died.

Jeremy, who performed the Caesarean section for Mrs Olumati, did his best to show that he was back to his normal jovial self, but in fact, he was utterly devastated. They were all eating slowly and silently, so Jeremy tried to lighten up the atmosphere a little. He leaned over towards Rachel, the medical student, who was sitting next to him and said, 'Rachel, these vegetables on your plate look as if they have been eaten before a couple of times.'

Rachel stared at her obviously over-cooked mixture of vegetables with a disgusted expression on her face but then couldn't help laughing as she said, 'Yes, they do, don't they?'

Alison shouted at Jeremy, 'Don't be so disgusting, Jeremy. We are all trying to ignore the state of this awful meal.'

Mohammad Khan, the other registrar, said while chewing a mouth full of food, 'Do not be so ungrateful, you lot. At least it is hot and cheap.'

To him, the cost of anything was of paramount importance. He had a wife who did not work and two small children. Trying to make ends meet on a registrar's salary was a daily struggle, and for this reason, he was always grateful to have a hot meal for a couple of pounds, irrespective of the quality.

Jeremy replied, 'Cheap? They should be paying us to eat this garbage.'

Samy was silently moving the food on his plate around with his fork without eating any. He was obviously thinking deeply without paying much attention to what was going on around him.

It was inevitable that the tragic death of Mrs Olumati and her baby would be brought into the conversation at some point, and it was the medical student, Jack, who opened the subject.

'I wonder what Mr Stewart will say now about psychiatry. Mrs Olumati died because of a psychiatric condition, postnatal depression. Will he now believe that psychiatry and mental health are as important as any other branch of medicine?'

Unusually, Alison, who was never the one to defend Mr Stewart, promptly responded, 'I do not think that he is as dismissive of psychiatry as he sounded the other day. Remember that although he saw Mrs Olumati only once and only for a brief period, he made the correct diagnosis of postnatal depression and tried to get the relevant help for her.'

'A lot of good this did her! He made the correct diagnosis of postnatal depression, but nothing was done in time to save her.' said Rachel with a shaky voice as if she was about to cry.

Jeremy winked at Jack, the other medical student, and said, 'So, hurry up, Jack and become a psychiatrist so that you can sort this mess out.'

Mohammad Khan, who was never known for his tact, suddenly asked Jeremy, 'How do you feel yourself about all this, Jeremy? After all, you did her Caesarean section. Do you feel guilty?'

Alison looked angrily at Mohammad and said, 'This is a very unfair question, Mohammad. Why should he feel guilty? The decision about the operation was made by the patient herself after being counselled in detail by several doctors and midwives over a long period of time. The complications that she had after the operation are common in the best and most experienced hands. She did not die from the complications of the operation; she died from postnatal depression. In all probabilities, if she did not commit suicide, she would have recovered fully from all her Caesarean section complications.'

Jeremy smiled at Alison in gratitude and said, 'I feel awful for Mrs Olumati and particularly for the baby, but I do not feel guilty. I looked back very carefully at my involvement with her, and there is nothing I could have done differently during the operation that would have made any difference to the outcome in this case.'

Alison said, bringing this discussion to an end, 'I think the main culprits here are the system's inadequacy and the awful circumstances of Mrs Olumati. Well, enough of this. We all need to go to our afternoon activities.'

The first to leave the cantine were the two medical students, Rachel and Jack. As they approached the canteen's exit, they held hands, and Rachel leaned with her head on Jack's shoulder.

The forever observant Jeremy Bell said as he saw this intimate interaction between Rachel and Jack, 'Oh, I didn't know that these two were an item.'

Mohammad Khan replied, 'Indeed they are. They are childhood sweethearts. I understand that they grew up together from early childhood as their families were neighbours and close friends. They went to the same schools and joined the same clubs and activities. They have always been inseparable all their lives.'

Jeremy nodded as he said, 'This explains why Rachel failed to succumb to my charm and sex appeal.'

Alison said as they all stood up to leave, 'You really are hopeless, Jeremy. You believe that all women must find you totally irresistible and just submit to your every whim and desire. What you need is a certain operation to help you control your urges.'

Jeremy put his arm around her shoulders and said, 'Can you do this operation for me, darling? Please, please, please!'

Alison pushed him away as they all burst out laughing, except Samy, who was still deeply immersed in his own thoughts. Since Mrs Olumati's suicide, he had not been able to stop thinking about what had happened, why it happened and whether he could have personally done something to prevent her suicide. For him, it was a tragic and totally unnecessary loss of two lives that should have been avoided.

As they walked back to the labour ward, Alison said to Samy, 'I see that Mrs Olumati's death has affected you a lot, Samy, which I can fully understand. However, there was nothing you or I could have done to change things.'

'This is what I am not so sure about. Unfortunately, I am no stranger to women dying during or after pregnancy, having worked for some time in the remote parts of upper Egypt where healthcare provisions are very sparse. Over there, a maternal death or two every few weeks is not unusual because of poverty, chronic diseases, lack of healthcare facilities and backward social traditions. But here, in England, one of the richest and most advanced countries in the world, what is the excuse?'

Alison searched in vain for something helpful to say in response, but as she could not find anything meaningful or relevant to say, she just remained silent.

****

That day, Samy was on-call for the overnight shift in the labour ward. Maria Nichos was the SHO (senior house officer) who was on-call with him, and Sister Smith was in charge of the labour ward overnight. Sister Smith was the one organizing the duty rota for the midwives, and she made sure that her shifts in the labour ward corresponded with Samy's as much as possible. At every opportunity, she tried to talk to him, charm him and try to find a way to his heart. She also made sure that he was made aware of her physical attributes, mostly in subtle ways but sometimes blatantly. When she talked to him, she always stood very close to him, and whenever she could, she brushed her body against his as if by accident. When she sat opposite him, she crossed her legs and let her uniform ride up her thighs to give him a bird's-eye view of her sexy legs. Samy seemed to be very slow on the uptake, but she was determined to persevere until he was well and truly trapped in her net.

It was a quiet start for the labour ward shift. Samy and sister Smith were sitting on their own in the labour ward office. Sister Smith started the conversation, 'This feels like the calm before the storm. It is never that quiet for long around here.'

Samy smiled and replied, 'I am ready, willing and able. Bring it on.'

Sister Smith decided to steer the conversation towards intimate matters before anyone came into the office, 'Now, Samy, confession time. It is the hospital's policy that the registrar on-call must tell the sister in charge of the labour ward all about his love life. I want to know all about your past history, your love affairs and all your deep-seated dark secrets.'

Samy laughed and said dismissively, 'I would be delighted to tell you everything about the history of my love life, but sadly, I do not have one, so there is nothing to confess.'

'Come on, Samy, you can confide in me. I am the best agony aunt in London.'

Samy laughed again, even louder this time, and replied, 'Trust me, I am the saddest case an agony aunt would ever come across. I will be thirty years old in a few weeks and have never been in love or even just come close to falling in love. I seem to have spent my whole life thus far trying to just survive and work on my education and training, so I never had time or energy for relationships. Moreover, wherever I have been, women seemed to ignore me, and I can't say that I blame them.'

Obviously, Samy was less than honest with sister Smith because he was certainly falling deeply in love with Alison, but he was trying his hardest not to admit this to himself, let alone to anyone else. Coming to England to complete his training was a once-in-a-lifetime opportunity for him to come out of his miserable and deprived existence to a bright and successful future, so he could not afford to have anything that might force him to deviate from his one and only goal. Moreover, he always thought to himself that at this stage in his life, he had nothing to offer any woman.

Sister Smith's eyes widened in disbelief, 'I find this very hard to believe, and I can assure you that the women in this hospital are certainly not ignoring you; quite the reverse. You should hear what the girls here say about you behind your back.'

Samy started to feel uncomfortable about where this conversation was going and was about to try to change the subject, but Sister Smith was like a dog with a bone, determined not to let go, 'Do you mean to tell me that all the time in the medical school in Egypt, none of the Egyptian girls chased you around the campus? What about the nurses and midwives in the hospitals you worked in over there and those in Manchester?'

'There was never an opportunity for any chasing from my end or theirs. I was too busy with my work, studies and training most of the day every day. Any spare time I had, and at the weekends, I worked as an assistant at a local pharmacy or a general dog's body at a grocery store to earn a bit of extra cash to help with my expenses as my only income was the excellence grant that the government was paying me every month because of the high scores and the distinctions that I achieved in my exams every year. I never had any time to socialize or make any close friends, let alone have a girlfriend. In my current circumstances, I have absolutely nothing to offer any girl.'

Samy then got up to put an end to this conversation and said, 'I better go and see what Maria is up to. Thanks for the coffee.'

Sister Smith sat quietly on her own, thinking deeply about what she had just heard from Samy. She was amazed that someone as attractive, intelligent and sweet as he was had never fallen in love or had a girlfriend. She had a wicked smile on her face as she thought to herself that it sounded as if he was a virgin, both physically and emotionally. Well, he was in the perfect place to have this put right. She was going to ensure that he would fall in love with her and also lose his virginity, not necessarily in that order.

Chapter 5
Something good out of something really bad

It was a Monday morning when Jeremy Bell, the senior registrar, entered the antenatal ward's office, where the midwife in charge was waiting for him. He sat on one of the chairs, obviously out of breath and said, 'What is the matter? You sounded very worried on the phone.'

The midwife replied, looking and sounding very worried indeed, 'I am very concerned that there is going to be a riot on the ward if something is not done about the delayed inductions of labour. We have fourteen women waiting for their labours to be induced, and the list is growing all the time. Some of these women have been waiting on the ward for four or five days, but the labour ward has not been able to take any of them because they have been very busy with so many women in spontaneous labour and also with a constant flow of emergencies. When there are rooms available on the labour ward, there are no available midwives to look after the women because of staff shortages.'

Jeremy replied impatiently, with a hint of anger in his voice, 'You brought me running from the other end of the hospital because some women are having to wait a bit for their labours to be started off? If there are no vacant delivery rooms in the labour ward or there is a shortage of midwives, then people will just have to wait. There is nothing we can do about it, and they have to understand that.'

'Would you like to go and say that to these women and their partners? Myself and my colleagues are now becoming rather worried that we may end up being at the receiving end of a violent reaction from a frustrated, angry patient or her equally frustrated and angry partner.'

Jeremy replied sharply, 'Why haven't you informed one of the managers, the consultant on-call or the midwifery matron to come and sort this out? This is a management job for them and not for me.'

The midwife replied as she started to get angry herself, 'They all said that they are tied up and cannot come. Mr Stewart, the consultant on-call today, is in the operating theatre and cannot come. He also said that if midwifery staffing shortages are the cause for the problem, then the midwifery matron or one of the midwifery managers should come and sort it out because this is their business and not his.'

Jeremy was about to say something in support of his boss's statement when the midwife added, 'All the senior midwifery managers, including the matron, are in a regional managers' meeting in central London. They will be there all day, and of course, all their mobile phones are switched off for the duration. This problem cannot wait until the matron becomes available; maybe tonight, maybe tomorrow, who knows. You are the next senior doctor after the consultants, so I thought that you were the only one who could help.'

The midwife's statement that she considered him to be the next in command after the consultants appealed to Jeremy's vanity, and he mellowed straight away, especially as he started noticing how pretty this midwife was.

'Alright then, I will sort this out just for you. Let me first go to talk to sister Smith on the labour ward to see what the situation is there, and I will then come back to talk to your angry women and their partners.'

He then winked at her as he added, 'But there will be a fee to pay for this service, and you will have to pay it in full.'

The midwife's demeanour also changed to a more agreeable and appreciative one. She clearly did not mind Jeremy's flirting because she had always admired him from afar. She smiled and replied, 'You are a star. I knew that you would save the day. I will be happy to pay any 'reasonable' fee; just hurry back before one of us gets punched or kicked by someone from this angry mob.'

Jeremy went to the labour ward and instantly sensed that it was full to overflow, with harassed-looking staff rushing from one room to another and no one having time to talk to him. One midwife was rushing with a trolley full of delivery instruments into one of the rooms, while another was running towards a different room with bags of blood which were to be transfused to a bleeding patient. Two midwives were pushing a bed on which a distressed patient in labour was being taken to the operating theatre. Sister Smith was shouting down the phone to get some of the midwives from the antenatal and postnatal wards to come and help in the labour ward. As soon as she finished talking on the phone, she ran into one of the rooms to help deliver one of the women, totally ignoring Jeremy.

One look at the activity board in the labour ward's office confirmed to Jeremy that the labour ward was utterly and totally full, with all the rooms occupied by patients who were either in active labour or having an emergency of one kind or another. He also noticed from the board that some of the midwives were looking after two or three women, which should never happen in any labour ward where one-to-one care is supposed to be mandatory.

Jeremy murmured to himself, 'Oh, dear! There is no room at the inn.'

The registrar on-call for the labour ward, Mohammad Khan, came out of one of the delivery rooms, looking hot and sweaty, with his scrubs heavily soaked in blood and other fluids of unknown origins.

Jeremy asked him, trying to sound friendly and kind, 'Is everything alright, Mohammad?'

'Only just.' Replied Mohammad as he passed Jeremy quickly and rushed into another delivery room, obviously to see to another urgent case.

Jeremy kept looking around for anyone to inform him about the overall situation in the labour ward and when it was likely for any of the patients on the antenatal ward waiting for induction of labour to be able to come to the labour ward. He knew the answer, but he was keen to have it confirmed.

Sister Smith finally appeared out of one of the delivery rooms, pushing a trolley on which various blood-stained instruments and a placenta were spread. She had obviously just delivered a baby in that room, and Jeremy followed her to the sluice room, which is the special room where contaminated instruments were washed.

He said in a joyful voice, trying in vain to cheer her up, 'Melanie, sweetheart. How is it going?' and he put his arm around her shoulder as she was clearing the trolly.

Sister Smith gave him a fierce stare as she said through gritted teeth, 'Not today, Jeremy, unless you want to have a freshly delivered placenta shoved up your …'

Before she completed the sentence, he quickly removed his arm from her shoulder and moved a step back. He knew from past experiences with sister Smith when to beat a hasty retreat.

'Sorry, darling. It is obviously one of those days on the labour ward.' Jeremy said in a soft, sympathetic voice.

'It has been like this all week. There are too many babies to deliver and not enough midwives to look after them. Today, I have each trained midwife looking after two and sometimes three women at the same time. Two patients are being monitored by student midwives on their own without any supervision or support, which is not good for the women or for the students.'

Jeremy quickly explained to sister Smith the reason for his visit as she continued to clear the trolley. She listened to him until he finished painting a picture of the antenatal ward with its angry women and worried midwives because of the delayed inductions of labour.

Sister Smith did not say anything for a few moments, trying to contain her feeling of utter rage and was about to explode in Jeremy's face. However, she knew that he was just trying to help, and it was not fair to take her stress and anger out on him.

She took a deep breath, tried really hard to control her anger and frustration, and replied decisively, 'To be honest, Jeremy, I do not give a damn about the antenatal ward and its problems as I have more than enough to cope with here. I neither have a free delivery room nor a spare midwife to take any inductions of labour, and I do not anticipate that the situation will change this shift.'

'But I see that you delivered one woman, and Mohammad has delivered another. Doesn't this mean that two rooms will be available soon once you move these two women to the postnatal ward and …'

Sister Smith turned round to face Jeremy with a stare like daggers from her beautiful eyes, 'You should know by now that after a delivery, we have to wash and change the woman, following which the room has to be thoroughly cleaned. Then we have to enter all the details of the delivery on the computer, which must be done immediately after the delivery. All this usually takes at least an hour and a half per patient.'

Jeremy asked innocently, 'On a very busy day like this, can't we leave the paperwork and computers for later and get on with the deliveries? I think that …'

This time, Jeremy knew that he had pushed his luck too far as sister Smith exploded in his face, 'Say that to the managers and the idiots who run the maternity services. They know how short-staffed we are, and yet they keep piling on us mandatory data collection, endless online form filling, details of times and motions, the list is endless. All these details are of no value whatsoever, and nobody looks at them or benefits from them except those managers who have too much time on their hands, which they use to produce coloured charts, graphs and tables to look at in their endless meetings. Entering these details into the system immediately after delivery is a non-negotiable rule, according to our bosses. Now get out of my face if you want to live.'

Jeremy bowed and said as he almost ran out of the room, 'Yes, your majesty.'

Jeremy went back to the labour ward office, where Mohammad Khan, the registrar, was sitting at the desk, entering on the computer the details of the forceps delivery, which he had just done. He looked flustered and tired. Jeremy sat opposite the desk, watching Mohammad as he typed furiously while looking at the computer screen, totally ignoring Jeremy's presence. Jeremy did not want to interrupt him, but he was hoping to get some more information from him before he returned to the antenatal ward. He thought that asking about how he was coping would be a good opener.

'What a crazy day, Mohammad! How are you getting on? Are there any outstanding problems that still need sorting out?'

Mohammad did not respond, obviously too immersed in what he was entering on the computer. Eventually, he said, 'Sorry, Jeremy, what did you say?'

Jeremy repeated the question. Mohammad said, still typing as he responded, 'This is the third forceps delivery I have done this shift. Earlier on, I had taken one patient to the operating theatre because her placenta was stuck, and I had to remove it by hand under anaesthetic, following which I had to take two other women who delivered but tore badly and needed to have stitches inserted in theatre.'

Mohammad then took a deep breath and added, 'At the moment, they are getting a patient ready in the operating theatre for a Caesarean section, which is my next port of call. Over and above all this, I do not know anything about the women in rooms 5, 9 and 10 as I did not have time to review them.'

Jeremy got up and left, returning a few minutes later with a cup of coffee and some biscuits for Mohammad, who thanked him profusely.

Jeremy asked, 'Can I help at all? Is there anything I can do to ease the pressure? I was just doing the ward rounds on the gynaecology wards and the antenatal ward, so I can leave that for later on and come to help if you need me.'

Mohammad shook his head in the negative and said, 'There is a plan in place for everyone in active labour at present, and I assume that the three women I have not seen do not have any urgent problems; otherwise, sister Smith would have told me. So, we are okay at the moment, but if we get stuck, I may have to take you up on your kind offer.'

As Jeremy got up to go back to the antenatal ward, Mohammad said with a resigned smile on his face, 'It is on days like this that I wonder why I am training to be an obstetrician. What was wrong with dermatology, sorting out skin problems only? I would have been sitting in a comfortable clinic looking at zits all day and prescribing some creams or pills. The pay would have been the same.'

Jeremy laughed and said, 'I also have these feelings every now and then, but we both know that however hard some shifts are, it is only obstetrics for us. We love it in spite of everything. We are that mad.'

****

Jeremy returned to the antenatal ward empty-handed. He could not see what he could say to the women and their partners to alleviate their distress, anger and frustration. This was one of the many very busy spells on the labour ward, which could last for many days with emergencies piling up and staff shortages totally disrupting planned work, such as inductions of labour or planned Caesarean sections. More importantly for Jeremy was the concern that he would have to disappoint this pretty midwife who believed that he would be able to sort the problems on the antenatal ward.

As soon as the midwife in charge of the antenatal ward, Patricia, saw him, she hurried towards him with a hopeful look on her face. Had he returned with good news about spaces on the labour ward for at least some of the inductions of labour? Had he thought of a solution for this backlog that no one else had considered before?

All her hopes were quickly dashed as soon as he explained to her the situation in the labour ward. Jeremy then said, 'I think it is time to think outside the box. There are so many maternity units in and around London. We should ring around and see if any of them have a spare capacity to take some of our inductions. I am sure that the patients will be happy to travel further in order to get on with their inductions rather than wait indefinitely for a space on the labour ward here.'

He thought for a moment and then added, 'If we find another unit that is willing to help us, I will then need to get the permission of Mr Stewart to go ahead with this. Neither he nor the hospital's management will be pleased with this solution because it will give the impression that our unit is not coping with its workload, and also, the hospital will lose the money we get paid for delivering each of these women, but I do not care. If anyone else can find a different solution, then good luck to them.'

Both Jeremy and the midwife in charge spent over an hour ringing all the maternity units in and around London to see if they could take any of these women, but to no avail. The units that had available delivery rooms did not have enough midwives, and those with enough midwives were full to capacity with labouring women and emergencies. They were all in the same boat as St Luke's.

When they finished phoning, they both looked at each other silently for a few moments and then Jeremy said, 'Well, that is that for London, but we haven't tried the Shetland Islands yet.'

They both burst out laughing in despair. Jeremy then, with a serious look on his face, said, 'Let us go and face the music. Don't worry, I will do all the talking.'

Jeremy stood in the part of the common corridor of the antenatal ward where the rooms of the women waiting for induction of labour were and called loudly, 'Ladies and gentlemen, may I have your attention, please.'

He then waited for a short while as the women and their partners came out of the different rooms and stood around him. Jeremy moved back to leave more space for others to come closer but also to get away from a rather large and aggressive-looking partner standing with his wife at the front of the group.

'My name is Jeremy Bell. I am the senior registrar in this unit. I am very sorry about the delay in starting your inductions of labour, and I fully understand how stressful this must be for all of you, but for the last few days, the number of emergencies and urgent cases that have flooded the unit has been unprecedented. All the staff are working flat out to create spaces on the labour, and as soon as we possibly can, we will get on with your inductions. I have just returned from the labour ward, and it is unlikely that any inductions will be possible during the day today, but the situation may change during the night. We have phoned all the maternity units in and around London to see if any of them can take some of our inductions, but unfortunately, they are all in the same situation as we are.'

Jeremy then paused for a moment, trying to gauge from the facial expressions of his audience how they felt about what he had just said. He then took a deep breath and continued, 'I do not see any need for keeping you locked up in the hospital when we know that nothing is going to happen for a good while. So, I suggest that you all go home, and we will ring you to come back when a room becomes available for you in the labour ward. You will all be prioritized according to the reason for your induction and how urgent it is.'

An angry voice of a partner standing at the back interrupted, 'What is this rubbish? I have taken a week off work for this induction and the delivery of the baby, and four days of the week have been utterly wasted waiting for you to get on with it.'

Another woman shouted, 'I have left my two little children at home now for so many days, which is upsetting them a lot, and for what? I have been stuck on this awful ward, and every day, I am told it may be later on today.'

Before Jeremy could respond, one of the partners said, 'It is not fair on the staff to be blamed for these delays. It is the lack of staff and physical space in the labour ward that is the problem. They can only work with what little they have. We should be appreciative of their efforts and show more understanding of the circumstances because I am sure that this situation is as difficult and frustrating for them as it is for us.'

Only a few of the women and their partners nodded in agreement; some shook their heads in anger and frustration, and the rest just stared at Jeremy expressionlessly. One of the partners obviously had aggressive intentions towards Jeremy and went for him, but two of the other partners restrained him and dragged him away.

They all dispersed and went back to their rooms, while Jeremy went back to the office on the antenatal ward, with Patricia, the midwife in charge, following. Her facial expression spoke volumes of her admiration and gratitude, which was, of course, duly noted by Jeremy.

As soon as they sat down in the office, Jeremy said sarcastically, 'That went well. I better leave the hospital tonight through the back door in case some of these partners are waiting for me in the car park.'

The midwife said with a warm smile, 'You were magnificent. I do not know how I would have coped with this lot on my own.'

Jeremy laughed and said, 'Before any of them goes home, make sure that they all know that I have a black belt in karate, and I always carry a loaded gun in my briefcase.'

'Wow! I always thought that you looked the dangerous type, but a loaded gun?'

Jeremy was delighted to see that she was obviously flirting with him as much as he was flirting with her, so his efforts to keep the peace on the ward were not wasted after all. He felt confident that he would be getting his well-deserved reward from this beautiful midwife, but there was some work to be done first.

Jeremy said to Patricia with a serious tone of voice this time, 'Let us review the case notes of all these inductions to make sure that there is nothing really urgent about any of them. They must all have the baby's heartbeat monitored before they go home and also as soon as they come back to the ward.'

Jeremy and Patricia spent another hour checking the case notes and were pleased to see that all the inductions of labour in this group of women were not for urgent reasons. When they finished reviewing all the notes, Jeremy sank into his chair and sighed, 'All done at last. They can all go home until further notice, but they must come to have the baby's heartbeat monitored every day until they have their inductions.'

Jeremy was delighted to see that Patricia had been warming up to him more and more, so he felt confident that he would be able to cash in on the investment of time and effort he had made. Patricia was not a midwife that he had noticed before, but after this encounter with her, he was determined to add her to his long list of passionate affairs.

As he stood up to leave, Patricia said, 'Thank you very much, Mr Bell. You are my hero.'

'Oh, please call me Jeremy, Patricia.'

He then paused, looked at her expectantly and said, 'Now you have to pay my fee for the services rendered. Can I take you out to dinner tonight?'

She blushed and nodded, accepting his invitation, and they arranged to meet up in West Hampstead in the evening.

True to form, Jeremy first took the midwife to his favourite Italian restaurant in West Hampstead, where they had a nice romantic meal with wine flowing freely. He then took her back to his fashionable flat in St John's Wood 'for coffee'. Of course, drinking coffee was the last thing on their minds because as soon as they got into the flat, they dived into each other's arms and started kissing passionately. They did not waste much time on foreplay as they were both desperate to make love to each other. Besides, they were both too tired after a long, hard day at work and too drunk to want to waste whatever was left of their energy on foreplay.

The two of them lost count of how many times they made love throughout the night. They would fall asleep for a while, and then the one who woke up first would provoke a new episode of sexual intercourse. It was as if they were both going for the record of how many times a couple can make love in one night.

In the morning, as Patricia was about to leave, Jeremy kissed her passionately and said, 'I would love to see you again, Pamela.'

She stared at him, obviously disappointed and said, 'It is Patricia, Jeremy. My name is Patricia and not Pamela.'

Jeremy quickly said with a big smile, 'Of course I know your name, Pat. I was just joking.'

He wasn't really joking, but she chose to believe him.

This was the start of a tumultuous affair which neither Jeremy nor Patricia were going to forget in a hurry!

Chapter 6

A life changing experience

Samy and Alison were sitting in the hospital's canteen having lunch on their own. Alison had not seen Samy for a few days because the duty rota sent them to different places or they were on-call on different nights. She was delighted to see that he was as happy to see her as much as she was to see him. In the short period of time they had known each other, their feelings for each other were developing at the speed of light. As much as their duty rota allowed, they both spent their breaks during the working day together and big chunks of their time off, too. In spite of the huge gulf that separated them financially, socially and culturally, Samy and Alison were falling in love faster than either of them could have ever imagined.

They often went after work for walks on Hampstead Heath, which was a beautiful setting for their growing romance to thrive, away from the prying eyes of their colleagues at the hospital. The more time they spent together, the more overwhelming their love for each other became.

Samy was very different from anyone Alison had gone out with before. He had a very strong personality but, at the same was also down-to-earth, sensitive and kind. He was self-assured and confident but without any hint of arrogance.

He treated everyone with care and respect, always endeavouring to be helpful to all, irrespective of the time or the effort required. He was not ashamed of his poor background or the difficult life he had and always spoke about them openly. All these personal qualities, combined with his exotic good looks and his sexy athletic body, made him irresistible to Alison and to many others.

Samy's attitude to falling in love with Alison was more complicated because he could not ignore the huge differences between them. However, he could not help but fall in love with her totally, madly and deeply, as his heart succumbed to her despite all his mind's objections. Her exceptional beauty, her obvious intelligence, irresistible charm, her effervescent warm personality and her wicked sense of humour eradicated all his defences. Although his mind kept telling him that they were totally unsuitable for each other and he did not stand a chance with her, his heart felt the complete opposite.

As Samy and Alison sat next to each other on a bench in the rose garden of Hampstead Heath, Alison started the conversation, 'So, what have you been up to today, Samy? You seem rather pensive and thinking deeply about something.'

'I spent the morning in the antenatal clinic.' Samy said and then paused for a moment before adding, 'One of the cases I saw in the clinic today bothered me a lot, and I did not really know what could be done for the best to help her.'

Alison looked very interested as she looked at him intently and said, 'Oh, tell me more, tell me more.'

'She was a thirteen-year-old girl who was thirty weeks pregnant. It was impossible to communicate with her in any shape or form. She seemed to be totally detached from the reality of her situation. Her mother was with her today, and she seemed far too busy being angry with her to be able to offer her any understanding or support …'

Alison interrupted, 'Is the girl's name Brenda Hutchinson?'

Samy looked very surprised and asked, 'Yes, it is. Do you know her?'

'Everyone knows Brenda because she has such a complicated history. Her mother, who, by the way, is only thirty years old, is very cross with her not only because she got pregnant at such a young age but also because her stepfather is the one who got her pregnant. Have you ever come across such a messy situation?'

'This is why I am so upset. Brenda reminded me of a girl of almost the same age in Egypt who was pregnant by an unknown man as she always refused to reveal who he was. The big difference is that the Egyptian one was murdered by her much older brothers to cleanse the 'family's honour'. Although I half expected this to happen to her, I was not able to do anything to save her. The police did not take me seriously when I warned them about her possible murder, and the social services could not care less. They all thought that she was a piece of worthless trash and did not deserve any help from anyone.'

'How dreadful! At least here, no one gets killed for getting pregnant at any age. Sex is free for all. It is in our constitution.'

Samy sighed and said, 'This is really sad. Sex is supposed to be the most special way for a man and a woman to express their absolute love and total commitment to each other. If one really loves another person, he or she would give the loved one the most precious thing one has: one's own body. This gift should only be given to the life-long partner. Sex should never be a casual pastime.'

Alison laughed sarcastically and said, 'You don't really believe that Samy, do you? Sex can certainly be very special if one is deeply in love, but it can also be done just for the physical enjoyment of it and not necessarily for eternal love. It can be great fun even if there wasn't any emotional involvement.'

Samy frowned and looked at Alison disapprovingly, 'I do not agree. Sex is supposed to be 'making love', which means that love must be present before sex is contemplated.'

'Come on, Samy. Have you never had sex without being in love?'

Alison's question shocked Samy not just because it was so personal but also because it suggested that Alison herself had had previous sexual experiences, which she was happy to declare so openly and without hesitation. He did not know how to respond for a few moments and then said hesitantly, 'I have never had sex because I have never been in love. I know that I neither had the opportunity to fall in love nor for having sex, but this has nothing to do with me being a virgin. It is a matter of principle and religion.'

Now, it was Alison's turn to be shocked. She put her hand on her cheek in amazement as she whispered, 'Samy, you are still a virgin?'

Samy blushed and looked around to make sure that no one could hear this rather intimate conversation. He then whispered, 'What is so strange about this?'

Alison saw that she had embarrassed him, so she quickly said, 'Nothing strange at all. It is just very unusual these days when boys and girls start experimenting with sex and relationships from their early teens or even before.'

It was clear that Samy was getting very uncomfortable talking about this subject, so it was time for Alison to change the topic of conversation. However, now that she knew that Samy held such views about relationships and sex, she was determined to get him to change his mind. Poor Samy now had two women after his 'virginity', sister Smith and Alison.

Alison said, completely changing the subject, 'Are you ready for the teaching sessions tomorrow?'

Samy looked relieved to get off the subject of sex and relationships as he asked Alison, 'Oh yes, I meant to ask you about this. What does this day of 'mandatory teaching' entail? What are we expected to do? Do we need to prepare anything?'

Alison laughed loudly and replied, 'Nothing to prepare and nothing to do. It is a 'day off' really. The whole day is spent attending what they call the 'mandatory courses' which all doctors, midwives and nurses must attend annually, supposedly to make us all better informed and up to date. Sadly, as you will see for yourself tomorrow, none of us learn anything of use from these stupid courses.'

'Surely, one might learn a few things that can be useful. These courses cannot all be useless.'

'You will soon find out.'

****

The next morning, Samy and Alison went into the lecture theatre in the education centre at the back of the hospital. Before Samy could go in, Alison grabbed his arm and said, 'Wait a minute. We have to sign the attendance register first; otherwise, we will not get the lovely attendance certificate. This is what it is all about, the attendance certificate. Also, you must remember to sign the register at the end of the day to prove that you have been a good boy and have attended the whole day. What you do between these two signatures is your own business.'

They both queued to sign the register and then went into the lecture theatre. This large hall was already almost two-thirds full, with a mixture of all types of health professionals of various degrees of training and seniority.

Samy and Alison went to sit in one of the middle rows of seats where most of the maternity staff were sitting. Sister Smith got up from her seat at the far end of the row and asked the midwife sitting next to Samy if she could swap seats with her as she wanted to talk to Samy about a patient. Obviously, she did not really have anything to discuss with Samy, but this was her way to get to sit next to him.

Jeremy was sitting next to the new woman in his life, Patricia, in the row behind Samy and Alison. From time to time, his hand would brush against her knee or her arm, and she, in turn, reciprocated. Neither seemed to care that a lot of the staff sitting around them could see what they were doing.

Mohammad Khan, the other registrar, rested his head on his hand and fell asleep, snoring loudly. Alison, who was sitting between him and Samy, elbowed him in the ribs to wake him up as his snoring annoyed her. She then said to the startled Mohammad, 'If you are going to sleep, sleep quietly; otherwise, your snoring will keep waking me up.'

Mohammad rubbed his eyes and said, 'Very sorry, Alison, but last night, my bloody kids kept me awake all night. I do not know which is worse: a night with my annoying kids or a busy night on the labour ward.'

Alison softened and touched his hand sympathetically and said, 'Alright then, I forgive you. You can go back to sleep, but if you start snoring again, I will keep waking you up and remember that our bosses, who are sitting in the back row, should not see you sleeping during this stimulating educational meeting.'

Mohammad mumbled as he closed his eyes again, 'Do not worry about the bosses because I know that they will be more deeply asleep than me.'

Samy, who was sitting between Alison and sister Smith, found it difficult to cope with the two of them at the same time because they were both vying for his attention, talking to him simultaneously about various subjects, which put him in an awkward position because he did not know who to respond to first. Unfortunately for Samy and Alison, neither of them noticed that they were being closely watched from the back of the lecture hall by an increasingly angry consultant, Mr Stewart. His obsession with Alison meant that he disliked immensely seeing any man getting close to her in any shape or form.

Samy noticed that all the consultants from the different departments chose to sit at the very back of the lecture theatre, and this impressed him because he thought that they were leaving the front seats for the younger trainees who needed this teaching more than themselves, but Alison quickly shattered his illusions.

'This has nothing to do with being considerate to the trainees. Notice how they all have with them their laptops, mobile phones and briefcases full of paperwork. They are here to go on the internet, read and respond to e-mails and do paperwork while pretending to listen to these bloody lectures. This sort of teaching day is as utterly useless to them as it is for us, but it is mandatory, so they have to attend because the hospital administration, the general medical council and the Royal Colleges of the different specialities decreed that they must attend to refresh their memories and update themselves. It is just a box they have to tick.'

At nine O'clock, the first speaker entered the lecture theatre and started his lecture about audit and clinical governance, which took a whole hour. The second lecture was about confidentiality and online security of health records, and the third was about protecting vulnerable adults. It was noticeable that at the end of each lecture, there were no questions from the audience to the lecturers. It seemed that all the attendees were just keen to get to the coffee break which followed these three lectures.

During the break, Samy, Jeremy, Mohammad, Maria and Alison were standing outside the lecture hall drinking their coffee and tea. Mohammad said, 'This was the best sleep I had for such a long time. I wish they would make us attend more of these mandatory teaching days.'

Samy said, 'I must say that I found that the value of these three lectures was very limited. The facts they presented were rather too basic, and I am sure that any health professional of any kind would not need to be reminded that keeping accurate records of what we do is important, the confidentiality of the patients is paramount, and one should not abuse vulnerable adults.'

Jeremy put his arm on Samy's shoulder and said, 'If you thought that this morning's lectures were useless, wait until you see the rest because they are even worse.'

He then added sarcastically, 'But to rub salt into the wound, over and above today's rubbish, we have to do another lot of online courses, which are all mandatory as well. If you do not do them on time, you will get warnings and threats from management, who will threaten you with disciplinary action if you persist in ignoring these courses.'

Jeremy left the group to go and talk to Patricia as he wanted to fix with her a date for another session of good food followed by a night of mad, passionate sex.

****

After the tea break, there were lectures about safeguarding children, fire safety, management of waiting lists for operations, the financial situation of the hospital and the need to cut costs of treatments. The number of people dozing off in the various parts of the lecture hall steadily increased as the day progressed. Alison started to fall asleep as well, and her head tilted to one side until it rested on Samy's shoulder, so he gently touched her hand to wake her up. She whispered an apology and sat up straight. This little interaction between them ignited Mr Stewart's jealousy and anger even more. He had not been doing any paperwork, nor was he listening to the lectures, as his gaze was totally transfixed on Samy and Alison all the time.

Another angry person in the lecture theatre was sister Smith, who felt that Samy was paying more attention to Alison than to her. She started to think of more effective ways of drawing Samy to her, fair or unfair.

During the lunch break which followed this second group of lectures, all the trainees sat together at a large table in the Canteen and were joined by sister Smith and some of the midwives. Sister Smith, who again made sure that she was sitting next to Samy, said to him, 'Well, Samy, what is your impression so far about these lectures? Have they changed your life? Do you feel as if they made you a better doctor?'

Samy smiled and replied quietly, 'I don't know about any life-changing experiences today, but I think they are trying to pitch the lectures at a level that suites all the very different groups of health professionals, with all their different roles, different educational needs and different stages of training. Of course, this is just impossible. How can a lecture be suitable for a junior trainee who has just qualified from the medical school and at the same time be suitable for someone like the consultants, Mr Stewart or Mr Stout, with all their vast knowledge and expertise?'

Mohammad Khan said with a wicked smile on his face, 'You just have to make the most of the day in your own way. These mandatory teaching days are just wonderful rest days.'

Alison laughed and said, 'Oh yes, you certainly made the most of it, Mohammad, catching up on your sleep.'

Alison got up to go to the toilet, and all the others were busy talking amongst themselves, which gave sister Smith a chance to talk to Samy without interference or interruption from anyone else.

Sister Smith said to him, 'Are you any good at DIY?'

Samy was puzzled and did not seem to understand why she was asking such a question, so he replied hesitantly, 'I don't know about being 'good' at DIY, but I can do some carpentry, basic electrical work and decoration. I learnt all this from my uncle when I used to work with him in his convenience store. We had to fix everything ourselves to save cost.'

Melanie quickly said, fully aware that this was a rare and very brief opportunity to have all his attention to herself, 'This is exactly what I need: some elementary carpentry. I have bought a wardrobe online which needs to be put together, and I am afraid I made a mess of it. Can you come to my flat and help me? I am sorry to ask you to do this, but I am desperate.'

'Of course, sister Smith, I will be delighted.'

'Wonderful. Thank you very much. I will certainly make it worthwhile to you.' said sister Smith while trying to stop herself from jumping for joy.

When she managed to get her overwhelming elation under control, she said, 'Would this Saturday's lunchtime be convenient for you? I checked the rota, and you are not working this weekend.'

Samy thought for a moment and said, 'This will be fine. You can give me the address later on.'

'I certainly will. I will cook a nice lunch for you. It is the least I could do.'

The rest of the day continued in the same way. Boring and irrelevant lectures, with the audience keeping themselves busy by talking to each other, texting and reading e-mails on their mobile phones, or just dozing off. The one obvious difference which was noticeable in the afternoon session was the fact that the number of attendees dropped significantly, as many of them did not bother to return from their lunch break. However, half an hour before the day ended, they all returned to the lecture hall so that they could sign the register again to confirm that they attended the whole day.

****

The whole group from the maternity unit left the lecture theatre together at the end of the meeting and queued to sign the exit register so that they could receive the all-important 'attendance certificate' later on.

Mohammad Khan, the registrar, said, 'I feel so refreshed after all this sleep. Thank you 'mandatory courses'. May you increase in number and duration.'

Jeremy gave him a serious look and said, 'I hate to spoil the enjoyment you had from such a good sleep, but you need to know that Mr Stewart has noticed that you slept throughout the whole day, and I am sure that you will be hearing from him tomorrow.'

Mohammad looked horrified to hear that, but before he could ask for more details, Alison said, 'Stop being wicked, Jeremy. Do not worry, Mohammad; he is just making this up. Mr Stewart disappeared after the morning session and only returned as the meeting was coming to an end to sign the register. Even if he did see you sleeping, it would not have bothered him in the slightest because he knows better than anyone how useless these mandatory courses are.'

Jeremy then turned round to pick on Samy. Unbeknown to sister Smith and Samy, Jeremy had heard them arranging the wardrobe-fixing date, so it was time for him to tease Samy about it. He tapped him on the shoulder and whispered softly in his ear, making sure that Alison, who was walking next to Samy, heard what he was saying, 'Samy, I also have a wardrobe that needs fixing. Could you please come to my place to fix it for me after you finish helping sister Smith with her wardrobe? I promise to cook a lovely dinner for you.'

Samy blushed as he knew straightaway what Jeremy was alluding to. Alison frowned and looked puzzled, not understanding fully what Jeremy was on about, but hearing that Samy was going to be helping sister Smith alarmed her.

Jeremy then added, 'What I want to know, you crafty devil, is how you managed to fix a date with the gorgeous sister Smith at her place so quickly. What is your secret? Is it your after-shave? Is it your exotic foreign accent, or maybe your natural tan?'

Samy looked embarrassed and blushed even more as he said, 'This is not a date. She asked me to help her fix a wardrobe that she bought online, and that is all there is to it.'

Jeremy laughed loudly and said, 'You fool! I bet this wardrobe is in the bedroom.'

Samy's embarrassment increased, and he started getting angry with Jeremy, 'Stop talking rubbish, Jeremy. This is not funny. I am just being helpful to a colleague and no more. I am sure that she looks at this in the same way that I do.'

Alison asked sharply with a very angry frown, 'You are going to sister Smith's home to fix a wardrobe for her?'

Samy was startled by Alison's obviously furious reaction, and he replied hesitantly, 'Yes. Is this a problem?'

Alison shook her head and said, 'No problem at all. Of course, you are free to do whatever you want.'

This response from Alison provoked a mixture of concern and surprise in Samy's mind. He was sorry to have obviously upset her, but at the same time, he was also pleased to see that she was jealous and angry about his visit to sister Smith. Could he dare to believe that a girl as wonderful and unique as Alison had fallen for someone like him? They both stared at each other in silence, and their eyes spoke the truth. They were well and truly falling in love with each other, but neither of them was ready to admit it.

Jeremy, who was observing their interaction, frowned as their silence spoke louder and clearer than any words. He said, 'Hello, you two. I am still here. Enough staring at each other. Snap out of it.'

The two turned round to face Jeremy, and Alison said, 'Sorry, Jeremy. I just don't think that Samy knows what sister Smith is really like.'

Jeremy laughed and said, 'He may enjoy finding out. It could be fun.'

Samy became very annoyed with Jeremy, and he replied angrily, 'I really do not understand what the problem is. Sister Smith is a colleague whom I respect and admire. She has been very kind and very helpful to me since I started working here, so offering her some help with this wardrobe is the sort of thing I will be happy to do for her as much I would be for any friend or colleague, even for you, Jeremy.'

Jeremy, who was one of the many in the department who noticed how Alison was keen on Samy, looked very serious as he said to Samy, 'Are you really that sweet and innocent, or are you just pretending? Sister Smith is planning to eat you alive, you stupid boy. Unless you are really keen to be devoured by this man-eater, I suggest you run for cover and do not go anywhere near her flat.'

'You are talking nonsense. There is absolutely no chance whatsoever of anything happening during this wardrobe-fixing expedition from my side or hers. Credit me and sister Smith with some common sense and maturity.'

'Alright then. But do not come crying to me the next day.'

With that, Jeremy left, leaving Samy and Alison walking slowly in the car park towards the main building of the hospital.

Samy hesitantly asked Alison, 'Why are you so upset about me going to sister Smith's place?'

Alison stared at him with her beautiful eyes, and his heart started beating faster. She said nothing, but she grabbed his hand and led him to where her car was parked. Without saying a single word, she threw her arms around him and held him in a tight embrace. Once Samy got over his initial shock, he responded by embracing her just as tightly. They held on to each other for what felt like an eternity, with neither of them wanting to let go of the other. Eventually, the embrace turned into a passionate kiss that lasted for a long time. This was what Samy dreamt about for a long time and what Alison wanted to do for an even longer time. This kiss told them both what they were not able to say to each other in words.

✷✷✷✷✷✷✷✷✷✷✷✷✷✷✷✷✷✷✷✷

Samy and Alison went from the hospital to Hampstead Heath. Although this was the first time they declared their love to each other, neither felt the need to say much. They were just happy to be so close to each other, holding hands and walking around the rose garden. With Alison sitting next to him on one of the benches, Samy felt that he was on top of the world. At that special moment, he wanted nothing else, and nothing else mattered to him. All his reservations and inhibitions were nowhere to be seen. His heart had finally defeated his mind as he surrendered completely to the power of love. From that day onwards, his life would never be the same again. This was the real life-changing experience that happened on that momentous day.

Alison also experienced feelings that she never knew existed. She always thought that she had been in love several times before, but none of these past episodes came close to how she felt for Samy. In just a few weeks, he seemed to have got into her heart and her mind, totally possessing them. She realised that this was the first time she had fallen in love for real.

Samy eventually started the conversation, 'I cannot believe what has just happened today.'

Alison smiled reassuringly and said, 'I can very much believe it. This is what I wanted to do for a long time, but I was not sure whether you felt the same or not.'

Samy raised his eyebrows and said, 'I had very good reasons for holding back. Not in a million years would I have believed that the most fantastic girl I have ever met, a gorgeous princess through and through, would have bothered with a peasant from Egypt, let alone kiss and embrace him.'

'You are no more a peasant than I am a princess. I did not plan to fall in love with you, but it just happened from the first day you appeared in the labour ward. I could not control my feelings for you, neither did I want to.'

Alison rested her head on his chest while he had one arm around her shoulder, and they both closed their eyes. They wanted this closeness to last forever, but the park's guard had other ideas. He shouted from a distance, 'Hello there. It is time for you two to go home because it is well past the park's closing time.'

They were both startled by the guard's shout and amazed at how late it was. As they walked past the guard, Alison smiled at him, and Samy apologized politely. Still holding hands, they both walked back to the hospital's car park, which was very quiet at that time of the evening. When they reached Alison's car, another long embrace and a passionate kiss followed.

Alison said, 'I think I need to say it first. I…'

Samy quickly put his index finger on her lips to stop her from completing the sentence and said, 'No. It is I who needs to say it first. I love you very much, more than you will ever know.'

Alison embraced him again and said, 'And I love you too, very very very very much, more than I have ever thought I could love anyone or anything.'

Samy opened the car door to her, but before she got in, she asked, 'Are you really going to sister Smith's place to fix her wardrobe? I am really worried about what she has in mind for you.'

Samy frowned and said, 'I think you are not being fair to her. I believe that she genuinely just wanted some help with her wardrobe. She obviously trusts me and knows that I will never take advantage of her.'

Alison shook her head and said, 'It is her who will try to take advantage of you. I will not argue with you about this because, after all, you are a free agent.'

'After this evening, I am anything but a free agent. If this is how you feel about sister Smith's wardrobe, I do not want to go. It is just a question of how to let her down without offending her, but never mind, I will think of something.'

Alison smiled happily and kissed him again, a long lingering kiss. She drove off, and Samy stood there, watching her car until it disappeared from view. He walked slowly towards his room in the Doctors' residence, deep in thought. He murmured to himself, 'Did all this really happen today, or was I just dreaming?'

For the second time that day, unbeknown to Samy and Alison, a furious Mr Stewart, mad with jealousy, witnessed clear evidence of the intimacy that was developing between Samy and Alison. He was sitting in his car in a dark area of the car park, taking a call on his mobile phone and had a bird's eye view of all these kisses and embraces. His utter obsession with Alison stopped him from having any hostile feelings towards her, but for Samy, he now had nothing but seething hatred and a crazed desire for revenge. Not only did Samy manage to steal Alison from him, but he also managed to achieve that in record time. Samy would have to pay a massive price for daring to snatch the love or 'the lust' of his life from his clutches. He had to erase him completely from the scene professionally, personally and, if necessary, physically. Alison was his and his alone, and he was determined to make sure of that one way or another.

Chapter 7

Battling for a lost cause

Samy phoned Mr Stewart at home just before midnight to discuss with him a case in the labour ward because it was a complicated one.

'I am sorry to disturb you, Mr Stewart, but I need your advice. I have just admitted a thirty-five years old woman in her first pregnancy. She is twenty-five weeks pregnant, and her water has broken. The neck of the womb is 3 centimetres dilated, with one of the baby's legs protruding through the neck of the womb into the vagina. The water that she is draining is rather smelly, and the blood test showed raised inflammatory markers, suggesting a degree of infection in the womb. I scanned her, and this confirmed that the baby was coming as a breech. The baby's measurements are consistent with a weight of just above a pound. The baby's heartbeat is regular at 140 beats per minute. The patient does not seem to be in active labour at the moment.'

Samy paused for breath and then continued, 'I have given her the first dose of the steroid injection to help the baby's lungs in case she is delivered soon and started her on intravenous antibiotics. My question is: what will be the definitive management plan? Delivery because of the infection that may kill the baby in the womb or try to treat the infection and wait with the aim of prolonging the pregnancy to give the baby a chance to grow a bit more? Also, if she is to be delivered, will that be a vaginal breech delivery, or should we do a Caesarean section which is less traumatic for the baby, although the baby might not do well anyhow?'

'What did the neonatal team say to her about the baby's prospects?' asked Mr Stewart, sounding very sleepy.

'They were rather neutral in their assessment and, after a lot of ifs and buts, they concluded that if the baby is delivered soon, the outcome will be very unpredictable, but everything is possible. The baby could survive intact and be completely normal, survive and have a mild disability, survive with severe cerebral palsy and brain damage, or the baby may die. It was all rather vague and confusing for the parents.'

Mr Stewart sounded as if he was getting out of bed as he said, 'The usual rubbish from the neonatologists. The baby is extremely premature, infected, and presenting as breech, which means a traumatic delivery even if we did a Caesarean section. These circumstances mean that this baby is almost certainly doomed. I will come to discuss the options with her myself. At the end of the day, she will be the one to make the final decision as she will be the one who will live with the result of such a decision for the rest of her life.'

Mr Stewart then put the phone down without saying goodbye or waiting for Samy to respond.

Samy was waiting for Mr Stewart in the labour ward's office. Mr Stewart arrived within half an hour of Samy's phone call. He was obviously in a very bad mood because of having to come to the hospital at such a late hour. As soon as he entered the office and without greeting any of those present, he asked where the patient's case notes were. Samy handed him the notes, and Mr Stewart flicked through them and looked closely at what Samy had written about her current history.

'Which room is she in?' asked Mr Stewart impatiently.

Samy answered, 'Room seven, sir.'

'I will see her on my own with her midwife. These situations are best discussed privately.'

'Of course, Mr Stewart. Can I make you a cup of tea or coffee for afterwards?' asked the midwife in charge of the labour ward that night.

Mr Stewart said as he turned to go to the patient's room, 'No, I need to go back to bed as soon as possible because I have a very busy long day tomorrow.'

As he walked in the corridor towards room seven, he mumbled to himself, 'These bloody cases only come after midnight. Why do they never happen during the day?'

Mr Stewart introduced himself to the patient and her partner. He then said, as he was looking at her observation chart, which was hung at the bottom of her bed, 'What are your thoughts on what should be done, Miss Stapleton? I understand that my registrar and the baby's specialist discussed with you the various options. We can just wait and do nothing to see what happens, allowing labour to start naturally whenever this is. Alternatively, we can get you delivered because of the infection by induction of labour or by a Caesarean section.

Looking at your observation chart, your temperature has been rising steadily in the last two hours, and this, together with your blood tests and the foul smell of the fluid that you are draining from the womb, indicates that you are developing a significant infection in the cavity of the womb in spite of the antibiotics that you have been given. This can be very dangerous for you and for the baby if the infection takes hold. So, this suggests that delivery is really what is indicated in this situation, and the only question we need to consider is whether we should induce labour to deliver you vaginally or do a Caesarean section.'

The patient and her partner looked at each other with their tears flowing freely. It was a little while before the partner replied, 'We would like to do what is best for the baby. This is our absolute priority.'

Mr Stewart looked at them sympathetically and said, 'I can fully understand that, but Miss Stapleton's safety and her prospects in future pregnancies must also be taken into consideration as well. If you ask me what will be the mode of delivery that will give the baby the best chance of survival, then I will have to say that it is a Caesarean section as the baby is presenting as breech and not as head-first, which means that delivery through the vagina could be extremely traumatic, especially at this very premature stage. However, Caesarean section at 25 weeks of pregnancy could be very difficult to do and will carry increased risks of haemorrhage or damage to the womb. This could compromise Miss Stapleton's prospects in future pregnancies for a baby that is unlikely to do well.'

Miss Stapleton looked very frightened as she asked with a touch of anger in her voice, 'But why will a C-section be a problem for me? A lot of my friends had their babies that way without any problem.'

Mr Stewart responded calmly, 'You are absolutely right. Caesarean sections are very commonly done, and, in most cases, there are no complications or difficulties. As a matter of fact, one out of every three babies in England is born by Caesarean section.

The difference in your case is that you are only twenty-five weeks pregnant, which means that your womb is still very small, so when we do the section, we will have to open the womb in its upper part and not in the lower part of the womb because the lower part of the womb at this stage is too narrow. The risk of haemorrhaging from the upper part of the womb is much higher and may not heal up as well as the lower part of the womb. Also, in future pregnancies, the risk of the C. section scar in the womb bursting open is much higher if the womb was opened in a previous pregnancy in the upper rather than in the lower part of the womb. So, you see, C-section at 25 weeks is very different from C-section at full term.'

He then quickly added, 'I must say, though, that whatever you decide, the prospects for this baby are very poor. The combination of extreme prematurity and infection is a very serious one, and the chances of a good outcome are very slim indeed, especially as the baby is presenting as breech, which means that such a vulnerable baby will have a complicated and traumatic delivery.'

The patient turned to her partner, who put his arms around her, and they both hugged each other as they burst into uncontrollable fits of crying. Mr Stewart stood there silently, not wanting to interrupt the outpouring of their emotions. After a few minutes, he said, 'Would you like me to leave you for a little while to talk about this on your own, following which we can discuss the situation further?'

Miss Stapleton disengaged herself from her partner's arms, wiped her tears, and said, 'I am sorry, sir, but you sound far more pessimistic about the baby and the operation than your registrar and the baby's doctor. You sound as if you want us to write off this baby.'

Mr Stewart responded calmly without the slightest hint of annoyance or anger, 'Not at all. The baby is still alive, and the heartbeat has been stable throughout, but infection is now taking hold which makes a very big difference to the baby's chances. The colleagues that you saw earlier did not see the last temperature reading which is now over 39 degrees despite the antibiotics. The baby will still have a chance of surviving the delivery, but in what condition and what sort of handicap he or she may have are totally unpredictable.

The odds of a good outcome are small, which means that we will be putting you through a difficult and complicated major operation for a baby whose chances of a normal life, or even just a life of any kind, are very limited. I am sorry to be so blunt. You need to know the facts about this very stressful and complicated situation so that your decision is based on a clear understanding of how things really are. We will certainly do what you want, but you must think very carefully about all the factors involved. We will do the Caesarean section for you if this is what you want, but I suggest that you take time to discuss this with your partner on your own, and I will then come back to see what you wish to do.'

Mr Stewart walked out calmly with the midwife following. He said to her while shaking his head, 'The odds are certainly stacked against this poor baby. It is very hard for them to come to a decision, but I am afraid we cannot decide for them. They have to make up their own minds about this and quickly because the longer the baby is left in an infected womb, the worse the outcome.'

He then sighed and said, 'I must say though that Caesarean section in this case will be madness. She can end up having serious complications and permanently ruin her prospects of a successful pregnancy in the future for a baby that is very unlikely even just to survive.'

Mr Stewart returned to the labour ward office where Samy and Maria, who was the Senior house officer on-call with Samy, were waiting. He sat at the desk and started writing in the patient's notes the main points of discussion with the couple. While he was writing and without looking at Samy, he said to him, 'You really messed this one up, Samy.'

Samy looked very upset at hearing this statement from Mr Stewart and asked anxiously, 'I am very sorry to hear that, sir, but why is that? What did I do wrong?'

Mr Stewart continued writing in the patient's notes. He ignored Samy's question for a few minutes. Then he said, 'You seemed to have given the patient very unrealistic expectations about this baby's prospects when, in fact, the situation is almost totally hopeless. Thanks to your inadequate counselling, the couple is likely to ask for a Caesarean section. The baby is likely to die as a result of the lethal combination of infection, extreme prematurity, and a traumatic delivery, even if it is delivered by C-section. Even if it survives the delivery, it is likely to be severely damaged with cerebral palsy, blindness, deafness, etc.'

As Samy was about to respond, Mr Stewart continued, 'Even if none of these complications was obvious in the early stages of life, this poor couple would have to watch this child for the next fourteen or fifteen years to see if he or she will have developmental, educational or behavioural problems, over and above the physical handicaps. Does any of this justify putting such a young woman through an upper-segment Caesarean section with all the possible complications that may ruin her chances of a successful pregnancy in the future?'

Samy could not take all this without a response. However, before he could say anything, Maria interfered in a loud and obviously angry voice, 'I do not know what this woman said to you, sir, but Samy was not positive at all about this pregnancy, and if you look at his entry in the patient's notes when he admitted her you will find that he had actually listed for her all the complications that you have just mentioned and more. The problem, I think, came from the neonatologist's team because although they talked to some extent about the complications and the possible poor prospects for the baby, their main emphasis was on the procedures and the treatments they would be giving the baby when it is born. They were the ones who gave her false hopes because they kept talking in generalities rather than explaining to her what was specifically relevant to her own situation.'

Mr Stewart was taken aback by Maria's unexpected intervention on Samy's behalf, but he could not help but smile as he said, 'Well, Samy, I handed it to you. Whatever happens to you, there is always a charming young lady ready to come to your rescue. One day, you will have to tell me what your secret is.'

Maria and the midwives in the room laughed, but Samy looked coldly at Mr Stewart without saying anything.

Miss Stapleton's partner knocked at the door of the labour ward office and said, 'Excuse me, sir, my partner would like to have a word with you on your own.'

Mr Stewart got up to go back to room seven and was surprised to see that the partner did not follow him but carried on walking towards the exit of the labour ward.

Mr Stewart called after him. 'Aren't you coming with me? In this situation, your input will be as important as hers.'

The man turned round and looked at Mr Stewart with a very sad and exhausted face. He replied in a soft and shaky voice, 'She doesn't want me in the room when she talks to you, and I must say that this has come as a great relief to me. I really want to leave the final decision entirely up to her because I don't know what to do for the best. Of course, I want everything done to give the baby the best chance, but not if this means exposing her to serious surgical risks. She is the one who will go through with whatever procedure, so it is only fair that she should be the one to decide.'

He looked intently at Mr Stewart and asked hesitantly, 'This is really feeble, isn't it? You must think that I am just an indecisive, unsupportive wimp.'

Mr Stewart looked at him warmly and shook his head as he said, 'On the contrary, I think you are showing a lot of care and understanding. This is a very difficult situation, and the choices are all unpleasant and complicated. For this reason, it is always best, as you said, to leave it to the one who will go through with it. I am a great believer in the accuracy of women's instincts, and I am sure that she will choose what is best for all concerned. You go and have some fresh air, and we will talk again later.'

As Mr Stewart entered room seven, he was surprised to hear Miss Stapleton ask the midwife who accompanied him to leave the room as she wanted to talk to him completely on his own.

Mr Stewart sat on the only chair in the room next to her bed. Her tears were flowing freely as she started talking. 'I do apologize about asking the midwife to leave, but what I am about to tell you should remain a secret between us and should not be discussed with anyone else or get documented in my case notes in any shape or form. Can you promise me that?'

Mr Stewart nodded calmly and said, 'Absolutely. In my job as a doctor, confidentiality is absolute, and it is not uncommon that there are some details patients do not want anyone else to know.'

This gave Miss Stapleton a lot of comfort as she felt that she was not the only one who had secrets of which she was ashamed. She paused for a few moments and said, 'I want to have a C-section, in spite of all the facts that you explained, because I want to give this baby the best chance of survival, irrespective of the personal cost to me or the significant possibility of the baby dying.'

She paused again while watching Mr Stewart's face for any reaction, but he continued to look at her calmly without any expression.

'This is a very much-wanted baby, as we have been trying for it for over four years, but this is not the main reason for my decision to have the section. The main reason for this decision is the fact that between the ages of 14 and 17 years, I had five surgical terminations of pregnancy. My partner knows absolutely nothing about this. The last two terminations were very complicated with haemorrhage and infection, which meant that I had to be taken back to the operating theatre to have the womb cleaned further. In the last operation, they said something about a large tear in my neck of the womb, which they had to repair. I think all these terminations of pregnancy caused the infertility problems that I had for the last four years and the complications I am now having in this pregnancy. I am right about this, aren't I?'

Mr Stewart replied with a low, soft voice, 'I fully understand how difficult terminations of pregnancies can be, with all the physical and psychological scars they leave behind. However, you must remember that there is no way of being sure that what happened in this pregnancy is a consequence of the terminations that you had as a young teenager. Five terminations are a lot, and the long-term risks obviously increase as a result. However, premature breaking of the waters and extreme prematurity are problems we see in many women who have never been pregnant previously. So, you should not keep blaming yourself and feel guilty about what happened so many years ago when you were very young. You must try to forgive yourself and move on.'

It was now Mr Stewart's turn to look closely at Miss Stapleton's face, searching for a reaction to what he had just said, but she just buried her face in her hands and continued to cry loudly.

Mr Stewart paused for a few moments and then added, 'What happened in the past should not be the basis for deciding on the present.'

She lifted her head and looked at him, with her tears still flowing copiously, and tried to respond but was unable to talk. So, Mr Stewart continued in a very positive and encouraging voice, 'Once this pregnancy is over, the fertility side of things can be looked into, but it is very encouraging that you conceived spontaneously, albeit after four years of trying, so, the prospects of another pregnancy at your young age are still very high.

As far as any damage to the neck of the womb as a result of the termination of pregnancy, this can be easily diagnosed and cured in any future pregnancy. A torn cervix can be treated by putting a stitch in it in early pregnancy to keep it tightly closed and prevent the breaking of the water. This is a very successful treatment, and most women will be able to continue with the pregnancy till full term without any problems.'

Mr Stewart then paused again and said, 'Would you like more time to think about all this and to talk to your partner? We will have to get you delivered tonight because of the escalating infection and fever, so time is limited, but we can give you a little bit more if you need.'

Miss Stapleton looked at him and smiled quietly. 'There is no need for waiting because my mind is mad up. I want a Caesarean section.'

She sighed and then continued, 'I feel very guilty about deliberately wasting five babies before when I had all these abortions. I will do what is best and safest for this baby and fully accept that what will be will be. Even if this baby dies in spite of having the section, I would have done for him all there is to do.'

Mr Stewart smiled at her and said as he stood up, 'That is fine. I will go and make the arrangements for the operation. I must thank you for confiding in me, which certainly gave me a better understanding of the situation and how you really feel. When you have recovered from all this, I suggest that we arrange for some confidential psychological counselling, which will help you cope with all the feelings that you obviously still have from these terminations. We can also look into the fertility side of things and assess that tear in the neck of the womb.'

Miss Stapleton was sobbing and did not respond as Mr Stewart left the room. He met the partner in the corridor and said to him, 'She decided to have the section.'

The partner nodded as he continued walking towards room seven and said in a resigned voice, 'I thought she would.'

Mr Stewart performed the Caesarean section under spinal anaesthetic so that the patient remain awake throughout to see the baby with her partner. Samy and Maria were assisting Mr Stewart, who could not hide his hostility towards Samy throughout the whole operation.

Miss Stapleton's partner was probably far more nervous than she was. Throughout the operation, he held her hand while she kept her eyes closed. As expected, it was a very complicated affair because she had extensive scarring inside her abdomen and pelvis, probably as a result of the infections that she had after the terminations of her previous pregnancies. The bowels and bladder were stuck to the womb, and Mr Stewart spent a long time stripping them off carefully to get to the womb.

On top of that, the baby was delivered with great difficulty as the womb had clamped down on the body of this tiny baby. After giving the couple a very quick glimpse of the baby, he was handed to the neonatology team in a very poor condition. The baby boy was so small he fitted in the palm of Mr Stewart's hand.

Mr Stewart took a long time to repair the womb, which was badly torn because of the difficulty in getting the baby out. The blood loss was also significant, and she needed a blood transfusion.

At the end of the operation, Mr Stewart explained to the couple what happened and the complications of the surgery. He left it to the neonatologists to tell them about the baby's condition and his prospects.

Away from the patient, Mr Stewart said to the patient's midwife, 'You will need to watch her very carefully because she has a very high risk of further haemorrhaging. If there is any deterioration in her condition, make sure that the intensive care team comes to review her to see if she needs to go to the intensive care unit to be closely monitored for a while.'

The neonatal team was still working on the baby, who had little tubes and fine catheters inserted everywhere into different parts of its tiny body. The baby was also being vigorously ventilated through a tube that was inserted down his throat and into the windpipe. When the consultant neonatologist noticed that Mr Stewart was standing next to him, he said, 'The baby is in a very poor condition. He is very difficult to ventilate as his lungs feel very solid. His heart rate is also unstable. I suspect that he has a severe infection on top of his prematurity problems.'

Mr Stewart shook his head in despair and said, 'This should have been predicted and explained to her from your end as well as ours. She should not have had this operation as the situation was obviously hopeless, but here we are.'

With that, Mr Stewart left the operating theatre in an even worse mood. He did not acknowledge or thank Samy, Maria, the anaesthetic team, or the scrub nurse for their assistance in the operating theatre, which did not come as a surprise to any of them.

In spite of the efforts of the neonatologists throughout the night, the baby died six hours later.

****

The next day, Samy went to the postnatal ward and asked the midwife looking after Miss Stapleton to see if she would see him, having learned of the baby's death. He wanted to offer his personal condolences to the couple and see if they wanted to discuss anything about what had happened. Miss Stapleton and her partner gave their permission for him to come and see them. Although they were both very stressed and very upset, as to be expected, they talked to him politely and respectfully.

Before Samy could say anything, Miss Stapleton said in a very quiet and tired voice, 'Thank you for all your effort during the night. It is very much appreciated.' Her partner nodded in agreement.

This was the last thing Samy would have expected: gratitude from a couple who had just lost their baby. He took a few moments to think of what to say.

'I am very sorry for your loss. I wish we could have done more.'

Miss Stapleton shook her head and said, 'You have all done your very best, but it was hopeless from the start. Mr Stewart said as much beforehand, but I insisted on having the section.'

She paused for a moment, then sighed and said, 'I am sorry to have wasted everyone's time and effort for such a lost cause.'

Samy said straight away, 'You have not wasted anyone's time because this is what we are here for. I think you are very brave because you have given the baby all the chances he could have ever had against such bad odds, so you can never look back and wonder whether you should have decided differently.'

****

As Samy was leaving the ward, he met Alison in the corridor. As soon as she saw him, her face lit up, and with a beaming smile, she asked him, 'Lovely to see you, Samy, but I thought that you would be tucked away in bed after the very eventful night that you had.'

Samy was very pleased to see her, but he had a lot on his mind with the death of baby Stapleton and Mr Stewart's criticism of his role in her management. With a tired smile, he said, 'I couldn't sleep for long, so I came to see Miss Stapleton, who lost the baby earlier this morning.'

Samy then said something that really worried Alison: 'This episode with Miss Stapleton last night confirmed for me something I suspected for a while. Mr Stewart does not like me at all, and I think he is out to get me. For a while now, he has been so hostile and aggressive with me for no obvious reasons, more so lately. He has been either ignoring me or being condescending and critical. He blamed me for

Miss Stapleton's decision to have a Caesarean section when her baby was not expected to survive, which is very unfair. Fortunately, Maria was with me when I counselled the patient, and she tried to put him right about this. Why do you think he hates me so much? What have I done to earn all this hostility?'

Alison blushed and froze for a few moments because she knew the answer to Samy's question but could not tell him about it. Mr Stewart's infatuation with her was at the root of his animosity to Samy. He always acted as if he was mad with jealousy at the sight of any man coming close to her. He must have seen and heard enough evidence of her admiration and affection for Samy. This worried Alison a lot because Mr Stewart's hatred for Samy could have very serious implications for Samy's position at St. Luke's Hospital and his future career.

Alison could not offer Samy any comfort and just said, 'He is a psychopathic monster. You have seen how he treats the medical students, his ex-wife, and many others. Just ignore him and keep doing all the clever things that you do at work, and he will not have a chance to give you any grief.'

'I will certainly do my best to get out of his way and leave him alone, although I know that this is not always easy to do.'

Chapter 8

Two very different worlds

As Samy was about to exit the postnatal ward to go back to his room, leaving Alison to finish her shift on the ward, Alison said to him, 'I will finish the shift at 6 O'clock, so if you are not busy, I would like to take you out to dinner. My treat.'

Samy smiled and was obviously delighted with Alison's suggestion. He replied cheerfully, 'What a brilliant idea. I could certainly do with a night out in your charming company.'

He then frowned, pretending to be making a serious statement, and said, 'But it will be my treat and not yours. Where I come from, the man always pays.'

Alison laughed and acquiesced readily to his demand. 'This is very old-fashioned, Samy, but I like it.'

'Alright then, it's a deal. You choose the restaurant, and I will pick up the bill.'

Alison volunteered to do the driving, and they arranged to meet up at 7 O'clock in the hospital's car park. At exactly 7 O'clock, Samy was walking towards Alison's parked car when she stepped out of her car to meet him. The way she looked took his breath away, and he froze a few yards from her to stare with his mouth wide open. She looked absolutely stunning and very sexy in her skimpy, figure-hugging red summer dress, which showed a generous portion of her shapely thighs. She was also wearing an expensive gold necklace with a matching bracelet and earrings, which complemented her dress and the elegant high-heel shoes. Her hair was tied in a neat bun, and, as usual, she had minimal make-up on. When one is that naturally gorgeous, make-up is not really needed.

Samy's eyes widened as he gasped and said, 'Wow, Alison, wow, wow, wow! You look absolutely gorgeous. I better sit down before I pass out.'

Alison was very happy to hear Samy talk to her in those terms for the first time. Obviously, the time and effort she spent preparing for this evening had the desired effect. She laughed and said, 'Thank you, Samy. Let us go. I hope you are as hungry as I am.'

Samy, who by contrast was dressed in a simple white open-neck shirt and cheap black trousers, replied, 'Seeing you looking like this has made me even more hungry. I just feel so very under-dressed for the occasion. I should go back to my room to change into my one and only Marks and Spencer suit, but I do not think that this will improve the situation much.'

They both laughed as Samy went round the car to open the driver's door for Alison. He then waited for her to sit and put on her seat belt before he gently closed the door. Alison did not make any effort to prevent her dress from riding even higher up her thighs for Samy's benefit, but he never once looked in that direction.

Alison drove to central London and parked the car in a private car park near Oxford Street. Samy enquired, 'This is a private car park for the residents of this luxurious block of flats, so why are you parking here? You may get clamped or have a penalty ticket.'

'I have a parking permit for this car park because Daddy owns a flat in this block. He has to come to London a lot for business meetings, and for this reason, he bought this flat many years ago.'

'What does your dad do?'

'He is a banker, runs a group of investment companies, and acts as an adviser to several government departments, plus a lot of other jobs that I do not really understand.'

Samy already had some idea about how rich Alison and her family were, and this current outing with her was to make this point even more obvious to him.

Alison walked with him to a French restaurant close by. A handsome formally dressed waiter opened the door for them and said, 'Good evening, Dr Richardson. It is very nice to see you again.'

Alison smiled warmly at him. 'Good evening, George. Which table have you got for us tonight?'

The waiter promptly replied, 'Your usual table, of course.'

As they walked behind the waiter, Samy could not fail to notice that everything about this restaurant had to do with opulence, exclusivity, and sheer class. The décor, the furniture, the chandeliers, and the paintings on the walls made him feel that he was entering a palace or a stately home and not a restaurant.

As they sat down at a corner table in what was obviously the best spot in the whole restaurant, Samy whispered to Alison, 'What an amazing place. You are obviously very well-known here.'

Alison replied casually, 'This is by far the best French restaurant in London. My parents have been coming here for many years, and Pierre, the owner, is a close friend of theirs.'

Samy looked around in awe at what he was seeing around him, and he started to worry about how much this meal was going to cost him. He regretted leaving the choice of restaurant to Alison, who obviously did not have a clue about his very limited finances. If he was the one to choose, he would have taken her to the Indian restaurant just round the corner from the hospital, where a meal for two would have cost him less than twenty pounds, with a generous tip included.

His worst fears were confirmed when the waiter brought the menus. The cheapest starter cost eighteen pounds, and the prices of the rest of the menu just got higher and higher.

There was no way he could pay for even a part of the cost of this meal.

Alison noticed straight away that Samy's face had dropped as soon as he looked at the menu. He was getting paler, and his lips were trembling as if he was talking to himself.

Alison leaned over to him and whispered, 'By the way, we are not paying anything for this meal today. This restaurant gives its regular customers a free meal if they have come for four meals within one month. My parents have come for four meals already this month, so this is the fifth free meal. Why do you think I brought you here tonight? Neither of us could afford that on our NHS salaries.'

Samy looked as if a massive weight had been removed from his shoulders. His face lit up, and with a broad smile, he said, 'What a relief. I was going to nip to the kidney transplant centre at the hospital to see if I could sell them one of my kidneys just to pay for the starters!'

They both laughed and started looking at the menu again. After a few minutes, Samy said, 'This is rather embarrassing, Alison, but I do not really know what I am looking at. It is all in French.'

Alison smiled and said, 'There is nothing to be embarrassed about. Most people who come here feel the same as you. This is really a French thing; they always feel that everyone should speak their language, even in England.

The best thing is to leave it to George, the head waiter, who will know what the best choices on the menu are tonight.'

The waiter came, and rather than choosing them, he gave them a clear description of each dish on the menu. Although Samy knew he was not going to pay anything, he still chose the cheapest dishes on the menu to be on the safe side, not that he could have afforded even those.

After they ordered the food, George asked, 'And which wine would you like tonight, Dr Richardson?' as he handed her the wine list. She tried to pass it to Samy, but he smiled and passed it back to her, saying, 'I'd leave the choice to you, Alison.'

Alison did not have to look at the menu and just said to George, 'Let us have Daddy's special red then, George. This is the best of French, isn't it?'

George smiled and replied, 'The best in the world, Dr Richardson. Excellent choice.'

Once the waiter went out of sight, Samy laughed and said, 'My knowledge of wine is only equalled by my knowledge of French food, one big fat zero.'

He then paused for a moment and said, 'I hope you don't mind, but I do not drink alcohol of any kind. I am an absolute teetotaller.'

Alison looked worried and said, 'Oh Dear, I am so sorry, Samy. I should have known that as an Egyptian Muslim, you never drink alcohol.'

Samy smiled and replied, 'I am Christian, Alison. A fifth of the population in Egypt, almost twenty million people, belongs to the Coptic Christian faith, and although drinking alcohol is not exactly prohibited, it is not encouraged. For this reason, many Coptic Christians choose not to have any.'

Alison started to worry about how the evening was going. Her aim was for them to have a romantic meal in one of London's best restaurants so that they got closer to each other. However, all she had achieved thus far was to make him feel very uncomfortable and totally out of his depth in a luxurious environment that he was obviously not used to. Unintentionally, she had shown him clearly how very different their two worlds were.

Samy watched the head waiter as he went towards the kitchen and said, 'I am sorry if you feel that I am staring at you every now and then, but you really look absolutely stunning.'

Alison looked relieved as he was still in this admiring, affectionate mood. She laughed happily and said, 'Thank you, Samy. Please feel free to stare at me as much as you like. This is good for my morale.'

''I don't think that your morale needs any boosting. I am sure that you are the centre of admiration and attention wherever you go. I feel that I need to pinch myself to make sure that I am not just dreaming. Not so long ago, I was struggling in Cairo, working all hours under the sun for peanuts and living in a grotty bedsit. Now I am working in a prestigious London hospital and having dinner in a most luxurious restaurant, with the most beautiful English rose. How did all this happen?'

Alison looked at him lovingly and did not say anything, as she did not want to interrupt the flow of his loving thoughts. Samy's facial expression suddenly changed to a very serious one as he frowned and said, 'It all just feels too good to be true, and I am afraid that this new world in which I am a total stranger will come crashing on my head at any moment, especially as Mr Stewart, for some unknown reason, seems to hate my guts.'

Alison's face went red with anger as she said through gritted teeth, 'This monster is causing a lot of grief to so many people. As I told you before, just ignore him. He is not worth the bother.'

'I noticed that he is always nice to you, so what is the secret? What should I do to make him give me the 'Alison treatment'? Would you tell me?'

Alison replied with a frankness that Samy did not expect, 'He is just a randy bastard.'

Samy's face expressed both amazement and shock in equal measures, but he did not want to let her explain further. He quickly changed the subject. 'Let us leave Mr Stewart and everything to do with work behind. This is such a beautiful evening which I am spending in the company of a gorgeous princess, waiting to eat French dishes the names of which I cannot even pronounce, let alone pay for, so let us just enjoy the moment and leave all our troubles behind.'

'I second that. Down with St Luke's and Mr Stewart.'

They spent three hours talking about their lives and their families while George, the waiter, kept providing them with various dishes, which they consumed very slowly because they were talking so much. By the end of the evening, they both knew almost everything to know about each other. The more Alison knew about Samy's difficult circumstances, his very poor background, and what he had to go through to reach this stage of his life, the more she admired and respected him, especially as he did not seem to be ashamed or embarrassed in any way about such a poor background. Alison was careful not to give him the full details about her family's fortune and their social status to avoid frightening him away. She was quite frank about her past love life and the three fairly serious boyfriends she had over the years. She was pleased to see that this did not seem to bother Samy at all. He obviously did not wish to pry or ask any searching questions about her previous relationships. He acted as if her past was none of his business.

At the end of the meal, Alison went to the toilet, and on her way back, out of Samy's sight, she signalled to George, the head waiter, to come to her. She thrust a twenty-pound note in his hand as his tip and whispered, 'Please put the bill on Daddy's account, George.' She obviously had invented this story about a free fifth meal!

Alison drove Samy back to the hospital and parked the car at a convenient spot close to the doctors' residence, where his room was. Samy released his seatbelt, stepped out of the car, and said to her with a very warm smile, 'Thank you very much for a most fantastic evening. I must say that this has been the best meal out I have ever had in the grandest restaurant I have ever seen.'

Alison smiled back and released her seatbelt while saying, 'I am glad you enjoyed it. I must say that my preference is for Indian or Chinese restaurants, but I thought that this is a special evening and we should go to a very special restaurant.'

She was obviously trying to make him realise that her taste is mostly down to earth and not always that extravagant. She was hoping to make him realise that her world was not really that different from his, but in vain. The differences between them financially and socially were too vast for Samy to ignore in spite of the fact that he was madly in love with her.

Samy laughed and said, 'You know, tonight's outing reminded me of the children's story 'The Princess and The Frog'. Do you know it?'

'Of course I do. I believe that in the end, the princess kisses the frog, who turns out to be a very handsome prince, and they live happily ever after. Although you are no frog, I still have to kiss you, so be warned.'

Alison walked round the car to where Samy was standing, and before Samy could say or do anything, she threw her arms around him and kissed him passionately on his lips. He was surprised and hesitant because they were in the middle of the car park and could be seen by anyone. However, his hesitation lasted for only a very brief moment, following which he became an active and very willing participant.

When they finished kissing, Alison was very disappointed because he did not invite her up to his room or try to take matters further. She was desperate to make love to him, and she knew that he wanted the same because she could feel his erection against her pelvis as he hugged her. However, he gently disentangled himself from her arms, planted another brief kiss on her cheek, and said, 'Good night, my love.'

And with that, he walked towards the block where his room was. He did not look back until he was about to enter the block, then he turned around and waved to her. Alison sat in the car for a while and was very confused. The night seemed to have ebbed and flowed in different directions, some good and some not so good, because at times she felt that Samy got very close to her, but at other times he was drifting away. However, the most important thing she felt was his last words to her: 'Good night, my love.' She could now be confident that Samy was as much in love with her as she was with him.

✱✱✱✱✱✱✱✱✱✱✱✱✱✱✱✱✱✱✱✱

The next day, Samy and Alison were scheduled to be the on-call team for the labour ward from 8:00 am. Alison arrived at the labour early and went to sit in the labour ward's office, where sister Melanie Smith was already sitting at the desk talking to a couple of midwives. Alison had an irresistible urge to have a dig at sister Smith because she was obviously trying to entice Samy to her flat with the flimsy excuse of helping her put up a wardrobe. Alison believed that Samy was by then well and truly hers, but she did not like the idea of sister Smith trying to tempt him away, albeit unsuccessfully. The romantic dinner of the previous night gave Alison a very satisfying sense of victory over sister Smith, and she wanted to celebrate this at her expense.

Alison said to sister Smith with a wide, sarcastic smile on her face, 'Tell me about this new wardrobe that you got, sister. Where did you get it from? Was it from Ikea or B and Q?'

This unexpected question clearly rattled Sister Smith. She blushed, fiddled with her hair nervously, and replied, 'Wardrobe? What wardrobe?'

161

Alison persisted, obviously enjoying sister Smith's discomfort. 'The new wardrobe that Samy is going to help you put up. Surely, you haven't forgotten.'

'Oh, that. It is just something I ordered online from an internet company. It looks too complicated for me to put up on my own, and Samy has kindly volunteered to help me.'

She then tried to get off the subject by asking one of the midwives sitting in the office to go and check on one of the women in labour, but Alison was never going to let her off that easily.

'You know, I need a new wardrobe myself for my flat. So, it may be useful for me to come to your place too to help you and Samy put it together, which will give me the opportunity to see if this is the kind of wardrobe I need for my flat. So, can I come too?'

Sister Smith's face got even more red, and her lips trembled without saying anything. Alison found it very difficult not to burst out laughing, but she managed to contain herself and, with a serious expression on her face, asked, 'When did you say Samy was going to come to your place?'

Sister Smith froze for a moment and then mumbled, 'Saturday. He is coming on Saturday lunchtime.'

Alison thought for a moment and then pretended to be very disappointed as she said, 'Oh, this is really disappointing. Sadly, I cannot make it this Saturday because

I will be flying with my parents to Jersey on Friday night for a family wedding and will not be back till Sunday night. Well, it was a nice thought.'

Sister Smith's immense relief was obvious. She sighed loudly and said, 'It was a nice thought indeed. You would have been very welcome to come.'

Alison thought for a moment and then said, 'Maybe I can get out of this wedding and come with Samy to your place. I think I can probably do that.'

She sounded serious, and sister Smith's horrified look returned as she quickly said, 'You sacrifice a weekend in Jersey attending a wedding in order to put up a wardrobe? Are you mad? You can always come by later on, and I will be happy to show you the wardrobe if you want.'

Alison smiled again and said, 'This is very kind of you, sister. I will do that, and if I like your wardrobe, I can order a similar one and get Samy to help me put it up.'

Chapter 9

The breech in the toilet

At 8.00 O'clock exactly, Samy walked into the labour ward office, but before he could greet the staff gathered there, suddenly, there was a lot of noise in the corridor as the ambulance team wheeled in a woman who was screaming loudly. She was obviously in a lot of pain, pushing and straining, indicating that she was in a very strong labour. Between her contractions, she was shouting obscenities at the ambulance staff and cursing hospitals and all those who worked in them.

The woman screamed from the top of her voice, 'My womb is about to explode, you morons. Get this baby out of me before it kills me.'

Sister Smith directed them to delivery room two, but before they could take her in that direction, the woman suddenly jumped off the trolly as soon as she saw the toilet door in the labour ward's corridor. She shouted, 'No one will touch me until I move my bowels. I feel they are going to burst if I do not have a good shit right away.'

She pushed the ambulance's paramedic out of the way and went into the toilet with sister Smith following.

One of the paramedics said to Samy, 'This is a thirty-eight years old woman in her fifth pregnancy, having had four normal deliveries before. She is 37 weeks pregnant and has been having vague abdominal pains overnight, which got a lot worse this morning and now she feels that she is in a very strong labour. There is no bleeding or any other symptoms. The baby's heartbeat is fine. She refused to let us examine her internally before we transferred her to the hospital because she said she was sure it was labour, and she did not want to be poked and prodded by useless paramedics. After four normal deliveries, she believed that she knew best about these matters.'

Suddenly, sister Smith screamed from the toilet, 'Samy, come quick! She is delivering in the toilet, and the baby is breech.'

Samy and Alison rushed in. The woman was half-sitting on the toilet with the baby's feet protruding from her vagina.

Alison could not help but say loudly, 'Shit! It is really a breech.'

Delivering a baby that was coming feet first could prove very complicated and dangerous for both the baby and the mother, especially if the size of the baby was large, the baby's back was coming towards the mother's back, or if the arms or legs were entangled within the woman's pelvis. For this reason, if the baby was known to be in a breech position before labour started, a thorough expert assessment was needed to see if vaginal breech delivery was feasible and safe; otherwise, a planned Caesarean section would be performed to avoid the baby being asphyxiated, damaged, or the mother having serious tears or haemorrhage from a difficult and complicated delivery. In this woman's case, a breech presentation was not suspected before labour started, which meant that these assessments and plans for the delivery were not made in advance of the labour. This delivery had 'trouble' written all over it.

There was no time for Samy to assess the size of the baby or how its back, arms, or legs were coming. Samy said to sister Smith, 'We cannot bring the trolly here to transfer her to a delivery room as the door to the toilet is too narrow. Get a stretcher quickly, and we will carry her manually.'

The woman, who was by then lying flat on her back on the floor with her legs wide open, shouted, 'There is no time to move me, you idiot. The baby is coming right this minute, and you will have to deliver me here and now. Stop wasting time and get on with it.'

As soon as she said that, another contraction started, and the patient screamed loudly while pushing down as hard as she could. With her pushing and straining, Samy could see that the baby's legs were slowly and steadily coming out of the vagina. His heart sank because the way the legs were coming suggested that the baby's back was towards the mother's back, which was the worst possible position for a vaginal breech delivery.

Samy asked Alison and sister Smith to hold the woman's legs up, effectively acting like a pair of stirrups, so that he could examine her internally. He also told one of the other midwives to call the neonatologist, the baby's doctor, to come urgently in case the baby needed resuscitation and also inform the anaesthetist just in case she needed to be taken to the operating theatre if the baby could not be delivered in the toilet. With great difficulty, Sister Smith and Alison squeezed into the narrow cubicle to hold up the patient's legs, one leg each, as Samy had requested. Samy knelt on the floor between the woman's legs and put his hand into the vagina to assess the situation.

The assessment was very difficult because the contractions were frequent, and the woman could not help but push very hard with each contraction. To make matters worse, she kept closing her legs on Samy's hand, making it impossible for him to examine her properly. She also kept moving in one direction or another all the time with Samy's hand trapped in her vagina.

However, eventually, Samy confirmed that the baby's back was towards the mother's back, indicating that this was going to be a very complex breech delivery, which he would have to conduct on the floor of a toilet with the patient being as uncooperative and aggressive as she could have ever been.

With colossal effort, Samy managed to turn the baby the right way so that it was no longer 'back-to-back'. The woman continued pushing and straining like mad in spite of Samy's and sister Smith's pleas to her not to. Her response to them was a mixture of swearing and screaming while continuing to push and fight against Samy's efforts to deliver her.

She kept shouting at them, 'You try and have this big lump coming out of your arse and see how you would cope. Hurry up and get this baby delivered, you useless lot. I cannot take this anymore.'

In spite of the fact that the woman was behaving like a constantly moving target, Samy managed to deliver the baby's legs and trunk, albeit with great difficulty. As soon as he did that, his heart almost stopped because he saw that he was now facing a much bigger problem: the baby had its arms raised above its head, which would cause the baby's head to be jammed in the pelvis. There would be no chance of the baby's head being delivered unless the arms were disentangled and delivered first to free the head from its impacted position in the pelvis. This nightmare of a delivery was getting worse and more stressful by the second.

The baby's body was becoming blue rather than the normal pink, suggesting that he was getting asphyxiated because of the delay in getting the head out.

The woman was screaming so loudly, Samy had to shout to get her to hear him, 'Listen to me now. There is a big problem with the way the baby's arms and head are impacted in the pelvis. I will have to turn the baby in certain ways to gain access to one arm at a time to bring them out before I will be able to deliver the head. This will be very uncomfortable for you, but we do not have time to take you to the operating theatre or to put you to sleep because the baby is getting very distressed. We must get him out in the next few minutes, or the baby will be damaged or even lost. So, please help me by lying still and calming down for a few minutes, and it will all be over. I cannot do this without your cooperation.'

The way Samy shouted at the woman made her realise the seriousness of the situation, so she calmed down to some extent and said in a disgruntled voice, 'I will do my best, my lord and master. Just stop shouting at me.'

Delivering the arms and the head of the baby involved several complicated manoeuvres, which were extremely uncomfortable for the woman who screamed uncontrollably all the time. However, she eventually managed to let Samy complete the delivery. She was swearing at Samy and cursing the hospital for employing him throughout the whole process.

The baby was delivered in a very poor condition. Samy quickly clamped the umbilical cord and cut it. The baby was passed out of the toilet cubicle to the waiting neonatal team, who were ready with all their equipment and the resuscitation machine in the corridor just outside the toilet.

Samy was breathing heavily and sweating profusely. He was covered in a mixture of blood, urine, and faeces because as the woman was pushing so vigorously, she moved her bowels and emptied her bladder on him to add to the inevitable bleeding from the womb that had already soaked Samy's scrubs.

The woman shouted at Samy, 'What the fuck have you been doing down there all this time? Why did it take you so long to deliver the baby? You obviously know nothing about breech delivery or anything else for that matter.'

The woman's criticism of Samy in those rude and disrespectful terms shocked all the staff in the toilet and the corridor, especially sister Smith and Alison. Samy was shaken to the core, and before he could gather his thoughts to respond, the woman's tirade continued, 'You had your hands up my vagina for so long, why was that? Are you some sort of a pervert?'

This last remark was just too much for sister Smith and Alison to take. They were both still holding the woman's legs up in the air while waiting for the placenta, the afterbirth, to come out. They both looked very angry and started to shout at the woman at the same time, but Samy raised his arm in a gesture that indicated to them that he did not want them to interfere on his behalf. He then said to the woman calmly but firmly, 'I am sorry, madam, for your discomfort and pain, but your baby was coming out in a very complicated way. It would have been difficult enough if we were delivering you in the operating theatre, on a special table, and with a general anaesthetic. However, you forced us to deliver you on the floor of a toilet with you fighting me all the way with all your moving, pushing, and straining, which made the delivery almost impossible. There was no way and no time for doing anything else with the baby half in and half out of the vagina. I had to persevere, although I knew that it was very hard for me because the baby was getting asphyxiated. I am very sorry for your suffering, but we could not have done anything different once you have refused to be moved to the operating theatre.'

He then paused for a moment and said, 'You should have let the ambulance team examine you at home so that we would have known about the baby coming as a breech well in advance and how far into labour you were. In addition, you should have let us take you to the operating theatre or a delivery room as soon as you arrived in the labour ward instead of insisting on going to the toilet first. I know that you had four normal deliveries before, but this was the first time you had a breech delivery, which is very different from what you have experienced in your previous deliveries. In spite of all your stress and suffering, you should still have listened to what we were saying to you instead of fighting us all the way. I am sorry to be so blunt, but you need to consider all these factors before you start hurling accusations and criticisms.'

The woman stared angrily at Samy for a few moments while he looked back at her expressionlessly. She then said, 'So, it is all my fault.'

Samy responded in the same calm voice, 'It is nobody's fault. The difficulties you had with your breech delivery are all well-recognized. For this reason, many women choose to have the baby turned around to head first position if the breech was diagnosed before labour started. Many others will choose to have a planned Caesarean section rather than a vaginal breech delivery. In this day and age, only very few breeches are delivered vaginally because of the associated risks to mother and baby.'

Alison and sister Smith put the woman's legs on the floor. They both felt sorry for Samy and struggled not to tell the woman off for her aggressive and rude attitude, but he obviously did not want them to do that or add any more to what he had just said to her.

****

A midwife passed a syringe with a drug called syntocinon to sister Smith, who said to the woman, 'I am going to give you an injection into your thigh which will help deliver your afterbirth and reduce the risk of bleeding. Is that OK with you?'

The woman nodded in agreement with obvious reluctance, and the sister gave her the injection. As soon as she finished injecting, the womb contracted vigorously, and the afterbirth almost flew out of the woman's vagina and landed on Samy's lap as he was still kneeling on the floor between the woman's legs. Both Alison and sister Smith could not help but burst out laughing loudly. The woman joined in the laughter at the sight of Samy covered in a mixture of water, blood, faeces, and urine with a placenta on his lap. Samy slowly stood up to avoid dropping the placenta on the floor and then burst out laughing himself. He put the placenta in a dish that one of the midwives held up for him. All the other people standing outside the toilet and in the corridor joined in the laughter once they saw Samy's state. He walked slowly towards the changing room, leaving behind him a trail of the mixture of fluids that had saturated his clothes.

The woman refused to go on a stretcher or a trolly, insisting on just walking to a delivery room. Once in the room, she said to the sister, 'This chap who delivered me has obviously got a very long way to go before he knows how to deliver babies. He needs much training before you can let him loose on the unsuspecting public.'

Sister Smith turned round with a very congested, angry face, but before she could say anything, the woman added, 'He took such a long time to deliver the baby. He was rough and inconsiderate. Was he a vet before he became an obstetrician?'

Sister Smith was lost for words. She did not respond for a few moments until she could control her anger and then said, 'Mr Samir is the best registrar we have ever had. You were having a very complicated breech delivery on the floor of a toilet, refusing to move to a delivery room. You were not exactly cooperative while he was trying to deliver you in these awkward circumstances. Despite all this, he managed to deliver your baby without causing you any tears. Many doctors would have failed to achieve this, so you should thank your lucky stars that you came in when he was around because I am sure that if any delivered you of the other trainees, the outcome would have been very different.'

The woman was about to respond, but sister Smith continued, 'Most obstetricians, whether they were trainees or consultants, would have insisted on removing you from this bloody toilet and forced you into going to an operating theatre to put you to sleep before trying to deliver the baby. The baby might have been lost while all this was being done because the baby was already half in and half out of the vagina for such a long time, but that would have been the expected procedure that most obstetricians would have followed, irrespective of the patient's wishes or the risks to the baby.'

The woman was taken aback by sister Smith's rather aggressive response, but she saw that sister Smith was not a woman to be crossed. So, she paused for a little while and said to her, 'Of course, you will have to defend him. You lot always stick together. I will lodge a formal complaint about this, and I may even sue the hospital. I have rights, you know.'

Sister Smith ran out of patience, so she said as she was leaving the room, 'You should do whatever you feel is right for you. I will send you the forms to fill if you wish to go ahead with lodging a formal complaint.'

Sister Smith left the room and slammed the door after her. She then paused for a few moments in the corridor, breathing heavily with an overwhelming feeling of anger directed at this ungrateful woman, coupled with a sense of frustration because her professionalism prevented her from responding to her aggressive comments and accusations appropriately, but that was health professionals' lot, while patients are free to say whatever they want about the care they receive, health professional could never respond in kind. It had always been and would always be a one-way traffic.

****

175

Sister Smith went into the changing room to wash her arms and legs from the blood and water that had splashed on her during the delivery. She also needed to change her heavily soiled uniform. Alison was in the changing room, having just finished cleaning herself and changing.

Sister Smith said to her, 'You wouldn't believe it, Alison, but this bitch we have just delivered in the toilet is going to complain about Samy. She wants to lodge a formal complaint and will also consider legal action.'

Alison could not believe her ears. 'Bloody hell, are you serious? After all that he has done for her?'

'Unbelievable, I know, but complaining and litigation are the order of the day in the NHS nowadays. I suggest that we both write comprehensive reports about what happened while the details are still fresh in our minds. I will get the ambulance team to do the same to show how awkward and uncooperative she has been throughout. Samy will also have to write a detailed report about all this in addition to his usual delivery summary.'

Alison asked, 'Shouldn't we wait to see if she will actually complain or not? Starting to write reports as early as this may suggest that we suspected that there was a case to answer.'

Sister Smith shook her head and said emphatically, 'Not at all. This is standard practice if a patient indicates that she is dissatisfied with her management. The detailed reports written by the attendants are then kept in a confidential legal file for future use if needed. The fact that they are contemporaneous notes will carry a lot more weight in a court of law, far more than reports written days, months, or years after the event.'

Sister Smith then sighed and said, 'I will have to go and tell Samy about this nonsense. I am not sure how will the poor chap cope with this?'

Alison's naughty streak sprang into action again as she saw that there was another chance to amuse herself at the expense of sister Smith. She replied confidently, 'I wouldn't worry about Samy's reaction and his ability to cope. If you knew what he had to cope with throughout his life, you would see that he is too strong a person to be bothered about this nonsense.'

Sister Smith could not ignore the way Alison was trying to provoke her. She stared at her angrily and asked, 'Oh, yes? And how do you know this?'

Alison replied with a cheeky smile on her face. 'For many weeks, we have been spending a lot of time together after work. We have become very close, and I mean very, very close. He is such a fascinating character, a really most wonderful man.'

With this, Alison left the changing room without looking at sister smith. If she did, she would have seen how angry and frustrated she looked. She was biting her lower lip, and her face was bright red because she knew at that moment that Samy had been snatched from her grasp by Alison. To her, this was not only disappointing but also insulting. She had always felt jealous of this exceptionally beautiful and very rich younger woman, but losing Samy to her added to these negative feelings an uncontrollable sense of rage and pure, unadulterated hatred.

Sister Smith's hostile feelings were directed towards Samy just as much as they were aimed at Alison. She felt that he had humiliated her by rejecting her advances and her obvious feelings for him to throw himself into Alison's arms. From that moment onwards, she was hell-bent on totally ruining him because if she could not have him, no one else would, least of all Alison.

****

The rest of the shift on the labour ward was very busy to the extent that neither Samy nor Alison had any time for a cup of coffee or even a glass of water. Alison could not help but feel concerned about how Samy was interacting with her during that shift. Although he was his normal, courteous, and respectful self, he seemed distant and pensive most of the time, which was not what she expected after what went on between them the previous night. She wondered if he was just worried about the expected complaint of the woman whom he delivered in the toilet. Could it be that he was just tired? Was it something to do with bad news from his family in Cairo or something else she did not know about?

As soon as the shift came to an end and Alison and Samy handed over to Mohammad Khan and Maria, who were the team for the evening shift, Alison rushed into the female changing room, got out of her blue labour ward scrubs in a flash and, just as quickly, put on her own dress and shoes. She wanted to catch Samy as soon as he came out of the men's changing room to see if she could find out what was on his mind.

Samy looked surprised rather than pleased to see her when he came out of the changing room. He said, 'Oh, Alison. You must have changed very quickly. What a shift this was.'

As they started walking together towards the exit, he added, 'Thank you very much for all your help today. You were wonderful.'

Alison was not terribly receptive to his compliment about her work on the labour ward as she had a far more important issue to sort out with him. 'Samy, what is the matter? You are not your normal self today? Have I done anything to annoy you?'

With a faint smile, Samy replied, 'You can never annoy me even if you tried. I love you too much for that.'

He then sighed and said, 'Let us get out of here because I need to talk to you. Should we go for a walk in Hampstead Heath if you are not in a rush, that is.'

'I am not in a rush at all. Would you rather go to have something to eat first? Neither of us had any food or drink all day.'

Samy shook his head and said, 'No, I do not want to eat, but of course, if you are hungry, we can meet later on. There is no hurry.'

Alison quickly said, 'I do not want to eat either. Let us go to the Heath and talk. I want to know what is bothering you.'

Samy did not say much as they walked towards Heath, which alarmed Alison even more, but she wanted to give him some space to sort out his thoughts, so she remained silent, too. They reached the rose garden at the bottom of Hampstead Heath, which was virtually empty at that time of the day. They chose to sit down on one of the benches in a secluded spot.

A couple of minutes passed, and Samy remained silent, staring into space. Alison tried to hold his hand, but he gently took his hand away.

Samy said, still looking straight ahead without looking at her. 'Alison, I wanted to apologize for my behaviour last night. I really feel awful about it.'

Alison looked very puzzled and could not make sense of what Samy had just said to her. She frowned and asked, 'I am not sure what you mean by this, Samy. What are you sorry about? You were your normal, lovely self, and I thought we had a fantastic evening. At least I know that I had.'

Then, with a very worried look, she asked, 'Are you trying to tell me that you didn't really love me and you did not mean anything you said to me last night?'

Samy was still looking away and did not respond, so Alison persevered. 'Maybe I did not make it clear yesterday, but I love you very much with all my heart. I thought the way I kissed you could not have left you in any doubt about my feelings for you.'

Samy turned his head towards Alison, and after looking at her sad and worried face for a moment, he said, 'Alison, I do love you more than I have ever loved anyone or anything. I do not know how this has happened, especially as we have known each other for such a short time. I have never been in love before and have always run away from any situation that might have, even remotely, resulted in the development of a romantic relationship of any kind. Then I met you and suddenly found myself in no time at all falling in love with you totally, utterly, and completely. The tight control I had all my life on my emotions disappeared without a trace, just like that. The kissing was but a sign of how my feelings for you have overwhelmed my heart and mind. I just couldn't help it.'

Samy paused for a moment and then turned to look at her and said, 'It is the increasing physical contact with all this kissing and touching that is the problem. My behaviour, especially yesterday, was way below the standards that I would have expected from myself. I should have behaved towards you with more respect and self-control. I can only apologize unreservedly. I really am very sorry.'

Alison's beautiful eyes widened, and she opened her mouth but could find the words for an appropriate response. She took a deep breath, and after a few seconds of hesitation, she said, 'I really do not believe my ears, Samy. I wanted to kiss you far more and for much longer than you did. With the risk of sounding too forward or too crude, I would say to you, in all honestly, that last night, I was desperately keen for things between us to go much further than just kissing.'

Samy raised his eyebrows, and it was his turn to be lost for words. Alison continued, 'I am not the sweet and innocent Miss Snow White that you think I am. I told you before that I have had boyfriends and lovers more than I care to remember. However, I can tell you with my hand on my heart that how I feel about you is something I have never experienced before, and I know that I will never again feel it for anyone else, even if I live to be a hundred!'

Samy looked at Alison adoringly for a few moments. He then smiled and said, 'Hearing you say this makes my heart dance with joy, but every brain cell in my head tells me that I am stupid and selfish because I know for sure that this relationship cannot go anywhere. I have nothing to offer any woman, let alone someone as special and wonderful as you are.'

As Alison was about to respond, Samy quickly added, 'There were some occasions in Egypt and also in England when I could have started or encouraged relationships with women, but I was always able to put an end to things before they could even begin, but in your case, I failed miserably. My feelings for you were like a tsunami that just totally overwhelmed me, although I am sure that I am totally unsuitable for you. The logical thing would have been for me to cut and run, but I do not have the desire, the will, or the strength to do that.'

Alison had heard enough. She put her hand gently over his mouth, moved closer to him, put her head on his chest, and wrapped her arms around him. Samy offered no resistance and just put his arms around her. Once more, his heart managed to stop his head from taking control of his relationship with Alison. They both had their eyes closed, remained silent, and completely lost track of time in each other's arms.

Chapter 10

The vicious storm

While Alison and Samy were having an intimate, quiet time in each other's arms in the rose garden, a vicious storm was brewing at St Luke's Hospital.

After her encounter with Alison in the changing room, it took sister Smith a long time to control her rage, jealousy, and the bitter sense of defeat. Eventually, she managed to leave the changing room with a plan to exact revenge on Samy and Alison, which made her feel a bit better.

She headed straight for the room of the woman who had the breech delivery in the toilet. The woman was sitting in her bed eating biscuits and drinking a cup of tea. Sister Smith smiled at her and asked in a friendly tone of voice, 'How are you feeling? Do you need anything?'

The woman looked at her suspiciously as the earlier encounter with sister Smith had ended on a hostile note. She replied while chewing a mouth full of biscuits, 'I am fine, no thanks to this fantastic doctor of yours.'

Sister Smith continued with the same friendly voice as her smile broadened, 'I am glad to hear that you are alright. How is the baby? I know that the neonatologist has taken him to the intensive care for observation overnight. Have they updated you on his condition?'

'They think the baby will be fine, but they have to watch him closely for at least 48 hours. He will also need to have some sort of scan to check his head and brain because of the difficult delivery.'

'This is just a routine, do not worry. It was a close shave, but he was a naughty boy for turning his bottom to the world and trying to come out feet first.'

They both paused for a few moments, with each of them trying to work out what the other was thinking, following which the patient said hesitantly, 'If you have come to butter me up because you are worried about the complaint which I said, I will make, don't. If the baby is going to be fine, I will leave it at that. Your useless doctor can carry on butchering other women, and I am sure that his incompetence will show up again sooner or later. He will eventually get what he deserves, of that you can be absolutely certain.'

Sister Smith's face attained a serious expression as she said, 'I had time to think about what happened, and I do think that this doctor has a case to answer. You must complain formally, or at least talk to the consultant in charge, Mr Stewart. We have to make sure that what the doctor did today was the correct procedure and the safest course of action for you and the baby. Mr Stewart, the consultant on-call tonight, is on his way to talk to you about all this and will investigate the performance and the conduct of Dr Samir. You must talk to him because he is a fair and very experienced man who will know how to judge these matters. I can reassure you that he will only have your best interest at heart, so just speak frankly to him about all your queries and concerns. He always takes the patient's side, and you will find him kind and understanding. If Dr. Samir did not handle your case correctly, Mr Stewart will be the first one to confirm this and advise you about your rights and the possibility of adequate compensation.'

The woman looked even more suspicious and hesitant. 'But I do not want to talk to no consultant. The baby is going to be fine, and that is what matters most to me. I do not want the hassle of investigations, having to answer lots of questions and fill endless forms.'

Sister Smith was very disappointed to see that the woman had changed her mind about complaining because she wanted to cause as much trouble for Samy as possible. She decided to try to force the patient to complain by whatever means, so she said, 'I hate to tell you this, but the baby's doctor cannot be 100% sure that the baby will be completely normal at this stage because subtle changes in the brain caused by the difficult delivery may not show up for many years to come. There could be long-term complications, such as educational and behavioural problems, not to mention risks of some chronic conditions such as epilepsy and hearing and visual problems. You must speak to the consultant, and he will explain to you more clearly about all these issues, including your right to compensation.'

On hearing this, the woman shouted, 'Bloody hell. So, I am supposed to sit and worry for years to come about how normal my son will be? Alright then, I will talk to that Mr Stewart and I will certainly go ahead with my formal complaint and the litigation.'

Sister Stewart nodded approvingly and had a satisfied smile on her face as she said, 'Mr Stewart will be here soon, and I am sure he will talk to you honestly and clearly about all this.'

As she turned to leave the room, the woman asked, 'Why have you changed your tune? Not so long ago, you were singing the praises of that doctor and defended him vigorously.'

Sister Smith replied, 'As I said, I had time to think about what happened, and on reconsideration, I think that he could have handled the situation better. In addition, I must confess that I did not like the way he talked to you at the end. Also, someone has just reminded me about another patient he had mishandled recently. Now I feel that my professional duty to my patients must override my loyalty to a colleague.'

Sister Smith went to the empty labour ward office, closed the door, and telephoned Mr Stewart at home. She lied to the patient when she said that he was already on his way to see her. She did not want to get him involved until she knew that the patient was ready to complain about Samy. Added to this lie, she had also invented the story about another case that Samy had mishandled not so long ago. No one had reminded her about such a case because no such case existed.

'I am sorry to disturb you at home, Mr Stewart, but there is a messy delivery that Samy did today, which I think you need to know about, especially as there is a strong possibility of a formal complaint and litigation.'

Samy's involvement in a 'messy delivery' was music to Mr Stewart's ears. He listened avidly to sister Smith's outline of the case. She made every effort to make Samy's actions sound inadequate, rough, and unprofessional. She also implied, without being too explicit, that some of his actions bordered on the inappropriate or immoral, which made the patient shout at him for the way he was touching her private parts.

Mr Stewart replied, 'The more I saw of that boy, the more I got concerned about his ability and his behaviour. He seems to be good at only one thing: charming women, which is certainly a dangerous character for a trainee gynaecologist. Do not let anyone talk to this woman until I see her. Was there anyone else with you witnessing this delivery? Can anyone else corroborate what happened? The more witnesses we have, the better.'

Sister Smith replied, 'Because all this happened in a narrow cubicle in the toilet, only Alison was able to see with me the dreadful way Samy was conducting this delivery, but she will never tell on him as they have been having a passionate affair for a long while.'

Sister Smith knew how obsessed Mr Stewart was with Alison, and for this reason, she was sure that confirming his suspicions about the relationship between Samy and Alison would stoke the fire of his hatred for Samy, which was what she wanted. It was clear to her that a very powerful and influential consultant could really ruin the career of a trainee, especially a foreign one who had not been in the country for long.

The fact that Mr Stewart remained silent for a long while after sister Smith's last statement, which spoke louder than words, confirmed to her that she had really got to him and managed to put the noose around Samy's neck. She hoped that Mr Stewart's wrath would be swift and terrible, which would be no more than what Samy deserved for rejecting her.

Eventually, Mr Stewart snapped out of his rage and said to sister Smith, 'I am on my way to see this woman. Just make sure that no one would talk to her until I see her.'

Sister Smith put the phone down and relaxed in her chair with a big smile on her face. She had a wonderful feeling of satisfaction with a job well done. She mumbled to herself, 'Well, Samy. You brought it on yourself. Enjoy!'

When Mr Stewart arrived in the labour ward, sister Smith took him to the woman's room and then stood outside the door to make sure that they were not disturbed. After nearly an hour, Mr Stewart came out and went into his office for a short while, following which he returned to the woman's room with a large number of forms and did not come out again for another hour. When he left for the last time, he looked very happy and excited as he thanked sister Smith for her sense of duty and dedication to the patient's welfare. He then went into his office, made some phone calls, and filled out some forms himself. He was very pleased with himself for having got Samy exactly where he wanted him. He felt like a hunter who had finally managed to trap his prey and was about to move in for the kill.

****

Samy and Alison were still in each other's arms, silent with eyes closed, very relaxed and very happy in each other's company in the rose garden of Hampstead Heath. Suddenly, they were both startled when Samy's mobile phone went off to indicate that he had a text message. Samy read the message and, with a grim face, passed the phone to Alison. The message was from Mr Stewart asking him to come to his office at 8 am the next day.

190

On his way to meet Mr Stewart the next morning, Samy went into the labour ward's office to inform the morning team that he would be late joining them because of this meeting. Only sister Smith and Mohammad Khan, the other registrar, were in the office as it was not 8 O'clock yet. As soon as he entered the office, a disgruntled Mohammad Khan said to Samy, 'Mr Stewart phoned me last night and told me that I would have to do your shift in the labour ward this morning, which means that I have to lose my day off because of you. I really needed this break, and if you are here now, why can't you do your own labour ward shift?'

The fact that he was not doing the labour ward shift was very much unexpected news to Samy, and his substantial worry about the meeting with Mr Stewart grew even more.

Before he could respond, Jeremy Bell, the senior registrar who was finishing his night shift on the labour ward, entered the office and looked very surprised to see Samy. He frowned and asked Samy, 'You are here? I thought that you were either ill or had to go back to Egypt in a hurry because Mr Stewart phoned me last night and asked me to take you out of the on-call rota for at least the next two weeks. What is the matter? Are you alright? You do not look ill, so what is the problem?'

A pale and obviously very concerned Samy replied in a shaken voice, 'I wish I knew what all this is about. I am on my way now to see Mr Stewart at his request, and hopefully, he will explain to me all these totally unexpected changes. I did not know that I was not going to be doing my labour ward shift today or about being taken out of the on-call rota for the next two weeks.'

Mohammad Khan and Jeremy Bell both looked worried for Samy because it became clear to both of them that Samy must be in real trouble for Mr Stewart to act in this way. None of them noticed that sister Smith, who was sitting at the desk looking really happy, staring gleefully at Samy with a wicked grin on her face.

As Samy turned round to leave the office, sister Smith said coldly, 'You should know why Mr Stewart wants to see you. It's about the breech you delivered in the toilet yesterday. Surely, you must have fully expected the patient to complain about what had happened.'

Samy, Jeremy Bell, and Mohammad Khan were all surprised at sister Smith's intervention, which was delivered in an accusing tone of voice that expressed simmering anger and hostility.

Samy looked at her inquisitively and said, 'If this the reason, then all that I need to do will be to just explain what happened, and he will see that I have done all there was to do in these difficult circumstances. I am glad that you and Alison were present throughout the whole episode and that you were able to observe closely all that I have done. Your testimony and Alison's will surely support everything I say on the matter.'

Again, sister Smith's response was totally unexpected by any of the three of them, least of all by Samy 'We will see about that. I can only testify to what I have seen. Whether this supports your side of the story or not is for Mr Stewart to decide.'

Samy looked shocked as he stared silently at sister Smith for a few moments, then without saying anything, turned round and left the room.

****

Samy saw that Mr Stewart's office door was open. He was sitting at the desk, and to his left was a middle-aged woman who Samy had never seen before. They were both looking intently at a file. Samy knocked at the door of the office, and Mr Stewart said without lifting his eyes from the file on the desk, 'Come in and close the door'.

'Good morning, sir. Good morning, madam.'

The woman looked at Samy, smiled, and nodded in acknowledgement of his morning greeting, while Mr Stewart just ignored it.

'Dr Samir, this is Mrs Sonia Goldberg, Head of the medical staffing department. I will come straight to the point because I presume that you know why I have called this

193

meeting. We have received a very serious complaint from Mrs Butt, whom you delivered in the toilet yesterday.'

Mr Stewart paused for a moment as if he was waiting to see how Samy would react to hearing the words 'very serious complaint.'

Samy looked very upset, and his face got paler, which filled Mr Stewart's heart with joy and satisfaction. He continued, 'The woman is accusing you of endangering her baby's life, risking serious injuries to her, and, in addition, touching her inappropriately in the process.'

Samy's heart almost stopped. He could have expected the first two accusations, but to be accused of touching her inappropriately was too much for him to bear. This woman was not only accusing him of incompetence and negligence but also of being a sexual pervert, which was the most serious crime a doctor could ever be accused of. His lips trembled, and he tried to respond, but words failed him.

Mr Stewart wanted to pile up the pressure on Samy without giving him any time to gather his thoughts. He handed him an envelope marked 'strictly private and confidential' and said, 'Here is a copy of her complaint, which you need to read very carefully and then respond to every point she is making. She is saying that the casual and uncaring way with which you delivered her on the floor of a cubicle in the toilet instead of taking her to the operating theatre or a delivery room was a serious mistake that could have been disastrous for her and her baby. She also believes that the rough and unprofessional way with which you conducted the delivery amounted to physical assault. More seriously, she felt that during the delivery, she was being touched inappropriately with your fingers. Her clitoris was rubbed repeatedly, you kept your hand in the vagina for long periods of time totally unnecessarily, and her anus was fingered several times, all of which amounted to a serious sexual assault. We will, of course, have to look into the clinical side of this complaint, but the sexual assault side may have to be passed on to the police and the General Medical Council.'

Mrs Goldberg saw that Mr Stewart was being very harsh and aggressive in the way he was talking to Samy before hearing his side of the story. He was acting as if the guilty verdict was a foregone conclusion before any investigation was formally started. She could clearly see that Samy, who was not invited to sit down, was becoming very distressed and was finding it increasingly difficult not to fall down.

She looked at Mr Stewart angrily, invited Samy to sit down, and said to Samy in a sympathetic tone of voice, 'We have read the delivery notes you made in the patient's file and your more detailed report that you put in the confidential legal file on the labour ward. Dr Alison Richardson, who was assisting you, has also written a helpful report which supports your side of the story. Sister Smith's report, though, is rather negative and seems to support, to some extent, some of the patient's accusations. We will need to get reports from all the others who were involved in this delivery, such as the ambulance team that brought her into the hospital, the other midwives who were present in the labour ward, and the neonatal team.'

Samy was in a daze, and his mind was struggling to process what Mrs Goldberg was saying to him. She felt that he was going to pass out and moved quickly to try to give him some comfort. She said calmly and reassuringly, 'So, as you see, nothing has been concluded yet. We will have to get all the details about everything that has happened before any decisions are taken.'

Samy asked with a trembling voice, 'With all due respect, Mrs Goldberg, conclusions seemed to have already been made and decisions have been taken. I have been taken off the on-call rota and have not been allowed to carry on doing my scheduled work in the labour ward today. I feel that I have already been found guilty before any investigation is made or my side of the story is heard.'

Mr Stewart interfered sharply, 'You are accused of serious professional misconduct and sexual assault, so, what did you expect? You are suspended without pay until …'

Mrs Goldberg had had enough of Mr Stewart's obvious hostility to Samy, so she interrupted him angrily, 'No, Mr Stewart. The suspension is with full pay until the investigation is completed, following which it will be the Hospital board who will decide on the appropriate action.'

She then turned to Samy and said, 'You will be given legal advice by our solicitors because this is a very complex and sensitive problem, but you have certainly not been found guilty of anything yet. This is still just a complaint and an unproven accusation. It is unfortunate that you have to be suspended, but when there is an accusation of a sexual assault, we have no choice.'

Mr Stewart looked disappointed because of Mrs Goldberg's intervention, which prevented him from making life as difficult as possible for Samy. However, he knew from past experience that Mrs Goldberg was not a woman to be contradicted.

Through gritted teeth, he said to Samy, 'You need to read the complaint very carefully and respond specifically in writing to each point the woman is complaining about. There is also a list of questions that I want you to answer in detail to help us understand why you handled this case so badly. In addition, you will find in this envelope a copy of sister Smith's and Alison's statements, which you need to comment on. I want your response to all this on my desk by tomorrow morning. You have twenty-four hours.'

Mrs Goldberg shook her head in a mixture of despair and anger before shouting at Mr Stewart, 'No, Mr Stewart. You know full well that there is no rush because we have to gather the statements from all the other people involved in this delivery. So, there is ample time for Dr Samir to get legal advice and support before submitting his response. '

She then turned to Samy and said, 'You can take as much time as you need, Dr Samir. I strongly recommend that you seek your own legal advice over and above the advice you will receive from the hospital's legal team. Are you a member of one of the medico-legal insurance companies such as the Medical Defence Union or the Medical Protection Society?'

Samy looked at her blankly and said, 'No, I am not a member of any of these organizations because I was told that as I am working for the NHS, my work is covered by Crown Indemnity, so I cannot be sued as an individual.'

Mr Stewart smiled sarcastically and said, 'If you think that you are innocent, then there is no need for the involvement of any of these organizations. Besides, none of the hospital's lawyers or the Medical Defence Union's lawyers will be keen to help with accusations of sexual molestation of a woman in labour. This will need a criminal lawyer and a very good one at that.'

Mrs Goldberg felt like telling Mr Stewart to just shut up, but her professionalism prevented her from saying that. She just ignored him and carried on talking to Samy as if Mr Stewart was not there. 'You must join the Medical Defence Union or the Medical Protection Society straight away and seek their advice on how to write a response to the patient's complaint. When you have had your response thoroughly reviewed by your lawyers and the hospital's lawyers, then you can drop it into my office on the fifth floor, but only when you are absolutely sure that your response is perfect in every respect because once you submit it, you cannot change anything in it.'

She then looked at him warmly and, with an encouraging smile, said, 'I am sure that the truth will come out in the end, as it always does in these matters.'

Mr Stewart laughed and said sarcastically, 'Do you hear that, Samy? The truth will always come out. Isn't this reassuring?'

Mr Stewart then stared at Samy with a very angry look and said, 'The reputation of this maternity unit and all its staff is at stake here. We do not want to be thought of as just a bunch of incompetent weirdoes and perverts. We need to clear this mess as quickly as possible before the newspapers get hold of it.'

Samy replied with a voice that could barely be heard, 'Believe me, sir, I am more anxious than anyone to clear this problem as quickly as possible, and I promise you that I will do my very best to achieve that.'

Mrs Goldberg asked, 'Is there anything you want to ask about or discuss in relation to the procedure or the investigation?'

Samy replied as he got up to leave, 'No, thank you, Mrs Goldberg. Thank you, Mr Stewart.'

As he turned around to leave, Mr Stewart shouted, 'You are suspended from any work in the hospital till further notice. You are not to come into any of the wards, clinics, or operating theatres. You are not to come anywhere near the patient or contact her in any shape or form. Do you understand?'

Samy nodded and mumbled as he left, 'Yes, sir. I understand.'

As soon as he disappeared from view, Mrs Goldberg tore into Mr Stewart. 'The way you treated this boy was inexcusable. I do not understand how someone with your extensive experience in medico-legal matters treats a very distressed and vulnerable young trainee in this harsh, disrespectful, and aggressive way before his situation is fully assessed and he is allowed to defend himself. You might as well have taken him out into the car park and shot him right away without bothering with any investigation.'

Mr Stewart was startled by Mrs Goldberg's attack, but it only took him a few moments to respond, 'If you knew about this registrar as much as I do, you would have asked to be the one to lead the firing squad.'

Mrs Goldberg said, with her angry voice getting louder, 'I do not care about your prejudices and premature judgement in this case. He is innocent until proven guilty, and the correct procedure in handling this complaint will be followed to the letter. If you are not prepared to do so, I will ask the chief executive of the hospital to get Mr Stout involved instead of you.'

Mr Stewart felt as if a bucket of cold water had just been poured over his head, and he had to immediately change his tone. For him, the thought of Samy slipping through his fingers and Mr Stout taking over the case did not bear thinking about. He looked at Mrs Goldberg respectfully and, with a warm smile, said, 'I am very sorry, Mrs Goldberg. This is such a serious complaint, and I am just anxious to conclude the matter as quickly as possible for the sake of the whole hospital and its reputation. However, you are absolutely right. As usual, we must follow the correct procedure exactly, and I promise that I will be calmer next time I face him. He is a 'bad apple,' and what I know about him makes me believe everything the patient has mentioned in her complaint. However, I will push all this out of my mind while I am investigating this complaint and will start from a totally neutral position.'

****

Mr Stewart wasted no time in trying to tighten the noose around Samy's neck. As soon as Mrs Goldberg left his office, he started making phone calls to all the senior midwives and nurses in charge of the various maternity unit's wards and clinics to inform them of Samy's suspension and the fact that he was banned from coming into any part of the department or the hospital for any reason. He instructed them all to inform their staff of this, and although he was not supposed to reveal anything about the accusations against Samy, he informed everyone he talked to about the details of the woman's complaint. He then added his own comments to give them all the impression that Samy's guilt was a foregone conclusion.

When Mr Stewart phoned Jeremy Bell, the senior registrar, to inform him about Samy's suspension, he told him to get a locum registrar from one of the medical locum agencies to cover Samy's duties and finished by saying, 'Make sure that you get a good long-term locum because Samy is unlikely to return to work with us again. The case against him is watertight, so we must prepare for life without him.'

This last statement horrified Jeremy to no end. He could not believe that Samy was such an evil deviant who molested a woman while delivering her baby with so many witnesses around him. Jeremy did not particularly like Samy and was jealous of him as he seemed to have grabbed the attention and affections of a lot of the female staff in the unit, which dislodged Jeremy from his position as the most attractive and sought-after man in the department. However, this accusation that Samy faced was so awful he would not have wished it on his worst enemy, least of all on such a pleasant and kind colleague who never did him any harm.

Chapter 11

No way out

With a smirky smile on her face, sister Smith took particular pleasure in informing Alison of the decision to have Samy suspended and banned from entering the maternity unit. She finished by saying, 'So you see, he is not such a good catch after all. You told me in the changing room the other day that you have become very close to him, so good luck with your pervert. He will certainly need someone to hold on to as his career and his whole future goes down the drain. I hope you two will be very happy together because you certainly deserve each other.'

Alison was shell-shocked to hear that Samy had been suspended, which she had never expected and certainly not so quickly. She burst into tears and ran out of the labour ward to go to Samy's room in the doctors' residence.

Samy was in his room, sitting on the bed in a state of shock, still holding on to the envelope that contained the documents he was supposed to read and respond to. His mind was paralysed, and he did not know what to do or who he should turn to for advice or help. He could not see any way out of this disastrous situation, especially as his chief defence witness, sister Smith, seemed to have turned into a witness for the prosecution for no reason that was obvious to him.

For the first time since his childhood, Samy started to cry. His Medical career was his whole life and the only thing that gave him hope for a better future and a way out from the tough and austere circumstances that he had thus far. He knew that if Mr Stewart had his way, he would be struck off the medical register in the UK, and no other country in the world, including his native country Egypt, would allow him to practice medicine because he would be labelled forever as a sex offender. A proven charge of molesting a patient had always meant an abrupt and permanent end to a doctor's career. And as if this was not enough, the patient or the hospital might report him to the police, and he might end up with a lengthy jail sentence followed by deportation from England back to Egypt in utter disgrace. Was there any way out for him from this deep hole? If there was one, he was unable to see it.

Samy was startled when Alison knocked at his door. In his current state, he did not feel able to face anyone, not even the love of his life. He kept very quiet, hoping that whoever was knocking at his door would go away thinking that he was not in. However, the gentle knocking continued with Alison's tearful voice, begging him to open the door, getting louder and more persistent. Samy got up and wiped his face with a towel in a vain attempt to hide the fact that he had been crying for a long time and opened the door.

Alison had one look at Samy and realised straight away the dreadful state he was in. As soon as she closed the door behind her, she threw her arms around him, buried her head in his chest, and carried on crying uncontrollably. It took her a long while to be able to calm herself down, following which she sat him down on the bed and sat next to him. Samy struggled really hard to stop himself from crying in front of Alison.

Samy did not want to talk at all, let alone give Alison the details of his desperate situation. However, he needn't have worried about that because she already knew enough about what was going on and fully appreciated the very serious situation he was in. For the moment, they just held on to each other as they sat very still, with neither of them knowing what to say.

Their silence was interrupted by a loud knock at the door, and without waiting for a response, Jeremy entered. In their distress, neither Samy nor Alison locked the door from inside.

Jeremy seemed surprised to see Alison and Samy in each other's arms. He paused for a few seconds and said, 'Ah, this explains everything.'

Samy frowned as he gently freed himself from Alison's arms and said, 'What do you mean, Jeremy? What explains everything?'

'Mr Stewart was clearly on the warpath and coming after you with such venom and determination, which made me wonder about the reason. The accusations of this woman are very defendable, but Mr Stewart seemed to have already decided that you are the devil incarnate, and he wants you erased from his little world at St Luke's.'

Samy still looked puzzled, but before he could ask again, Jeremy said, 'It is Alison, you moron. Everyone in the department knows that he is absolutely besotted with her, and he obviously knew that you two were getting intimate with each other. So, this is his way of getting rid of a rival.'

Samy looked at Alison blankly and said nothing. Alison felt awful because she knew that Jeremy was right and worse was to come her way.

Jeremy waved his arm dismissively and said, 'This is not important now. There is nothing we can do about an aging consultant who is unable to control his urges toward a girl less than half his age. What matters is how to refute this ridiculous complaint. Are you a member of the British Medical Association, the doctors' trade union?'

'No, I am not. I could not afford the membership fee. Any spare cash I had, I always sent to my struggling family in Cairo. I never thought I would ever be in a situation that would require assistance from a trade union.'

Jeremy thought for a minute and then said, 'This we can fix straight away. I will lend you the money, and you will join the BMA today. It is very important that you have them in your corner because they will help you from the employment and contractual points of view. In addition, you need to join the Medical Defence Union, which is a medical insurance organization to help you with professional issues and litigations. I will lend you the money for this subscription, too, and you can pay me back whenever you can later on.'

Samy looked uncomfortable at the thought of borrowing money from Jeremy. He replied hesitantly, 'Is all that really necessary? I thought that all NHS employees are covered by Crown Indemnity, which means that the hospital is obliged to defend its staff and provide them with legal advice. This is also what I heard from Mrs Goldberg, the head of medical staffing today.'

Jeremy shook his head and said sharply, 'This would have been enough if the hospital was backing you for real. Unfortunately, Mr Stewart has appointed himself as the chief prosecutor in your case, and he is a very influential man. If he says that you are guilty, then the hospital will settle the case out of court to avoid the huge legal expenses of defending the case and give the woman massive compensation. The hospital's management will certainly not love you for that and will certainly be coming after you even if the whole matter was settled out of court. Getting rid of you may even have to be a part of the deal to shut the patient up. Giving her money may not be enough to satisfy her as she may want your head on a plate as well.'

Samy still looked unconvinced, so Jeremy continued, 'But this is not your biggest problem. The bigger worry is about the accusation of sexual assault, which may get you permanently struck off from the medical register by the General Medical Council. This will be the end of your medical career and, in addition, may land you in jail if the police get involved. Believe me, you will need every bit of help you can get, so you must join the trade union and the Medical Defence Union right away.'

Alison interrupted angrily, 'We were with Samy throughout the whole episode in the cubicle in the toilet from start to finish, sister Smith and myself. There is no way he had molested the patient or touched her inappropriately. There are two witnesses who were very close to the delivery and saw everything. In addition, there were so many people standing just outside the cubicle and in the corridor, so would anyone in his right mind think that there was any chance for a sexual assault?'

Jeremy looked at Alison for a moment and then said, 'This is the main problem for Samy. It seems that sister Smith is actually a hostile witness who is supporting the woman's accusations, though not explicitly. Mr Stewart was the one who told me that. She is obviously out for revenge because she was very keen on Samy, but he ignored her and went for you.'

Jeremy paused for a moment, looked at Alison, and added, 'As for your supportive testimony, it is worthless because you are his lover, and everyone will assume that you are just trying to save him at the expense of the poor patient. In any case, as a senior and very experienced midwife, sister Smith's testimony would carry far more weight than yours because you are an inexperienced and non-specialized doctor who had never seen a breech delivery before.'

This upset Alison far more than it upset Samy because Alison believed that her teasing and provocation of sister Smith in the changing room was what prompted her to change her mind and become a hostile witness. Alison could not help but feel responsible for bringing this disaster to Samy.

Jeremy and Samy were so engrossed in their conversation that they did not notice that Alison went as white as a sheet and was struggling to prevent herself from bursting into tears.

Jeremy asked Samy, with obvious impatience, 'Are you going to accept my help or not?'

'Of course, I will. I am very grateful to you. Very grateful indeed.'

'Alright then. We can get you to join the British Medical Association and the Medical Defence Union now and pay the fees on the Internet. I know the BMA's area representative and will phone him to see how we can get you the appropriate legal advice before you submit your response to the patient's complaint and to Mr Stewart's list of questions that he added to the patient's complaint. He also has links to the Medical Defence Union, so he may be able to get one of the specialist lawyers with him.'

'I have already written a report immediately after the delivery, and they have it on file.'

Jeremy shook his head and replied, 'A report written for a legal investigation is completely different from a contemporaneous report written to just document the sequence of events and the actions taken. You must trust me on this. The wording and the way you explain your actions have to be spot-on if you are to come out of this quagmire alive. You need a lawyer on your side to talk in the right way to the lawyer on the opposite side.'

Samy nodded in resignation and said nothing, while Alison remained completely silent. Jeremy said as he was about to leave, 'I will go to get my laptop so that we can get you to join the British Medical Association and the Medical Defence Union online right away, and we can then start looking at the complaint and how to respond to it.'

'Thank you very much, Jeremy. Thank you.'

As soon as Jeremy left, Alison fell into Samy's arms and burst into tears. She was shaking so violently Samy thought that she might have been having a fit.

Samy tried in vain to calm her down, but she continued to cry even harder and louder. What made it worse for her was the fact that she did not feel able to tell him about her guilt and shame. She was sure that her teasing of sister Smith in the changing room was what provoked her hostility towards Samy, so he was paying such a high price for Alison's childish antics.

Eventually, Samy said, 'That is enough, Alison, or I will start thinking that you, too, see no way out for me from this mess.'

Alison wiped her tears, and with great difficulty, she managed to stop crying. 'Not at all, sweetheart. This is nothing but a vindictive and malicious accusation which will go nowhere. I am just upset because it is so unfair. This should never have happened to anyone, least of all to you.'

Samy smiled and tried to sound confident 'God willing, the truth will eventually come out somehow. Now, I will need to read carefully what is in this complaint and make a start on how to respond to it before Jeremy comes back. So, sadly for me, you will need to go home so that I can concentrate on this. Try not to worry, my love, and I will keep you posted.'

Chapter 12
Saviour or executioner?

While Samy was waiting for Jeremy to return, he started looking at the contents of the envelope that was handed to him by Mr Stewart and Mrs Goldberg. He read the patient's complaint time and again. The difficulty he could see was the fact that almost in all the points she made, it would be her word against his. Who would people believe?

His concern increased exponentially when he looked at Mr Stewart's list of questions, which were clearly designed to trap him and force him to make statements that could be interpreted in ways that would sink him even further. This was not a neutral investigator trying to get to the truth but a prosecutor fishing for evidence that would condemn a criminal he knew for sure was guilty. To make matters more difficult for Samy, some of Mr Stewart's questions were not easy to understand as some did not have a specific or straightforward answer, and some sounded irrelevant to what had happened with that delivery. Obviously, Mr Stewart was deliberately trying to get him to give vague or hesitant answers, which would give the impression of an unsure and unreliable defendant.

Jeremy did not come back to see Samy as planned because he was called to the labour ward to deal with one emergency after another, so Samy started writing on his own a report with as many details as he could remember about what happened and all the procedures he performed. He also tried to address the complaints that the patient made about his conduct during the delivery and responded to all Mr Stewart's questions as much as he could.

It was nearly midnight when his mobile phone went off. Samy thought that it was Jeremy, but to his utter amazement, he heard Mr Stewart's voice saying, 'Hello, Samy. I hope that I have not woken you up. How are you coping?'

Samy was shocked, not just because Mr Stewart was phoning him, especially at this late hour, but also because of the friendly tone of his opening sentences.

It took Samy a few moments to recover his composure and reply quietly, 'I am fine, sir. Thank you.'

There was another long pause before Mr Stewart said, 'I am sticking my neck out here because, as I am the chief investigator of this complaint, I am not supposed to contact you or offer you any advice, but I felt that I should tell you a few things which may be of help to you. However, you have to keep this strictly between you and me because if the fact that I have helped you got out, I will be in a lot of trouble, and this will also worsen your situation.'

Mr Stewart paused again for a longer while this time, fully expecting Samy to be unnerved and unsettled by this totally unexpected change in his attitude. It was only a few hours before in his office when Mr Stewart was like a grizzly bear attacking Samy with such venom and aggression, so why was he offering to help him now? What brought on this sudden change of heart?

Mr Stewart felt that it was necessary to repeat what he had just said to make Samy believe that the executioner was offering to defend the condemned man. He said to Samy, with his voice getting louder to make sure that Samy could hear him clearly, 'Samy, I am offering to help you defend yourself and refute the accusations of this woman.'

Samy did not know how to respond as his mind froze. He remained silent, which forced Mr Stewart to elaborate further.

'I intended to give you all the help I could from the moment I heard about this patient's complaint, but I had to look angry and aggressive with you in front of Mrs Goldberg so that she would not suspect that I was really on your side and will do my best to save you, something an investigator of a complaint should never do because he is supposed to be neutral and objective.'

This explanation just increased Samy's puzzlement because Mr Stewart was the last one on earth he would have expected to offer him help of any kind, especially after what Jeremy had said earlier. Furthermore, it was not just that morning Mr Stewart had been aggressive and abusive towards him but for many weeks before that. Samy remained silent, thinking that there must be a 'catch' somewhere in Mr Stewart's offer.

Mr Stewart continued in the same warm and friendly tone of voice, 'The first and the most important thing I wanted to point out to you is that in this situation, you must do your very best to sort out this problem as quickly as possible because the longer you take to respond to the complaint, the more guilty you will look because people will think that you are struggling to make up and fabricate an appropriate response. Also, any delay will make the patient's anger and frustration just grow and grow. Speed is of the essence in the handling of a complaint of this nature.'

As Samy continued to remain silent, Mr Stewart was forced to check that Samy was still listening to him. 'Samy, are you still there?'

He was relieved to hear Samy saying, 'Of course, sir. I am just listening very intently. I am certainly very grateful for any advice you may care to give me.'

Samy then sighed and added, 'I have already got my response to the complaint written up as well as the answers to your list of questions. I was just waiting for Jeremy to help me join the trade union and the Medical Defence Union to review and edit ......'

Mr Stewart interrupted sharply, 'This will waste a lot of time, which you cannot afford. As I said to you just now, a speedy response will go a long way to diffuse the situation because this will show clearly that you have nothing to hide and that you are confident in your innocence. Moreover, a speedy response will demonstrate that you are a caring and empathetic doctor who is keen to ally the patient's worries and fears as quickly as he can. I am absolutely sure that a brief and to-the-point response will quash this complaint in no time at all, but if you start involving lawyers and trade unions in such an uncomplicated case, the whole matter will be blown totally out of proportion, and the proceedings will take a very long time. This, of course, will upset the patient a lot and will increase her hostility and hatred when she could have been pacified and calmed down with a speedy and respectful response. Most patients are just seeking reassurance and explanation, not compensation. I am sure that this patient will drop all her accusations once she receives the appropriate response. I have spoken to her at length, and I am confident that we can get her to drop all her complaints if we approach her in the right way. Trust me, I know what I am talking about, having dealt with such cases hundreds of times over the years.'

There was another long pause, with each of them waiting for the other to say something. Samy eventually said, 'I am really very grateful to you, sir, for taking the time to advise me. This is very kind and generous. But I hope that you do not mind me asking you, although I am clearly innocent as you say, do you think that it is still worth getting legal advice and guidance from the Medical Defence Union about how to present my response, which is what Jeremy and Mrs Goldberg advised me to do?'

Mr Stewart replied impatiently, 'This would have been necessary if you were guilty and needed to dress things up with fancy lawyer's talk to hide your guilt. But we both know that you have nothing to hide, and all that is needed is just a simple and honest response. I will be very happy to review your response myself to make sure that it fulfils all the patient's expectations and the hospital's requirements. Ignore Jeremy's nonsense; he does not know anything about medico-legal matters. Mrs Goldberg is just a bureaucrat who would always insist on prolonged and convoluted procedures, multiple meetings, and the involvement of all and sundry for no reason at all. This is just the way her mind works, and in your situation, this will only make matters worse. Remember, I am the chief investigator in your case, so I will make sure that your response contains exactly what everyone expects to reach the right conclusion. However, we will have to do this very quietly so that no one knows that I have helped you in any way because this will be blatantly wrong and unethical in view of the fact that I am the hospital's chief investigator and I am supposed to be impartial. I cannot over-emphasize this point enough.'

Samy was getting even more confused by this sudden flood of sympathy and support from Mr Stewart, who had never had a kind word to say to him since he started working at St Luke's maternity hospital, but he found it impossible to turn down such an offer of help from his boss, who was exposing himself to serious professional risks if his help to Samy was discovered. He was frantically searching for a response, but he could not find anything adequate or logical to say. He did not trust Mr Stewart, but he could not ignore his genuinely friendly tone of voice or his readiness to risk his own career and professional standing in order to help him.

Samy's silence worried Mr Stewart, so he rushed to hammer the point home. 'You also need to remember that the longer this investigation goes on, the longer you are suspended from work, which is very damaging to your career and your reputation. More seriously, there is the risk of the patient reporting you to the police and the General Medical Council if she finds that our investigation is taking a long time. Just get your hand-written response to me, and I will review it and make the necessary adjustments. I will then have it typed and return it to you to see if you are happy with it, following which you can give it yourself to Mrs Goldberg. We can get this problem nipped in the bud before it becomes a major issue, but you have to act immediately if you want my help. You need to trust me, Samy, because I know what I am talking about. I have been involved in the handling of complaints and legal actions for decades.'

Although Samy felt very uncomfortable about the whole conversation with Mr Stewart, he felt that he had no option but to accept his advice.

'I have been working on my response all day, and I think I have covered all that is required, so I will be able to get it to you tomorrow if that is alright with you.'

'As a matter of fact, Samy, I have not gone home yet. I am still in my office at the hospital, so if you can get your response to me now, I will read it and edit it straight away. I will then have it typed by my private secretary first thing in the morning and get it back to you for review. This will enable you to hand it over to Mrs Goldberg in Medical Staffing tomorrow, and the whole matter will be over and done with. I bet that Mrs Goldberg, as well as the patient herself, will be very impressed with your speedy response. This will speak volumes of innocence.'

'But I need to write it up in a more organized way for you to read, sir.'

'Do not worry about that. What matters most is the substance and not the style or the appearance. The whole thing will have to be typed anyway, so just give me what you have done as it is, and I will do the rest. I keep telling you, speed is of the essence here, so let us not waste any time.'

Samy was unable to resist Mr Stewart's pressure, and he agreed to take his notes to him straight away. Mr Stewart sounded delighted that he had his way, and he finished the conversation by saying, 'It will be best if you do not come to my office at this time of night because this could raise suspicions if someone saw you there. My car is parked very close to the doctors' residence, so you can drop your papers to me there. I will keep my car's headlights on until you come. Please remember that this is strictly between you and me. No one should ever know that I had anything to do with your response, or we will both be in even bigger trouble. Do I have your word of honour on that?'

'Absolutely, sir. Thank you very much.'

****

Mr Stewart was standing by his car as Samy handed him the papers that contained his rough notes. Mr Stewart smiled warmly and said, 'There is no need for you to worry, Samy. You will be absolutely fine, I promise.'

As he sat in his car, he added, 'Once again, I am sorry that I had to act so aggressively with you earlier in front of Mrs Goldberg, but this was just a smoke screen so that she does not suspect that I am going to help you, which was what I intended to do all along. All this may seem unnecessary, but what I am doing to help you could be viewed as serious professional misconduct by the hospital or the General Medical Council, hence the need for all this subterfuge.'

Samy frowned as he was clearly uncomfortable with the thought that something illegal or unethical was going to be involved in conducting his defence. If he was innocent, as he knew for sure, why should he need such underhand, unethical, and even illegal ways to prove it?

Mr Stewart rushed to allay his fears before he left, 'There is nothing wrong with what we are doing, Samy. We are just trying to get to the truth quickly, which is what is best for the patient and for you. We are not falsifying any evidence or employing lies, fakes or false witnesses in your defence. This is just a short cut that will spare you and the patient a lot of distress and, in the process, save the hospital a lot of money that would have gone on lawyers' fees. Proving your innocence is not just important for you and the patient but also for the reputation of the whole department, the hospital and the NHS as a whole. So, I am not doing all this just for you.'

Samy watched Mr Stewart's car leave the hospital with a worried look on his face. He stood in the cold, dark night, wondering if what he had just done was the right course of action. Had he just made the wise decision by using Mr Stewart's generous offer of support in finding a quick escape route from a possible disaster that could ruin his life and his career? Or had he just helped Mr Stewart put his head in the hangman's noose? Only time will tell.

Samy had a sleepless night with his mind going round in circles, worrying about the sinister nature of the patient's complaint and the prospects of a guilty verdict that would label him forever as an incompetent, careless and unsafe doctor combined with an accusation of being a sexual deviant. Even if such charges were dismissed, he knew that it was not uncommon in these situations that many people would feel that there was 'no smoke without fire' and he would always have this black cloud hanging over his head wherever he went.

Samy also could not work out why Mr Stewart's attitude towards him had changed so much and whether his kindness and desire to help him were really genuine. Because of his trusting nature and his natural tendency to think the best of everyone, Samy tried to talk himself into taking what Mr Stewart said to him at face value. He also kept telling himself that Mr Stewart, as he said himself, had another very important reason to help him out of this predicament, which was to save the department's and the hospital's reputations. Mr Stewart was the one who appointed Samy to this post at St Luke's, and for this reason, he would want to avoid the blame and the responsibility of having appointed an incompetent pervert, so there was an element of personal self-interest in his desire to help Samy. Whatever his reasons were, Mr Stewart was now in-charge of Samy's fate, and it was too late for Samy to do anything about it.

****

Just before 7 o'clock in the morning, Mr Stewart rang Samy on his mobile phone and asked him to come down to the same place in the hospital's car park where they met the previous night. Samy rushed down, and Mr Stewart signalled to him to come and sit next to him in his car.

Mr Stewart smiled warmly at Samy and said in a concerned voice, 'You look tired, Samy. Have you had any sleep last night?'

Samy shook his head in the negative and replied, 'I could not sleep at all, sir. This situation I am in is an absolute nightmare.'

Mr Stewart looked at him sympathetically and said, 'This is very understandable. However, it will be over soon, and everything will go back to normal very quicky once we get your response to Mrs Goldberg. Here it is, all neatly typed and arranged in the right order.'

Mr Stewart handed Samy a folder and continued, 'I spent most of the night working on arranging your response in the right way, added a few points and deleted a few things to make it just perfect. I have checked and corrected your answers to the additional list of questions as well. I have then got my very disgruntled private secretary to type all this at dawn today, and here it is. You owe her a cup of coffee and a piece of cake in return for all her efforts.'

Samy started reading the documents with a racing heart, anxious to see whether his response sounded convincing now that it had been reviewed by Mr Stewart. The more he read, the more he was impressed with the professionalism and accuracy of the typing of the document, which impaired his ability to judge objectively the substance of what he was reading. On the whole, though, he felt that the response to the complaint in this form certainly looked much better and more convincing than his rough notes. Mr Stewart had not only rearranged and altered Samy's responses, but he had also re-written certain parts from scratch and deleted some paragraphs altogether. Samy started to believe that Mr Stewart was well and truly on his side, and he felt rather guilty because he had doubts about his sincerity. His sense of relief was immense.

Mr Stewart sat silently next to Samy to give him the opportunity to digest what he was reading. When Samy finished, he turned to Mr Stewart and said, 'I really cannot thank you enough, sir. This is fantastic. I could have never done this myself.'

Mr Stewart smiled and replied, 'It is all your own doing. I just arranged the paragraphs in the right order and changed a few sentences here and there. So, it is all your very own handy work, and you must always say that to anyone who asks. I was very pleased to see that you addressed all the issues in the patient's complaint so well and so clearly. Your response to my list of questions was just as impressive. I can tell you now with absolute confidence that you have nothing to worry about, absolutely nothing.'

Mr Stewart was obviously stressing the fact that his role in the writing of this response was a peripheral one. He was just an editor, and Samy was certainly the one and only author of this response to the complaint.

Samy shook Mr Stewart's hand warmly and said, 'I will never forget this, Mr Stewart. You are very kind, and I am eternally grateful for your help.'

'Not at all. There are two copies of your response in this folder. Take one to Mrs Goldberg in the medical staffing department and hand it to her yourself. Keep the second copy for yourself just in case there are any queries in future. Remember, not a word to anyone about my involvement in this. Not even to Alison.'

Hearing Mr Stewart mention Alison's name worried Samy to no end because it reminded him of what Jeremy said in relation to Mr Stewart's feelings for Alison. However, he said nothing and left the car.

****

At exactly 9 O'clock in the morning, Samy went to see Mrs Goldberg. She was surprised to see him so soon but greeted him warmly. She then said, 'Was there anything you wanted to discuss or enquire about, Samy?'

226

Samy shook his head as he handed her the folder which contained the response to the complaint that Mr Stewart had prepared for him.

'I have just come to give you my response to the patient's complaint and to Mr Stewart's list of questions.'

Mrs Goldberg frowned with a mixture of disbelief and concern as she said, 'You finished it all already? Have you obtained medico-legal advice or the trade union review, as I advised you yesterday? Do you want to discuss your response with one of the hospital's lawyers before you submit it?'

Samy replied calmly, 'I had all the advice that I need. I do not want this matter hanging over my head for any length of time. I believe that I am clearly innocent, and for this reason, I want this nightmare to be over as soon as possible. I need to go back to work and continue my training. This suspension is damaging my career, my reputation and my mental health.'

Mrs Goldberg's frown got even deeper as she said, 'Of course, it is up to you, Samy. I fully understand why you feel you need to proceed with all possible haste to clear your name and end your suspension, but these matters are always complicated and are best handled at the right pace to make sure that everything is thoroughly and very carefully dissected to ensure that the responses are exactly as they should be. There is no room for any errors, and rushing things can be very costly.'

Samy responded again in a calm but determined way, 'I appreciate the point you make, Mrs Goldberg, but I am sure that presenting my response to you now is the right course of action as this will save us all a lot of time. My defence is clear-cut, and my response will show that my actions were all appropriate, so there is no reason for any delay.'

Mrs Goldberg paused for a moment and then asked, 'You said that you had all the advice you needed. Can I ask you who had given you such advice?'

Samy looked uncomfortable and hesitant as he said, 'I am very sorry, Mrs Goldberg, but I cannot answer this question. Rest assured though that my adviser is very experienced in these matters, and he was the one who recommended that I should give you my response today without delay.'

Mrs Goldberg took the folder from Samy and said, 'Fine. I will read your response now and will then pass it on to Mr Stewart, as he is the chief investigator for the hospital. Depending on our discussion with our lawyers in the legal department, we will see if there is a case to answer which will determine the next step in the proceedings. Most patients who complain wait for the result of the internal investigation of the hospital before they approach their own solicitors to take the hospital and the doctors to court.

Lawyers for the patients usually would not take on a case formally until they have seen from the hospital's internal investigation that there is a reasonable chance of proving negligence. They only get paid if the patient wins, so they are always keen to see some evidence of shortfalls or mistakes in the patient's treatment documented by the hospital's own investigation, which will give them some idea about the prospect of winning compensation.'

Samy was not taking in most of what Mrs Goldberg was saying. He had not had any sleep the previous night and had not eaten or had any drinks for most of the previous day, as well as being physically, mentally and emotionally exhausted, which meant that he was just keen to get back to his room to crash out for a long overdue sleep.

He politely thanked Mrs Goldberg and hastened back to his room, where he threw himself on the bed, fully clothed with his shoes on. He could not think about anything anymore and just fell into deep sleep.

Chapter 13

The Suicide Note

It was lunchtime when Samy was awakened by a persistent knocking on the door. It was Alison and Jeremy on their lunch break, wanting to see how he was. Jeremy explained to Samy that several labour ward emergencies prevented him from coming to see him the previous evening as was planned. Samy looked at Jeremy expressionlessly and did not react to what he said.

Jeremy got fed up waiting for Samy to say something, so, with his usual crude sense of humour, he said, 'You look like something the cat had just dragged in from the rubbish tip. You need a bath and something to eat. I can help you with the latter, and I bet Alison would like to help you with the former, you lucky devil.'

Neither Samy nor Alison were in the mood for Jeremy's jokes. Alison said sharply as she went to hug Samy and kiss him on the cheek, 'Shut up, Jeremy. Samy does not need your not-so-funny jokes right now. Just give him the sandwiches you brought for him and keep quiet.'

Jeremy shrugged his shoulder and handed Samy a couple of sandwiches and a can of Pepsi, which he had got from the hospital's cantine. Samy took them reluctantly and just put them on the table, obviously not intending to eat or drink anything. He sat on the bed and looked at his watch. He was surprised to see that it was already lunchtime because he thought that he had just fallen asleep for a few minutes, but actually, he had been asleep for over three hours.

Jeremy said, in a serious tone of voice this time, 'We have a lot to do today, mate, so please have something to eat and drink because I need you to be fully alert.'

Samy did not respond and just looked at him blankly with an apathetic expression on his face. This irritated Jeremy, who was trying to help him and thought that Samy was not appreciating how much time and effort he had been putting in on his behalf.

Alison unwrapped one of the sandwiches, opened the can of Pepsi and forced them into Samy's hands as she said, 'Please, darling. Just do this for me. Eat something.'

Jeremy was relieved to see Samy responding positively to Alison, albeit reluctantly, as he started eating the sandwich slowly and sipping the drink. Jeremy started explaining the plan which he thought Samy would need to follow. 'First of all, I am sure you realise the seriousness of the situation because this woman's written complaint is dynamite. When I read it, I could not believe how well-written it was. It is clear, concise and to the point, listing the events chronologically and logically. It rang true, although I know for sure that it isn't.'

Both Samy and Alison were about to say something, but Jeremy raised his hand to signal to them that he had not finished. 'On the other hand, the contemporaneous statement you wrote on the day of the delivery is disorganized, rambling and vague. It is also written in 'bad English', which I do not blame you for because, after all, you are a foreigner, and although you speak excellent English, writing a legal report is a completely different matter. You need a lot of help with that, and the whole thing will have to be re-written from scratch.'

Samy replied in a low, monotonous voice, 'I have already had it re-written and submitted it to medical staffing earlier this morning.'

Neither Jeremy nor Alison could believe their ears. Alison was horrified, and Jeremy looked very annoyed. Jeremy shouted, 'Have you gone barking mad? I thought I told you very clearly yesterday that you must not do anything on your own until you get specialist medico-legal advice from the lawyers of the Medical Defence Union and the British Medical Association.'

Samy replied without reacting to Jeremy's anger, 'I have got specialist advice from someone who has extensive experience in these matters, and he reviewed my response in detail. All the corrections were made, and he had it typed neatly and professionally. He was the one who advised me to submit it to medical staffing straight away because a speedy response would make all the difference to my position in this mess. A copy is over there on the desk. Have a look, and you will see that it was very well done.'

Alison asked in a shaky voice, 'From whom did you get this advice, Samy?'

As Jeremy went to the desk to read the typed response which Mr Stewart had prepared, Samy replied to Alison, 'I am sorry, Alison, but I cannot reveal that to anyone. I have given my word to keep this confidential.'

Alison frowned and was unable to understand the reason for the secrecy. Jeremy shook his head in despair as he started reading the document. He was impressed to see the high quality of the typing and the general presentation. However, as he read page after page, his first favourable impression quickly disappeared to be replaced by a mixture of tremendous anger and utter frustration.

Alison could see the change in Jeremy's facial expression and realised that there was a serious problem with Samy's report. She knew that Jeremy, as the senior registrar and so close to becoming a consultant, knew a lot more about the handling of litigations and patients' complaints than Samy. For this reason, if Jeremy felt that there was a problem with Samy's report, then Samy must be in real trouble.

When Jeremy finished reading Samy's report, he sat silently for a few moments while gritting his teeth and clenching his fists. Samy's heart sank as he heard Jeremy's verdict.

'This is not a response to a complaint; this is a suicide note and a very long one at that. I do not care who is the idiot you got to review this rubbish, but you have managed to make a very serious situation even worse. You totally failed to explain the two main issues in the complaint, which are why the patient was delivered in the toilet and not taken to a delivery room or the operating theatre and why she felt that you were rubbing her clitoris and your fingers going in and out of her arse and her vagina repeatedly throughout the whole delivery. These were the main issues that you should have explained clearly and in detail rather than wasting time describing the technique of vaginal breech delivery and how you delivered the placenta. In addition, you did not discuss the woman's unreasonable behaviour and how she was the main reason for all the difficulties she had with the delivery.'

Samy protested, 'I did not want to sound like I am trying to blame her for what happened or make her look as if she was awkward, abusive or a liar, although she really was. My fingers never went into her anus or rubbed her clitoris, and I stated that clearly in my response. I thought that criticizing her a lot would have just provoked her anger and aggression even more.'

Jeremy stood up to leave as he was unable to control his overflowing anger and despair. He felt that there was nothing he could do to help Samy after he had handed this inadequate response to Mrs Goldberg in spite of what Jeremy told him the day before about getting the advice of the trade union and the medical insurance experts before doing anything.

Alison rushed to hold Jeremy's arm and pleaded, 'Please, Jeremy, just calm down and tell Samy what he should do now. You are far more knowledgeable and experienced in these matters than him.'

Samy, who was still holding a half-eaten sandwich in one hand and a can of Pepsi in the other, said in a very shaky voice, 'I am sorry to have upset you, Jeremy. I know you are trying to help, and for that, I am really very grateful, but this is what I was advised to do last night. My response was given the all-clear by that expert, and I was almost ordered to submit the report to Mrs Goldberg in medical staffing as soon as she arrived at 9 O'clock this morning.'

Jeremy was about to shout at Samy, but Alison, who was still holding his arm to prevent him from leaving, squeezed his arm firmly to stop him. Jeremy looked at her pleading, beautiful face and immediately calmed down.

He said, 'I do not understand why you refuse to tell us who advised you on this matter. It must be someone we know because you do not want us to identify him. He must also be someone from this hospital because you were able to see him so quickly. The only people I know who could advise you on medico-legal matters in this hospital are the two consultants, Mr Stout and Mr Stewart. It cannot be Mr Stewart because he is the chief investigator of the complaint, and he is supposed to remain completely neutral. He is certainly not supposed to take your side or give you any advice, and, more importantly, he absolutely hates your guts.'

Samy remained silent and kept his gaze fixed on the floor because he was concerned that his facial expression might give Jeremy a clue about who had advised him.

Jeremy continued, 'The other consultant, Mr Stout, is away this week, so you would not have had access to him. In addition, Mr Stout certainly knows far more than most about medico-legal issues, so I do not believe that he would have approved this dreadful response that you have submitted or advised you to hand it over to medical staffing so quickly. So, who could it be? I would not be surprised if this adviser was one of the cleaners or the kitchen staff.'

Samy was obviously not going to reveal the name of his adviser as he remained silent and stared at the floor. Jeremy waved his hand dismissively and said, 'Oh, hell. It does not matter anymore. The report has been submitted, and that is that. My question now is this: do you still want my help, or will you continue to follow the guidance of this stupid adviser who is taking you straight to the gallows?'

Samy replied, 'I do not think that there is any chance that I will be getting any more help from him, so I would very much appreciate your help, and I promise to follow your advice to the letter from now on.'

Samy looked so pathetic and downhearted, which forced Jeremy to mellow and feel sorry for him. He did not want to add to his misery and distress, so he changed subjects.

'We should still go ahead with registering you with the British Medical Association and with the Medical Defence Union. I am sure that they will both confirm to you my opinion on your miserable submission and its damaging effect on your situation. I am hoping that they will be able to suggest some sort of strategy to try to resolve the situation. I have already had a word with the British Medical Association's local representative and the Medical Defence Union's centre about your case, and a specialist lawyer, together with a BMA representative, will be coming tonight to discuss everything with you. We will need to e-mail them all the documents related to the complaint after obliterating the patient's personal details so that they have the chance to formulate some idea about the plan to defend you. We just have to hope that this woman does not get the police involved at this stage because this is certainly the most complex and the most serious aspect of the problem.'

This last statement seemed to upset Alison far more than it did Samy because it reminded her of her role in bringing this predicament on Samy. Her feelings of guilt were growing by the minute, and she felt utterly helpless and unable to do anything to save him. She wondered if it would have been better for this lovely, bright young man not to have ever laid eyes on her.

Samy stood up and shook Jeremy's hand as he said, 'I cannot thank you enough, Jeremy. To go through so much trouble on my behalf is overwhelming. I am just so shell-shocked and unhinged that I am unable to think clearly about anything. My training and work as a doctor are all I have in this world, and I stand to lose everything for something I did not do.'

Jeremy smiled reassuringly and patted Samy on the back as he said, 'Try not to worry too much. I am sure that the truth will come out eventually. We just have to fight for it in the right way. Just remember that you are not alone in this battle. There are a lot of people who like you and will help you as much as they can.'

He then suddenly frowned again. 'The one to watch, though, is sister Smith. She seems to enjoy seeing you in this predicament and is going all out to sink you. While trying to avoid being too obvious, she is spreading a lot of rumours and insinuations about what actually happened during the delivery of that woman. I assume that she is after your blood because you jilted her and rejected her advances. She clearly fancied this lovely Egyptian Casanova, but he was too slow to respond. You should have satisfied her lust for you long ago, you idiot. This would have saved you a lot of trouble. If

I were you, I would have devoured her given half a chance, just to keep the peace.'

Alison smacked his wrist and shouted, 'Not everyone thinks like you, Jeremy.'

Samy was not in the mood for this sort of talk. He said, 'I never felt like a Casanova and never will. I did not believe for a minute that she would decide to become my enemy because I did not sleep with her. She is a much better person than that.'

Alison and Jeremy looked at each other, and then Jeremy said, 'This just shows how much you know about women.'

He then asked, 'I am free this evening, so do you want me to come with you to this meeting with the BMA representative and the lawyer?'

Samy responded promptly, 'Absolutely. I would very much appreciate your support and your input. I am well and truly out of my depth here. I have never been involved in something like this, and I am concerned that I will mess things up even more. Obviously, I have already made my first big mistake with that report, which I submitted to medical staffing this morning.'

'Alright then, I will bring them to your room, and we will see what they will say. I better go back to work now.'

As Jeremy turned to leave the room, Alison jumped up, kissed him on the cheek and said, 'Thank you very much,

Jeremy. I do not care what they all say about you. I think you are wonderful.'

Jeremy smiled happily and said, 'You see, Samy, women just cannot help but attack me at every opportunity. I am totally irresistible.'

****

Alison did not leave Samy until he had eaten his sandwiches and drank the Pepsi can. She then left him to rest and have some sleep before his crucial meeting with the BMA representative and the lawyer. She made him promise to ring her as soon as the lawyer left to let her know what he said.

Alison walked slowly towards the labour ward with her mind in real turmoil. Although she did not have any experience in medico-legal problems or the handling of patients' complaints, she could see clearly that Samy was facing a possible catastrophe. His situation might have been less bleak if sister Smith supported him in her testimony or if Mr Stewart was not so hostile to him. However, thanks to his relationship with Alison, these two are aiming to ruin his career and even put him in jail.

Alison kept wondering if the problem would have been simpler if she had kept her relationship with Samy a secret, if she had not childishly provoked sister Smith's anger by telling her how Samy was getting close to her or if she somehow tried to keep Mr Stewart sweet rather than treating him dismissively and rudely rebuff all his advances time and again. Samy might have had a fighting chance then of coming out of this disaster unscathed. But as things were, Alison could see the writing on the wall for Samy, and she would have played a major role in his inevitable downfall. How could she live with herself if the most wonderful man she had ever known and the only one she had ever really loved ended up utterly ruined because of her?

By the time Alison reached the labour ward, her mind was made up. She got Samy into this mess, and she would have to be the one to get him out of it, whatever the price.

Throughout the day, Alison carried out her duties in the labour ward like a robot. She was doing the tasks asked of her slowly and meticulously with a grim expression on her face. She knew that her mind was not on the job at all, and for this reason, she was trying to be as slow and deliberate as possible to avoid making any mistakes. All the staff around her noticed that she was not her normal bubbly self, and no one was able to get her out of the black mood she was obviously in.

As soon as her labour ward shift ended, Alison rushed to her car and drove to her flat as fast as she could, ignoring red lights and speed limits. She had a serious decision to make, and there was no time to waste. She had to quickly find a way to help Samy out of this quagmire, but what could she do? Whichever way she tried to look at the situation, there was only one key that she could see to unlock this complex problem: Mr Stewart.

Alison dreaded having to approach Mr Stewart, but he was the only one holding all the strings, and no one else but him had any significant power or influence on the outcome of this investigation. But what could she say to him to get him to help Samy? How would he react to her trying to interfere in a very serious complaint such as this? She heard from Jeremy that Mr Stewart was supposed to be neutral and objective in his investigation, so it would be highly irregular to ask him to manipulate the investigation in Samy's favour. How would he react to her intervention on Samy's behalf, and would this make matters worse for Samy? Would it just ignite his jealousy and obsession further?

Alison sat in her flat staring at her phone, not knowing what to do for the best. Should she phone Mr Stewart, and if she did, what should she say? She was in floods of tears and totally unable to decide on a plan of action.

****

After Jeremy and Alison left Samy's room earlier that day, Samy, who was utterly exhausted, could not go to sleep straight away. He struggled to accept that Mr Stewart was just leading him down the garden path to oblivion by deliberately getting him to submit a 'suicide note,' as Jeremy described it, to the medical staffing department. Mr Stewart sounded so genuine, kind and supportive. Was all this just falsehood and deceit? Could a great consultant like him sink to this level? What should he do if Mr Stewart approached him again with more advice? Should he accept or turn down any more of his recommendations?

In the evening, the meeting with the BMA representative and the lawyer that Jeremy arranged confirmed Samy's worst fears. They both agreed that his response to the patient was totally inadequate, poorly worded and would complicate his situation a lot. However, they reassured him that the situation was not hopeless by any means and the battle was just starting. Everyone now had to wait for the result of the internal investigation of the hospital and the patient's next action once she saw the hospital's final report.

The next stage was likely to be a letter from a lawyer who would be employed by the patient requesting a copy of the full set of notes of her delivery and the statements from the various witnesses. This would indicate that the real fight was about to start in earnest. Samy was told in no uncertain terms not to take any further steps in this matter on his own. Everything, big or small, must be discussed with his lawyers before any action is taken.

The lawyer finished the session by saying, 'I have to be frank with you; you have a huge problem here. In most cases, when it is the patient's word against the doctor's, the scales tend to tip in favour of the patient, especially in matters of sexual assault, so we will have to proceed with caution and hope for the best.'

After they all left, Samy sat on the edge of his bed, motionless and in deep thought. What the lawyer said at the end made him realise that the deep hole he had fallen into was actually a lot deeper than he thought. Samy phoned Alison on her mobile phone to tell her about what went on with the lawyer and the bleak prospects he obviously predicted. Samy was so upset he failed to notice that Alison was falling to pieces at the other end of the phone and was struggling to respond to him.

Samy's phone call made the decision for Alison. She would have to approach Mr Stewart, come what may. This would be an 'all or nothing' gamble because Mr Stewart would either respond positively to her by doing his very best to save Samy or would be more determined to crush him to smithereens. However, there was no other way, and she had to act immediately.

****

It was 10 O'clock at night when Alison rang Mr Stewart at home.

'Good evening, Mr Stewart. This is Alison.'

There was a pause for a few moments, following which Mr Stewart responded coldly, 'Hello, Alison. I have been expecting your call.'

'I am very sorry to disturb you at this late hour. I have tried earlier, but you were out.'

'I had a private case to sort out. I think I know why you are calling.'

Alison was taken aback, and after some hesitation, she said, 'Do you? Tell me then, what do you think I want to talk to you about?'

His answer was one word: 'Samy!'

Alison was unsettled even further because he had worked out what her motives were so easily. This ruled out her plan to take a gradual and subtle approach to the subject.

Before she could find the right response, Mr Stewart added, 'You want to try to save your lover-boy. Isn't this what you have in mind?'

The sarcastic tone of voice of Mr Stewart upset Alison a lot, and she struggled to keep control of her emotions. The speech she had prepared seemed to have just vanished from her mind. She tried quickly to find something sensible to say but found it very difficult to get her brain into gear. With a shaken voice, she said, 'I was there when it all happened, Mr

Stewart. I saw everything from start to finish, and I cannot believe that the fantastic miracle he performed in such difficult circumstances could end up ruining his career.'

Mr Stewart replied impatiently, 'It is not just his career that is at stake here. He may end up going to jail for a very long time for being a sexual pervert.'

Before Alison could say anything else, Mr Stewart continued in the same authoritative, firm tone of voice, 'Anyway, the investigation is well on the way, and we will soon find if your lover-boy is a real hero or an incompetent doctor as well as a criminal pervert.'

This sent shivers down Alison's spine, and she became even more desperate to do whatever was needed to stop Mr Stewart from crushing Samy, as he was obviously determined to do.

She said while trying hard not to burst into tears, 'Please stop calling him my lover-boy. I just want to talk to you about all this because I know that you want to see justice done, and you are the only one who can get to the truth.'

Saying this in such a pleading, pathetic voice appealed to Mr Stewart's vanity and arrogance. He knew for sure then that he had her well and truly locked up in his trap. His anger calmed down, and he said quietly, 'I have seen your written statement about the delivery, so is there anything else you want to add?'

Alison replied in a suggestive way, 'There is a lot more that I can add to my written statement, but I prefer to talk to you face-to-face if that is alright with you.'

Mr Stewart paused for a few moments to prolong Alison's discomfort. Having chased her in vain for so long, seeing her grovelling and desperate to see him gave him a very satisfying sense of triumph and power. He remained silent for a while because he did not want her to think that she only had to snap her fingers, and he would fall at her feet and do whatever she wanted.

'Alright then. I will check my diary and see when we can meet in the next few days.'

'Please, sir, this cannot wait. If you are not too tired, I can come to your house now. I promise that I will not take a lot of your time.'

Mr Stewart smiled to himself as he kept her waiting for a reply for a few more moments. Then he said in a dismissive tone of voice, 'Alright then. You can come to my house now, and I will listen to what you have to say. I am just angry at the fact that I have invited you to come to my house so many times and you have always refused. Now that your lover-boy is in trouble, you are so keen on coming even at this late hour. It must be true love.'

Alison replied, still struggling to hold back her tears, 'I never meant any disrespect towards you at any time, and I have every faith in your ability and desire to get justice done for such a wonderful doctor. Nothing else matters.'

'Nothing else matters indeed. I will see you later on then, but I must make it clear that I am only interested in clear facts and solid evidence and not your emotions or feelings for him.'

'I would expect nothing else, Mr Stewart. Thank you very much, sir. I will see you shortly.'

As soon as Mr Stewart put the phone down, he jumped for joy like a schoolboy who had just scored a goal in a football match. He ran into the bathroom to have a shower and shave. He kept saying to himself, 'She is really coming. She is really coming. Thank you, Samy!'

Chapter 14

Desperate situations call for desperate measures

Alison had to ring the doorbell three times before Mr Stewart opened the door. He looked coldly at her as he said, 'Do come in, Alison.'

Alison gave him a radiant smile and said as she walked in, 'Good evening, Mr Stewart. I am very sorry to disturb you so late.'

Mr Stewart said nothing as he showed her into the sitting room. Alison sat on the sofa while he sat on the chair opposite. She waited for him to start the conversation, but he just sat there staring at her without saying anything. His face expressed a mixture of simmering anger and contempt, which made Alison realise that this was going to be even more difficult than she thought it would be.

Mr Stewart himself did not realise the extent of the anger and frustration that had built up within him because of all these months of chasing Alison without being able to get anywhere near her. He never knew whether his obsession with her was caused by overwhelming love, uncontrollable lust or a mixture of the two. As he had her in his house for the first time and obviously in a submissive mood, he found it difficult to know how to make the most of this advantageous situation. Should he show her his tender, loving side, or should he let his angry, vengeful feelings take over? The former did not get him anywhere with her in the past, so it may be that the latter should be what was indicated in the current situation. After all, she had rejected his many advances for so long only to give herself to an Egyptian immigrant. This must be pay-back time, he thought to himself. She would have to pay dearly for all the hurt and suffering she had caused.

Alison could see clearly that Mr Stewart was not in an agreeable mood, and for this reason, she tried hard to turn on the charm. 'I am very grateful to you for giving me the opportunity to talk to you tonight and ...'

Mr Stewart interrupted impatiently, 'Alison, it is rather late, and I am tired, so let us cut to the chase. What is it you wanted to say about Samy and that episode in the toilet? Do you have anything new to add to what I have already read in your statement?'

Alison froze for a few moments as she saw that her plan was falling apart. She thought that she only had to show up at Mr Stewart's house, and he would just melt in her hands and do whatever she asked. How wrong she was!

Mr Stewart was pleased that Alison was rattled by his rather aggressive attitude, and he wanted to make sure that the pressure on her was maintained. He continued, 'I will be frank with you and will tell you exactly the position Samy is in at the moment, but you must give me your word that you will not utter a word to anyone about this, not even to your lover-boy.'

Alison nodded and said quietly, 'Of course, sir. I promise.'

This time, she did not care that he was still calling Samy 'her lover-boy' although she had asked him not to. What mattered most to her was helping Samy, and for this, she was prepared to put up with whatever Mr Stewart was going to throw at her.

'There are two main points in this case which are indefensible. The first is his failure to take the patient to the operating theatre to deliver her in an environment which would have been much safer for her and the baby. He spent a long time delivering the baby in the toilet, which shows that there was plenty of time to take her to the operating theatre. This confirms his very poor judgement and clinical incompetence because he should have known that delivering a complex breech with the patient flat on the floor of a toilet could have caused serious damage to the mother and her baby.'

Mr Stewart paused for a few moments to build up the tension and then continued, 'The second point, which is certainly more sinister, is what the patient stated about him fingering her anus, her vagina and rubbing her clitoris repeatedly during the delivery for no obvious clinical reasons. Why would the patient make up something like this?'

Alison's face was getting paler with every word Mr Stewart was saying, and she looked increasingly upset, which pleased him no end.

'To be honest with you, Alison, Samy's fate is sealed. I have discussed all this with our legal experts and an independent medical assessor from the hospital's medical insurance company. They all agreed that Samy is clearly guilty on all accounts. Case closed.'

Of course, all this was a blatant lie. He had not discussed the case with anyone, and the investigation was certainly nowhere near its conclusion. Mr Stewart could see that his web of lies was really getting to Alison, so he continued along the same line that had been so effective thus far.

'The best-case scenario will be for the hospital to go to the patient with a huge compensation offer in return for her dropping the case, which may solve the problem from the hospital's point of view. The bigger problem for your lover-boy would be persuading the patient not to report the matter to the General Medical Council or to the police because she may decide to drop the case against the hospital but still continue with the action against Samy to have him struck off from the medical register and to get the police to investigate and prosecute his sexual assault charge. To be honest, I would not want to intervene on behalf of someone like this, neither should you.'

This last statement just swept away all Alison's defences and wiped out her ability to think rationally about the situation. Mr Stewart had overwhelmed her with the details of Samy's desperate predicament, which she believed was all because of her. Mentally, emotionally and physically, she was completely crushed. She could not offer any resistance to what was to come next from Mr Stewart.

Her tears started to flow, and she was unable to speak for a few minutes, during which Mr Stewart just stared at her with a grim and uncompromising expression on his face. He was enjoying her agony while getting ready to move in for the kill.

Eventually, Alison asked with a shaken voice, 'Is there no way out of this mess? Can you help at all?'

Mr Stewart paused for a while. 'To be honest with you, he is well and truly doomed. If the normal process is applied, he will lose his medical career for ever and will be going to jail for a very long time.'

Alison's crying became more of a wailing, and her body began shaking uncontrollably. This confirmed to Mr Stewart that his triumph was complete. It was time for him to collect the trophy for which he had been waiting for such a long time.

He said with a quiet and indifferent tone of voice, 'I am sorry to see you so upset about someone who really does not deserve all this affection from a girl like you. However, because of my feelings for you, I am prepared to help him, although this will expose me to a huge risk myself. I will be doing this for you and not for that scum bag.'

Alison lifted her head and looked at Mr Stewart with bated breath, with her tears still flowing freely. Her beautiful face and tearful eyes focused on him dealt a massive blow to Mr Stewart's domineering and all-powerful attitude. He could not help but mellow and soften his tone of voice.

'This is going to be very difficult and may compromise my position in the hospital and damage my career irreparably, but I am compelled to do that because of my love for you. This should show you what you really mean to me.'

Alison wiped away her tears and stopped crying. She continued to look at Mr Stewart eagerly without saying anything to avoid interrupting his train of thought as she was desperate to hear what he had to say about saving Samy.

'The only way to put an end to this complaint is by manipulating the investigation in a way that will convince the woman that she does not have a case against Samy. If the hospital's investigation into the incident concludes that there was no case to answer, no litigation lawyer in his right mind would take up the case for compensation because of the high probability of not getting any compensation and also ending up having to bear the huge cost of the failed litigation. I am sure that I can do that and have the whole matter shelved before it gets referred to any outside agencies, such as the General Medical Council or the police. However, this will mean some devious and dishonest manoeuvring, which I will have to do, so the personal risk to me is huge.'

Alison could not believe her ears. Her heart was pounding, and her breathing accelerated as she asked Mr Stewart, 'Can you really do that? Can you save him?'

'I am sure I can. I have talked to that patient at length and built up a good rapport with her, which makes me confident that I can convince her to withdraw her complaint or at least accept a modest financial compensation without any admission of liability, and the whole thing will just vanish. Of course, all this will be highly irregular, and if it were to be known that I have influenced the investigation in any way, I can be the one who stands to lose everything.'

He then took a deep breath and added, 'I have investigated so many complaints over the years, some of which were even more serious than this one, and I can tell you with great confidence that the chief investigator can always steer the investigation towards an innocent or a guilty verdict, irrespective of the evidence. It is difficult but not impossible.'

Alison looked at him intently, trying to make sure that he was not just kidding or toying with her. He stared blankly at her and waited for her response. She had no option but to believe him, as the alternative was too horrible to even contemplate. The silence lasted for a few moments, following which she wiped her face and regained her composure before saying quietly, 'You have no idea what this will mean to me. I was sure that if anyone could save Samy, that would be you. I am eternally grateful for your assistance.'

Mr Stewart's grim and unsympathetic facial expression returned as he said, 'I want a lot more than your eternal gratitude, Alison. This assistance is not for free. I will be risking my reputation and my career to save your lover-boy. You know full well what I want from you, and I expect to get it before I do anything. As they say in Latin, 'quid pro quo' a favour in return for a favour.'

Alison froze for a few moments as they both stared at each other in silence. Mr Stewart did not have to spell out for her what he wanted. Her mind went into overdrive as she had to think quickly about how she should respond. This was Samy's only chance of surviving this calamity which she brought on him, and she had to be the one to extricate him out of it. She had to admit to herself that when she contacted Mr Stewart, she knew full well what he would be expecting from her. The price she would have to pay for his assistance was to submit to his sexual desires. She had to surrender her body to Mr Stewart in return for saving Samy's future from utter ruin. This was a very high price to pay, but she felt sure that it was certainly worth paying to save the love of her life. After all, it was not as if she was about to lose her virginity to Mr Stewart or as if she had never in the past had meaningless sexual encounters and one-night stands with men she did not have any emotional connections with. So, one more meaningless sexual encounter should not really matter to her, especially if Samy did not know about it.

Even if Samy knew that she slept with Mr Stewart and broke up with her, this would be a better outcome for him than having his career and his life totally ruined because of her. She loved Samy so much that she was prepared to save him, even if this meant that he would break up with her as a result. It did not take long for her mind to be made up, and she accepted that Mr Stewart could exact his price from her.

Alison stood up and said quietly, 'Okay.'

Mr Stewart struggled to control the emotions that exploded in his heart. An effervescent mixture of overjoy, excitement and sexual arousal overwhelmed him, but he did not want to look overly keen, so he remained seated and looked at her coldly for a few moments, which made her feel very uncomfortable. He then got up and walked slowly towards her with the same cold stare. He led her by the arm to a large sofa at the far end of the sitting room. There was no kissing or foreplay of any kind because he was keen to make love to her before she changed her mind. He just laid her on her back on the sofa, lifted her dress up, pulled her panties off and then proceeded to make love to her. He was rough, intense and forcible. He was thrusting his penis inside her so hard Alison felt as if it was hitting against her tonsils. She was in a lot of pain but just closed her eyes and cringed, hoping that her ordeal would end soon.

Mr Stewart was not just making love to Alison; he was punishing her for all the sexual frustration, jealousy and unfulfilled passion he had endured for so long. Having had him dangling on a string for months and months, she was now well and truly his, and he was going to make the most of this opportunity.

When Mr Stewart finally climaxed, he had an overwhelming feeling of pleasurable fulfilment. He sat up on the edge of the sofa, puffing and panting. Alison remained flat on her back, crying silently. He got up without looking at her and went to the toilet. He returned to find Alison standing up next to the sofa and putting her panties on. He gave her a disgruntled look and said, 'You cannot do that. I have not finished with you yet.'

The look of horror on Alison's face showed how concerned she was about the prospect of another episode of this violent sex which she had just endured. However, she felt unable to object in any way, so she just said, 'May I go to the toilet first?'

He did not say anything and just pointed to where the toilet was. She seemed to take a long time in the toilet because she cried her eyes out for a while, not only because she was physically very sore from the rough sex which she was subjected to, but also because she was emotionally traumatised from having to sleep with a man she utterly detested. Her feelings of guilt because she brought nothing but ruin and distress on Samy's head were exaggerated further by the guilt for betraying him by sleeping with Mr Stewart.

When she came out of the toilet, Mr Stewart again led her by the arm, but this time to the bedroom. He then ordered her to lie in bed after taking all her clothes off. He stood close to her, watching her intently while he was taking all his own clothes off. Alison lay on the bed, flat on her back with her eyes closed, awaiting the second onslaught.

This second episode of sexual intercourse was very different from the first one because this time, Mr Stewart was very slow, gentle and deliberate. He spent a lot of time kissing not only her lips but her whole-body bit by bit, following which he proceeded to touch, massage and caress every single inch of her body, front and back, with special attention to the sensitive and erotic spots. As a senior gynaecologist and also as a man with many years of personal sexual experiences with several women, he obviously knew his way around a woman's body. The actual intercourse this time was gentle and brief. Alison felt no pain and actually struggled to prevent herself from getting aroused, but eventually, she had to succumb to his expert stimulation and climaxed fully to her own shame and to his utter delight. His triumph was complete.

Alison and Mr Stewart were both laying in bed, looking away from each other and not saying anything. They were both exhausted, not just physically but also mentally and emotionally. Although Mr Stewart was ecstatic about finally having Alison in his bed, a part of him was disappointed because she came to him under duress to help Samy and not because she had any feelings for him. He had always dreamt of having a loving and passionate relationship with her in which she would have been a willing partner who felt for him as much as he had felt for her. However, this was not to be, so he had to settle for just quenching his thirst for her from the sexual point of view. Not a bad second choice, he thought.

Alison lost all track of time and fell asleep. Hours later, she woke up when Mr Stewart started stroking her hair gently, following which he proceeded to make love to her for the third time. This took much longer time than the previous episodes because he was again trying to get her to climax in spite of her determined efforts to avoid that. In addition, he himself needed more time to summon yet another erection within such a short space of time. At his age, this was not an easy task.

Again, Alison failed to control her reaction to Mr Stewart's sexual manipulations as she climaxed for a second time. She had not had sex for a long time since she broke up with her previous boyfriend, and Samy rebuffed all her sexual advances, which meant that her resistance to Mr Stewart's sexual stimulation was less than what she would have liked it to be.

After they had rested for a short while, Mr Stewart asked, 'Can I get you a drink?'

'No, thank you. May I go home now?'

Mr Stewart looked disappointed and replied, 'At this time of night? It will be morning soon, so why don't you sleep here and then go home in time to get ready for work?'

'I would rather go now, sir, if that's alright with you.'

Mr Stewart sat up, looked angrily at her and said, 'Don't you think that you sound rather ridiculous when you call me 'sir' after what we have just done?'

Alison ignored him and got up to go to the toilet, following which she got dressed while he watched her without saying anything.

As he followed her to the door, he said, 'I will expect you here again tonight at nine O'clock. Don't be late.'

Alison turned round, looking horrified as she asked, 'What for? I thought that you have already had all you wanted from me.'

He stared at her coldly and said, 'It is for me to decide when I have had all that I wanted from you. Do you really think that one night will make up for months and months of yearning for you?'

Alison's face dropped, and she looked as if she was about to burst into tears, so he rushed to say, 'You should consider it a compliment that I do not look at you as a one-night stand. I have tremendous feelings for you, and I want to enjoy your company for a little while. Is this too much to ask? Do you appreciate the significant personal risks which I will be taking in order to save Samy's neck?'

Alison looked back at him with a mixture of anger and frustration as she said, 'I do not have a choice, do I? I will come again as you requested, but just make sure you fulfil your part of the bargain quickly.'

'Do not worry, I will. I am a man of my word.'

Alison looked at him with eyes like daggers, shook her head in despair and slammed the door shut behind her.

****

After Alison left Mr Stewart's house, she was unable to drive home straight away. She sat in her car, staring into the dark street ahead with her mind going into a dreadful spin. She was physically exhausted and in a turbulent state of utter confusion, mentally and emotionally. She wondered what exactly had happened to her throughout that night as the enormity of what she did started to dawn on her. Did she do Samy a great favour that would save his career and his future, or had she just broken his heart and ruined for ever his love for her, over and above ruining his career? Did she really have to totally succumb to Mr Stewart's desires in that way? Why did she allow herself to react to Mr Stewart's sexual manoeuvres and end up climaxing not just once but twice? Could she trust a man like Mr Stewart to really help Samy as he had promised, or had she paid him off too early before he could fulfil any part of his commitment?

She could not think about anything clearly or come to any conclusions except for one aspect of the whole situation. She was not going to tell Samy about what she had done with Mr Stewart, at least until he was out of this predicament. She felt that she had brought him professional ruin, and for this reason, she must do her utmost to avoid breaking his heart as well while he was still in the middle of this quagmire.

Although she felt very sad and depressed, she was well past shedding tears, so she eventually gathered herself and drove off. The deed was done, and she could only wait and see what would happen next.

Alison went home and rushed into the bathroom, where she stood under the shower for over an hour. She kept rubbing her body as hard as she could as if she was trying to purge herself from the filth that had penetrated so deeply into her skin after her night of sex with Mr Stewart. The more she thought about the events of that night, the more depressed she became. She went to the hospital at 8 O'clock as usual, wondering how she could cope with work in her current state of mind.

Chapter 15

The impossible dilemmas

Alison was scheduled to be in the labour ward for the whole day, and she dreaded having to face sister Smith. However, she could do nothing about this and had to just grin and bear whatever came her way from sister Smith.

As soon as Alison entered the labour ward office, Sister Smith smiled and said with a sarcastic tone of voice, 'Good morning, Alison. How are you feeling today? You look rather pale and tired.'

Sister Smith did not know anything about what went on between Alison and Mr Stewart the previous night, but the dreadful state Alison was in was not difficult to spot. Alison did not respond for a while and then said quietly as she sat down, 'I am fine. Thank you.'

'How is Samy? How is he coping with the suspension and the investigation? Have you seen him lately?'

Alison felt like bursting into tears but managed with great difficulty to stop herself. The other emotion she struggled with was the urge to strangle sister Smith, which was even more difficult to control. However, she chose to just look away and did not say anything.

Mr Stewart entered the office and greeted the staff cheerfully. After talking briefly with sister Smith about the state of the labour ward, he said to Alison, who remained seated and looking away from his gaze, 'Can I see you in my office now, Alison? There is something I need to discuss with you.'

Alison got up slowly and followed him down the corridor towards his office. As soon as they reached the office, he closed the door and tried to kiss her, but she pushed him away.

'What is the matter, Alison? I just want a good morning kiss.'

Alison looked at him with a mixture of hate and disgust as she said, 'I think I had enough of you to last me a lifetime, so fuck off.'

Mr Stewart was taken aback by her aggressive response, but he quickly regained his composure and said in an intimidating tone of voice, 'You better watch your behaviour, Alison. I have not saved Samy yet. I will leave you for now, but I expect you at my home tonight as we agreed earlier this morning, or else ...'

Alison just stared at him and left the office without saying anything. Mr Stewart sat at his desk feeling rather deflated because he hoped that Alison would start to warm up to him after their night of passion, which he thought she had enjoyed, except for the first part. However, he did not let her hostile reaction dampen his jubilant mood because, for him, having sex with Alison was what he had wanted most. Surely, her love and affection would have been the icing on the cake, but if he could not have these, he would be more than satisfied with just the sex.

As he stood up to go to the operating theatre to start his morning list, he had a big smile on his face. He was satisfied and happy with everything in his life at that particular moment. He felt as if the whole world was at his feet with a prestigious job, massive power and influence in his field of work, a huge income from his private practice and the most gorgeous girl in the world at his disposal; what else was there?

What made him feel even better was the fact that he was poised to crush his arch-enemy, the man he hated more than any, Samy Samir, who dared to try to steal his girl from him. For Mr Stewart, it really was a wonderful life, or so he thought!

****

Alison managed to avoid seeing Samy for a few days for fear of not being able to stop herself from telling him all about her affair with Mr Stewart. Mr Stewart insisted on her coming to his house every night, except for when she was on-call overnight. He would make love to her two or three times every session. She got better at preventing herself from climaxing in spite of his persistent and prolonged attempts at stimulating her. He also failed to improve their

267

communication during their nights together. Whatever subject he tried to talk to her about, she would refuse to engage with him. All her responses were mono-syllabic and abrupt. He had her body in any way he wanted, but not her mind or her heart. It was a war of attrition, which he was losing. He was trying his hardest to make the sex as gentle, as sensual and as varied as possible, in addition to talking to her about matters he thought would be of interest to her to show her that their relationship was about more than just sex. However, all his efforts were to no avail. He was well and truly whistling in the wind.

For her part, Alison made sure that she was clearly cold and indifferent towards him at all times, hoping that he would eventually get bored with her and release her from being his sex slave. She felt that she had no choice but to continue surrendering to him until Samy was saved from his disastrous situation.

Mr Stewart did not have any intention of doing anything to save Samy. Every time Alison would ask him about what he had done to solve the problem, he would make up one lie after another about conversations he had with the patient to try to persuade her to drop her complaint and about long meetings he had been having with the hospital's lawyers and advisers. His elaborate and very detailed fibs aimed to convince her that he was trying really hard to sort out a very complicated situation while, in fact, he was doing absolutely nothing. He was happy to let the current situation continue to drag on for as long as possible, helped by the fact that everyone knew that things usually move very slowly in medical staffing as well as the legal departments of the hospital. The wheels of bureaucracy in the NHS always turned at a snail's pace, especially in legal matters.

Alison kept phoning Samy most days, making up reasons for not going to see him, but as the days passed, she ran out of excuses, and she had to go to see him in his room at the hospital. She was pleased to see that he looked like his normal self. Gone was the sad, depressed facial expression, the black haloes around his eyes and the dropped shoulders to be replaced by a positive and cheerful face with a perfectly erect posture. He greeted her warmly, hugged her and kissed her on the cheek. Her reaction to his hug and kiss surprised him as she seemed to recoil from his touches rather than reciprocate as she had always done previously. She tried to smile as she sat down on the bed, expecting him to come and sit next to her, but he chose to go and sit on the only chair in the room well away from the bed, with his smile replaced by a serious frown.

'How are you, Samy?'

'I am fine. Thank you.'

They looked at each other, both wondering what to say next. To Alison's surprise, her affair with Mr Stewart seemed to have erected a massive barrier between her and

Samy, although Samy knew nothing about it. She was no longer able to feel so close to him; moreover, she felt that she did not have the right to do so. Samy could see clearly that there was a fundamental change in their relationship, although he did not know exactly what that change was or why it had happened. The silence lasted only a couple of minutes, but these felt like many hours to both of them.

'I am very sorry for not coming to see you for the last few days. I would like to explain …'

Samy waved his hand to interrupt what she was trying to say. 'There is no need for that. You do not owe me any explanation, and believe me, I fully understand why you have not been coming to see me.'

It was Alison's turn to frown and look puzzled when he added, 'I understand that in my current situation, I am not someone that anyone would want to be associated with.'

Alison looked shocked and was lost for words for a while. She then shook her head in disbelief as she said, 'What a load of rubbish. How could you think that? I just had some personal issues lately, which I will tell you about one day. You have enough worries at present, and I did not want to add to them.'

'I am not worried anymore. I have cut the problem down to size, and I feel fine now. I know that I am innocent, and I trust that the truth will always prevail eventually.'

'I wish I had as much faith as you do. We live in a nasty, messed up world, and the good does not always come out on top.'

Gone were her encouraging and supportive words, which she flooded him with when he last saw her, and he wondered what brought this on. He tried to remain positive as he responded to her pessimistic statement.

'My faith is more in God Almighty, who I know will see me through this one way or another. Throughout my entire life, I have been through many tighter and more desperate spots than this one, and things always turned out alright in the end.'

He then paused for a while, looking at her intently and trying to work out why she was behaving so strangely. She was obviously more worried and upset about something else, but he was not going to press her. He thought to himself that she would tell him about what was upsetting her in due course when she was good and ready. For the time being, he was just happy to see her.

Samy updated her on what was happening as far as his communications with the British Medical Association and the Medical Defence union. Their advisers and lawyers were still studying all the documents related to this complaint and would be getting back to him soon with a plan of action. For the time being, he was advised not to do or say anything until he heard back from the hospital about their internal investigation.

Alison suddenly got up and walked towards Samy, who was still sitting on the chair. She stood in front of him for a few seconds, holding his head between her hands, with her beautiful eyes staring longingly at him. She then sat on his lap, wrapped her arms around his neck and rested her head on his chest, and her tears flowed silently. The barrier she felt was erected between them because of her affair with Mr Stewart had suddenly vanished, and she felt close to him again. Her feelings for Samy were so overwhelming nothing could have dampened them for long, not even her affair with Mr Stewart.

✱✱✱✱✱✱✱✱✱✱✱✱✱✱✱✱✱✱✱✱✱

It was just after 9 O'clock in the evening when Samy's mobile phone rang. To his surprise, it was one of the consultant anaesthetists ringing him from the Caesarean section operating theatre in the labour ward.

'Dr Samir, we desperately need your help with a Caesarean section, which is being performed by your colleague, Dr Khan. He has been struggling to control the bleeding from the womb for over an hour. The patient had already been given twenty pints of blood transfusion, but she

272

continues to lose blood from the womb much faster than the blood we are pouring into her veins.'

Samy responded decisively, 'I am sorry to hear this, sir, but I am suspended, and I am not allowed to even just enter the department, let alone operate on a patient.'

'I have been told that, but we are desperate, and you are our last hope. The consultant on-call, Mr Stewart, is tied up with a complex operation in a private hospital in central London, and he cannot come for at least another hour or two. The other consultant, Mr Stout, is out of town. Jeremy, your senior registrar, left the hospital a few hours ago, and his phone is switched off. We have even tried to get one of the on-call general surgeons or vascular surgeons to help, but they are all tied up with multiple seriously injured cases from a major road traffic accident. You are our last chance to save this poor woman. Dr Khan said that you are very experienced, and he would trust you as much as he would trust a consultant.'

Samy had a very difficult dilemma to sort out, and he did not have much time to solve it as they needed him in the operating theatre immediately. So, what should he do? If he refused to help, which was what he should do from a legal point of view as he was suspended, the woman might die. If he went to help, he would be breaching a very strict suspension order, which could end up worsening his situation in his current predicament. Worse than that, if he failed to stop the bleeding and the patient died, he could be blamed for that, especially as his competence was in question after the breech delivery in the toilet. He could end up with a manslaughter charge to be added to the sexual assault charge he was threatened with.

In spite of the complexity of his situation, Samy ignored all these considerations and decided that whatever the personal risks were to him, helping a patient in a life-or-death situation was his absolute priority. He had to go and do his best for her and worry about the consequences afterwards.

Samy ran as fast as he could to the operating theatre after saying to the consultant anaesthetist on the phone, 'I am on my way, sir, but please make sure that they keep trying to contact Jeremy Bell or Mr Stewart to see if either of them could come.'

As soon as Samy entered the operating theatre, he could clearly see the very tense atmosphere that prevailed. There were too many people in the room, all with grim faces and eyes focused on the operating table where Mohammad Khan, the registrar, was sweating profusely while trying desperately to insert more stitches into the bleeding womb.

A huge pool of blood all around the operating table showed clearly the amount of blood the patient had already lost. Samy scrubbed and gowned, following which he stood behind Mohammad and whispered quietly, 'Can I have a look, Mohammad?'

The faces of the two midwives who were scrubbed with Mohammad lit up as soon as they saw Samy standing at the table. Mohammad let a loud sigh of relief when he heard Samy and said, 'Oh, Samy. I am so glad to see you. Please take over. I do not know what else to do. The more stitches I put into the womb, the more it bleeds. Everyone we contacted to come and help is busy elsewhere. You are my last hope, and I am sure you will sort it all out.'

Samy replied calmly as he stepped into Mohammad's place at the operating table. 'I don't know about that, but I will certainly do my best.'

He then turned to the consultant anaesthetist and asked 'How is her blood clotting?'

'We have been giving her all the clotting factors she needs, and we have managed so far to keep her clotting parameters within the normal range. She had fresh frozen plasma, tranexamic acid and platelets. She has also had all the drugs to make the womb contract and compress the bleeding vessels, but none of these measures managed to make any difference.'

Mohammad then intervened, 'The womb is well contracted most of the time. The bleeding is from the edges of the incision in the womb, which seemed to have extended outwards as I was delivering the baby out of the womb. I just cannot see clearly the source of the bleeding and have been inserting the stitches blindly and obviously failing to catch the bleeding vessels.'

The consultant anaesthetist, who was obviously a senior and very experienced one, said to Samy impatiently, 'I don't really want to tell you how to do your job, but this woman has been in the operating theatre under a deep general anaesthetic for over three hours and is still haemorrhaging heavily. There is no time for fiddling with this and that. Just do a hysterectomy to switch off this tap of blood because we cannot maintain her circulation for much longer. I have seen enough of these cases to know that she has reached the point of no return. It is hysterectomy or death!'

Mohammad shouted angrily, 'She is only twenty-two years old, and this is her first baby. It would be an absolute disaster if she lost her womb. She will definitely sue the hospital.'

The anaesthetist, who was getting even angrier, shouted back, 'I would rather have her alive to sue us than dead because of you being reluctant to do a hysterectomy.'

While the two of them were arguing, Samy was having a detailed look at the woman's abdomen to assess the situation. He inserted some large swabs around the womb to soak up the blood that was pouring out, as the suction tube that the nurse was using to remove the blood from the tummy was not coping with the amount of blood that was coming out. He then said to the midwife who was holding the suction tube, 'Please change the suction tube you are using to the larger size and also increase the suction power on the machine to the maximum so that we can remove the blood from the abdomen faster.'

Samy then felt the need to put an end to the argument between the anaesthetist and Mohammad, so he said calmly to the anaesthetist while exploring the woman's pelvis, 'I fully appreciate what you said, sir, and if there is no other way I will do a hysterectomy. However, I just need to see what is going on first and will then proceed to do whatever is appropriate as quickly as possible.'

His calm tone of voice and his show of respect to the anaesthetist took the heat out of the situation, and everyone seemed to have calmed down to some extent. Samy asked the other midwife who was handing the instruments to him. 'We need to get a wider access to the womb to see where all this blood is coming from. May I have the knife, please?'

The midwife on the other side of the table handed him the knife, and Samy extended the incision into the abdominal wall to gain wider access to the womb. He then put his hand into the woman's abdomen and lifted the womb out of the abdomen. These two manoeuvres enabled him to see more clearly what the problem was. He said to Mohammad, 'The cut into the womb has extended outwards on both sides, so most of the bleeding is actually coming from the torn blood vessels as they enter the womb rather than from the womb itself.'

Samy, assisted by Mohammad, Maria and the two scrubbed midwives, struggled to find the torn blood vessels on both sides of the womb. Eventually, he managed to get to them one by one and sutured them slowly and carefully. Finally, the bleeding was stopped.

The anaesthetist said, 'She seemed to be more stable now, and her observations are much better. You have obviously got all the bleeding vessels.'

Samy did not respond for a few moments because he was looking intently at the womb. He then said, 'We are not out of the woods yet. The situation is certainly better, but I can still see steady oozing from one side of the womb. Can someone phone Mr Stewart in the private hospital to see when he would be able to come because a consultant's decision about what to do next is needed here? Fortunately, the bleeding is now minimal, so we can wait for him to come if he will be available in the near future.'

Samy returned the womb into the woman's abdomen and covered the area with a warm towel. He kept checking the bleeding from the pelvis every few minutes while waiting to hear if Mr Stewart would be coming. The midwife who went to phone Mr Stewart returned with an angry and congested face and said, 'Mr Stewart refused to talk to me. When the nurse in his operating theatre at the private hospital told him that we needed to talk to him, he swore, cursed loudly and said angrily that he was still in the middle of a very complex operation and would not be coming for a long while yet. He then asked for a message to be passed on to the idiot who is doing this Caesarean section to use his judgement if he has any and seek help from elsewhere if he cannot manage on his own.'

Everyone in the operating theatre was shocked to hear Mr Stewart's response. The consultant anaesthetist was the angriest of all. He said, 'I will see to it that this bastard pays dearly for his attitude. He should not be doing private work while he is on-call.'

Mohammad said, 'I think the problem is because he thought that Jeremy, the senior registrar who is almost a consultant, was supposed to be on-call today and not me. However, Jeremy had something to do tonight and swapped the on-call with me, not knowing that Mr Stewart would be tied up elsewhere. If Jeremy was the one operating on this patient, I am sure that he would have coped with all this bleeding on his own and would not have needed Mr Stewart.'

The anaesthetist shook his head, his anger escalating. 'This is no excuse. A consultant should never do private work of any kind while on-call for the NHS, irrespective of which registrar is on-call with him. This is a contractual obligation.'

He then asked Samy, 'What do you think needs to happen now to resolve this case? Do you think that she needs to have a hysterectomy?

Samy took a deep breath and said, 'The decision is very difficult to make, and for this reason, I wanted a consultant's opinion. If we do not do anything to stop this slow oozing of blood, there is a possibility that the bleeding will increase later on, and she will have to come back to the operating theatre for a hysterectomy, which is very dangerous in her fragile state after all what she has been through. Alternatively, if we do the hysterectomy now, which will stop her from having any more children, this mild oozing of blood could turn out to be one that will settle down completely by itself. It is a real dilemma, and more senior input is definitely needed. A trainee should not be the one to decide on his own to remove the womb of a 22-year-old woman who has only one baby.'

He took another deep breath and continued, 'On balance, though, I will do a procedure called ligation of the iliac vessels, which is less drastic and will preserve her womb. This will mean that I will stitch the main blood vessels of the pelvis from which the womb's blood vessels arise, and thus, we switch off the tap at the source. It is a technically difficult procedure to do, and I have only done it a couple of times with a consultant assisting, but I am confident that I can do it. I would have preferred to have a consultant's blessing before doing this, especially as I am suspended at the moment, but here we are. Let us do that.'

The consultant anaesthetist said decisively, 'Dr Samir, you must do what you think is appropriate and rest assured that I will support you all the way if you are in any trouble afterwards. This patient has been through the mill today, and I am sure that she will not cope with another return to the operating theatre later on. The time to save her life is now or never.'

When Samy removed the swab that was covering the womb, it was obvious that the amount of blood oozing from the womb and the surrounding vessels was increasing, so he went ahead with the procedure of ligation of the iliac vessels, which took him the best part of an hour. He was very slow and meticulous because of the critical state the woman was in and also because of his limited experience in this particular procedure. When he finished, everyone involved was relieved to see that the procedure was a success, with the bleeding stopping completely and the anaesthetist declaring that the patient's condition was stable.

The patient was kept in the operating theatre until the anaesthetist decided that she was ready to be transferred to the intensive care unit. Samy walked with the intensive care team as they ferried the patient from the operating theatre to the intensive care unit on the top floor of the hospital and stayed with her for another hour. He did not leave until the intensive care team reassured him in no uncertain terms that the patient was very stable and promised him that they would let him know straight away if there was any concern.

When he got up to leave, the consultant anaesthetist shook his hand and said, 'You have done great, young man. You have certainly saved a life tonight, and I am sure that there will be nothing but praise for you from the hospital management about this. I do not know the details of your suspension, but from what I have seen from you today, I am sure that you are not the one in your department who should be suspended.'

Samy smiled politely and just said, 'Thank you very much for all that you have done for this patient, sir. The way you managed to maintain her vital functions gave us the time to do what was needed. I am very grateful to you, and I am sure the patient and her family would be too.'

****

Samy walked out of the intensive care unit, taking the long way around to avoid going close to the labour ward for fear of coming across sister Smith if she was working that night's shift. He hoped against hope that his involvement with this case would be kept quiet, but of course, there was little chance of that because what happened was the talk of everyone who was in the operating theatre and in no time at all, almost every member of staff in the maternity unit and also in most of the other departments of the hospital heard one version or another of this episode. Most people applauded Samy, but some thought that he was crazy to stick his neck out while suspended.

As Samy went out into the car park to go to the doctors' residence, He saw Mr Stewart running towards the hospital's main entrance. Samy could not avoid him, so he stopped and said, 'Hello, Mr Stewart.'

Mr Stewart looked very surprised to see him and stopped in his tracks. He frowned and gave Samy a fierce look as he shouted, 'What the hell are you doing here? You are totally banned from coming into the hospital while suspended.'

Samy replied calmly, 'I think you better go first to see your patient in the intensive care unit before you start on me, sir. She is in bed 8.'

Mr Stewart's frown got even deeper, and he asked with the same loud voice, 'And what did you have to do with this patient? You have not been involved with her treatment, I hope, or it will certainly be curtains for you.'

Samy had enough of being shouted at after such a prolonged and very stressful episode, so he walked away as he said, 'Just go and see your patient, sir. Maybe you will then have a better understanding of what has gone on.'

****

Mr Stewart went to the labour ward first to talk to Jeremy, the senior registrar, whom he thought was the on-call registrar but was shocked to see that it was Mohammad Khan who was on-call. Mohammad told him in detail what had happened. The more he talked about the deteriorating patient's condition and the repeated failed attempts to get help from Mr Stewart, Jeremy or consultants from other specialities, the more Mr Stewart's face got paler.

Mohammad finished by saying contemptuously, forgetting all about his usual morbid fear of Mr Stewart, 'I don't know about you, sir, but Samy today saved the life of a patient and over and above that, he also saved my career and probably someone else's.'

Mr Stewart ignored Mohammad's impertinent remark and got up to go to the intensive care unit. If he was angered by his registrar's rude remark, worse was to come his way because as soon as he stepped into the intensive care unit, the consultant anaesthetist who looked after the patient in the operating theatre spotted him. He immediately rushed towards him, and without responding to Mr Stewart's greeting, he pointed to a small office at the other end of the ward and said, 'I must have a word with you right now.'

Although that office in the intensive care unit was a fair distance from where the patients and their nurses were on the ward, the staff could clearly hear the anaesthetist shouting at Mr Stewart and using language that was never used between senior doctors. Eventually, the two consultants came out, both looking grim-faced and flushed, which made the staff wonder if they had engaged in a boxing dual in the office.

Mr Stewart went to see the patient, who was heavily sedated and on a ventilator to help her breathe. He looked at the charts which documented her progress. He was relieved to see that she was very stable and the drain which Samy left in her tummy had nothing in it, which meant that there was no further internal bleeding. He then spent some time reading what was recorded in her notes about the sequence of events from the time she came to the hospital in labour till she arrived at the intensive care unit. He was horrified to see that the midwife who phoned him at the private hospital had documented in detail what he said, including all the swearing and cursing, word-for-word.

This incident gave Mr Stewart a dilemma of his own. Samy obviously saved his bacon, but at the same time, he had broken the terms and conditions of his suspension. How should he respond to this? Would Samy's action give Mr Stewart even more ammunition to finish Samy off? Or would this be a way out for Samy from his predicament, which was, of course, the last thing Mr Stewart wanted?

Chapter 16
This is so unfair

Three days passed without Mr Stewart hearing anything from the hospital's management. He had expected that the Chief Executive would have summoned him for a serious telling-off after he failed to come to save a bleeding patient who nearly died during a Caesarean section. His position was particularly difficult because he was doing a private operation while on-call for the labour ward, which is utterly indefensible. He kept saying to himself that he was far too important to be taken to task about an incident such as this, especially as the patient had pulled through and recovered very well, albeit slowly. The Chief Executive would probably just mention this incident in passing the next time he saw him. He felt that he had certainly got away with it, and what a relief that was.

Mr Stewart was in his office, getting ready to go to his afternoon clinic, when his phone rang. His heart sank when the caller identified herself as the Chief Executive's secretary, asking him to come to his office at 6 pm. Mr Stewart tried to wriggle out of this meeting by explaining that he had an urgent commitment that evening which could not be re-scheduled. He tried to ask for another date in the next few days, but he got an abrupt rebuff. 'This is a very urgent matter that cannot be postponed. The Chief executive asked me to tell you in no uncertain terms that he must see you this evening, whatever your other commitments might be. He will not accept any excuses.'

This rather aggressive, uncompromising message from the Chief Executive of the hospital really unsettled Mr Stewart, and he had no option but to accept the invitation to this meeting.

Mr Stewart put the phone down and sank back into his chair, feeling very anxious and for a good reason. He was sure that the consultant anaesthetist who was involved with the poorly Caesarean section patient had reported him to the Chief Executive, but why had he not called him to this meeting sooner? Why had he waited for three days after the incident? Whatever the reasons were, Mr Stewart knew that he must be in real trouble with the hospital management.

He started to think about what he could say when the Chief asked him about what happened that night and why he failed to come to rescue the woman who was haemorrhaging during a Caesarean section. He kept making up different stories and inventing various false excuses, but he could not think of anything that was really convincing or even just slightly believable, especially as his whereabout that evening were clearly documented. He had to admit to himself that he was really cornered and started to think that honesty might be the best policy. He could just admit that this was an unintended mistake and accept a rap over the knuckles.

Surely, the Chief Executive would accept a simple apology and a solemn promise never to do this again. After all, the patient came to no harm.

This was not an easy thing for Mr Stewart to do. Admitting that he made a mistake and apologizing for it went against every grain in his body. An arrogant and over-confident high achiever like him did not apologise, whatever the scenario was. However, he had never been in this vulnerable situation before, and he must do his best to get this matter sorted out as quickly and as quietly as possible.

****

The afternoon's outpatient clinic ran as normal, but Mr Stewart was noticeably pensive and rather absent-minded. He had always been very energetic, sharp and on the ball, but not that afternoon. His mind was elsewhere because he was trying to get his story straight about why he was doing private work when he was supposed to be on-call for the labour ward. He was also trying to formulate an apology that did not sound too contrite or submissive. He must act in a way consistent with his senior status and superior standing in the hospital and in his professional field.

Mr Stewart finished the clinic just before 6 pm and rushed to make it to the meeting on time. His heart was pounding, and he had cold sweat running down his face because, for many years, he sat in judgment on others, but now he was to be the one to be judged, which was a totally unfamiliar experience for him.

The secretary ushered Mr Stewart into the Chief Executive's office and as soon as he went in he realised that the big problem he thought he had was actually much bigger. The Chief Executive had with him Mrs Goldberg, the head of the medical Staffing department, the hospital's Chief lawyer and Mr Stout, the other consultant in the Maternity unit. This was really serious.

Mr Stewart tried his best to look calm, cool and collected in spite of the initial shock of seeing this quartet, which could have only meant formal proceedings against him and not just a slap on the wrist.

The Chief Executive, who looked rather uncomfortable, said, 'Thank you for coming at such short notice, John.'

As Mr Stewart sat down, he said with a faint smile, still trying to make light of the situation, 'I would have come even sooner if I knew that I was going to be meeting such an illustrious company.'

The Chief executive ignored Mr Stewart's flippant remark and carried on talking in the same monotonous cold tone of voice, 'I think you know what this meeting is all about.'

Mr Stewart frowned and replied, 'Yes, indeed I know, and let me tell you straight away that I am very sorry about what happened on the labour ward when I was on call last, and I can promise you that this will never happen again. The most important thing is that the patient is fine and she will make a full recovery. I have been seeing her two or three times a day since she had the operation, and I am very pleased to say that she is progressing very well.'

The Chief Executive of the hospital and his three companions looked at each other for a few moments, and then the Chief Executive said, 'It is good to hear that the patient will be fine, but this was not the first thing we wanted to talk to you about. There is something even more serious.'

Mr Stewart's heart almost stopped in horror. What could be more serious than him doing private work while on-call for the labour ward, with a patient nearly dying as a result?

'We were going to discuss what happened to this patient with you next, but we first wanted to talk to you about what you have been doing with Samy Samir and the case of the breech that was delivered in the toilet.'

Mr Stewart was well and truly rattled to hear that he was being brought in front of this panel to be quizzed about Samy and his breech delivery. How could they consider this a more serious situation than the patient who nearly died because of his absence?

The Chief Executive continued, 'I will let Mr Stout explain to you what we found out about your involvement in investigating this case and the serious problems we have with your actions.'

Mr Stout was obviously not enjoying the fact that he was going to criticize a colleague he had worked with for so many years, but he had no choice. He started talking quietly while staring at Mr Stewart expressionlessly.

'The patient who had the breech delivered in the toilet by Samy Samir submitted a handwritten complaint the day after the delivery. Mrs Goldberg was surprised to see the high quality of the language and the technical terms she used in expressing her complaints about the delivery. For example, she described 'rhythmical movements', 'sacral pressure' and 'psychological trauma'. These are terms she could have never thought of herself because if you studied her background, you would find that she left school without any qualifications and she could hardly read or write. This was dictated to her by someone else who has extensive medical and legal knowledge. She submitted the complaint not so long after the delivery before she had the chance to receive any visitors to help her write the complaint, neither did she have the chance to seek help from a lawyer.'

Mr Stewart shuffled uncomfortably in his seat as Mr Stout continued, 'Mrs Goldberg was not the only one who suspected that this complaint was not as straight forward as it looked. Sister Morrison, who was the sister in-charge of the postnatal ward that day, also noticed something odd about this patient.'

Mr Stewart's distress shot through the roof on hearing the name of his ex-wife, sister Morrison, because there was so much bad blood between them, and her involvement in this matter could only mean disaster.

Mr Stout continued while looking at Mr Stewart sternly, 'Sister Morrison was expecting this patient to come to her postnatal ward from the labour ward, but that was delayed for more than five hours. When she investigated the matter, she found that you were in the patient's room twice in quick succession, each time for more than an hour. Fortunately, the patient seemed to have liked the midwife who was looking after her in the labour ward after delivery, and she told her all about what you were doing in her room all this time. You were telling the patient what to write down and even helped her with the spelling.'

Mr Stewart looked uncomfortable and anxious as he kept moving restlessly in his chair. Mr Stout paused for a few moments while continuing to stare coldly at Mr Stewart, following which he continued slowly, 'Would you like me to reiterate what the patient said about your involvement with her? I am sure you know all about it, so why don't you save us all some time?'

Mr Stewart replied hesitantly, 'I only tried to help her because I felt sorry for her, and I believed that Samy had put her and her baby in harm's way. I only assisted her in expressing her complaints in the right way for people to understand her grievances, nothing more.'

Mrs Goldberg responded sarcastically, 'This is very noble of you, Mr Stewart. However, you came to this definitive conclusion about Samy's guilt without examining any evidence, without talking to the accused registrar, and without gathering any information from those who were present at the time. You also appointed yourself a secret advocate for the patient, which breaks every rule in the book because you knew that you would be the chief investigator of this incident, which means that you must remain absolutely neutral while the matter is being examined. There are specific formal arrangements that protect patients' rights and enable them to get the help they need in such a situation, so there was no need at all for your intervention on her behalf. We have actually established from the patient that you pressurized her to go ahead with the complaint although she told you that she had already decided not to complain as the baby was going to be alright and also because, on further consideration of what happened, she thought that the doctor had done his best in a difficult situation. Your insistence on making her complain about Samy, as well as your promise of a huge financial compensation from the hospital if she added a claim of sexual molestation during the delivery, persuaded her to go ahead with what you wanted her to do.'

Mr Stout added, 'This patient is a simple woman with desperate social circumstances, and she thought that going along with your plan would not only help her financially but would also be an opportunity for her to take revenge on the hospital and Social Services with whom she had so many problems for so many years. Two of her children have been taken away from her by Social Services and adopted, and the other two who are still with her are on the Social Services at-risk register with a possibility of them being permanently removed from her care at some point in future. This fifth baby will also be on the at-risk register, so she has certainly got an axe to grind, and for this reason, she was almost boasting to the midwife about how she will make the hospital and the social services pay for all that she suffered at their hands over the years.'

The Chief Executive added angrily, 'Instead of trying to calm the patient down and explain to her the difficulty of delivering a breech on the floor of a toilet; you fanned the flames of her anger after she had already decided not to lodge any complaints. What is even worse is your attempt to get a trainee accused of sexual assault, which is just pure evil. Do you really think that a sexual predator, however stupid, would choose to molest a patient in these circumstances and with two witnesses watching closely and so many members of staff just outside the toilet?'

Mr Stewart protested, 'I admit that I helped the patient write the complaint, but I certainly did not tell her to invent the sexual assault. All I did was to help her express her complaints about the delivery in a language that was clear and orderly. Nothing more.'

Mr Stout gave him a disgusted look and said, 'I am sorry to tell you, John, that you are a liar. I have spoken to the patient myself, and it was not difficult to get her to admit everything. She confirmed what the midwife said to sister Morrison, which certainly included the lie about sexual molestation. You should have known that she was an unreliable witness, and if this case went to court, her testimony would have blown out of the water effortlessly. Your hatred for Samy blinded you to what was very obvious, which is the fact that a drug addict, a prostitute with several stints in prison and a failed mother four times over is not going to be believed when she makes a false accusation such as this.'

Mr Stewart tried to respond but could not find something meaningful to say. Mr Stout continued, while the other three members of the panel stared at Mr Stewart with mounting anger, 'I know this patient well because I have looked after her in her first three pregnancies. She is not exactly bright, and she obviously ignored your request to keep your involvement with her a secret. She told her midwife everything about your involvement with her, and I did not have any difficulty getting her to admit everything to me as well.'

Mr Stout sighed and shook his head. 'Because you were so intent on destroying that boy, you failed to notice the flaw in your sinister plot and the obvious character faults in this particular patient.'

Mr Stewart loosened his tie as he felt as if he was suffocating. He scanned the faces of all the four people sitting opposite him and felt as if they all had their hands on his neck and were strangling him slowly but surely.

The Chief Executive tightened the screw even more 'From the way you interacted with Dr Samir during the first session of your investigation; it was clear to Mrs Goldberg that you were out to destroy that doctor. I have never thought of you as a racist, but maybe I was wrong.'

For the first time, Mr Stout intervened to defend Mr Stewart 'I do not think that racism has anything to do with this situation. It is more of a personal problem between John and Samy, and there is no need to go into the sordid details.'

The chief executive looked at Mr stout inquisitively, but it was obvious that the latter was not going to give any more details on this matter. He then came to the second point that he wanted to quiz Mr Stewart about.

'Now we come to the second point, which is also very serious, your failure to come to help your registrar because you were doing a private operation although you were on-call for the labour ward. This is just unforgivable, and the patient could have died as a result of your absence.'

Mr Stewart was almost in a daze from that first assault on his integrity and professionalism, but he had to snap out of it quickly before the second onslaught began.

He said hesitantly, 'I have already apologized unreservedly for that. I have never ever done any private work when I am on-call in the past, but this was an urgent cancer case which could not be postponed, and it turned out to be far more complicated than I expected.'

The Chief Executive and his three companions again looked at each other in disbelief, and then Mr Stout shook his head and said, 'We have checked with the private hospital, and we know that the case you had, John, was a patient with infertility, and the operation you did for her was to open up her blocked fallopian tubes, which is absolutely a non-urgent operation. She bled excessively during the operation, not because she had cancer, but because she had extensive scar tissue in her pelvis, and this is the reason for the operation taking such a long time. However, all this is irrelevant because you should never be doing private work of any kind when you are on-call for the NHS. Moreover, it is not true to say that you have never done any private work when you are on-call. I do some private work in the same private hospital that you operate in, and I have seen in the operating theatre's register on many occasions lists of operations that you have done while on-call.'

The Chief Executive added, 'It is one lie after another, John. Where will it all end?'

There was then a long pause with all four of them staring at him silently. Mr Stewart then broke the silence, and with a despairing voice, he asked, 'Now what? Am I suspended? Am I fired? I will fight this tooth and nail. This is so unjust, so unfair.'

The Chief Executive shook his head in despair. 'I am sure you would fight to save your career, but where do you think this would get you? Either of these incidents would be enough to end your career in disgrace. You should lose your job and get struck off the medical register forever. You can fight this as hard as you wish, but this will only delay the inevitable.'

Mr Stewart mumbled, 'This is so unfair, so unjust. After all, I have done for this hospital and its patients, I end up being thrown on the scrap heap and for what?'

Mr Stout lost his patience with Mr Stewart, so he shouted at him, 'After all we have listed for you, you still ask what for? Forging statements for a patient with a view to embezzle money from the NHS, conspiracy to ruin the life and career of a bright young trainee, unprofessional and biased conduct of a serious investigation, neglecting your duty while on-call which nearly killed a patient, not to mention all the lies. Shall I go on?'

Mr Stewart looked at the floor and did not say anything. He could see that the die was cast. He was well and truly trapped. For him, there was no way out.

The Chief Executive then said in an authoritative and uncompromising tone of voice, 'This meeting is unofficial, and you would have noticed that I did not have my secretary sitting in on it to take notes of our discussion. Going down the official route will inevitably involve a lot of bad publicity, which will not be good for anyone, least of all for you. According to the legal assessment of the situation, we know that we can have your medical career ended for ever, but this will take a long time in industrial tribunals, courts of law and General Medical Council hearings. The legal fees will be colossal for both sides. More importantly, the hospital's reputation will be badly tarnished at a time when its permanent closure was being considered by the Department of Health in the move to re-organize healthcare provisions in London. So, we all agreed that we will give you the opportunity to resign as long as you promise never to work in the National Health Service again. In return for this, we will not take matters any further. Your work with the patients as a consultant gynaecologist has always been outstanding in spite of all your personality defects, so you should be able to work in the private sector in a much quieter environment and well away from trainees and junior doctors.'

He then said with a steely voice, 'Do not expect any references from anyone in this hospital, and if we ever hear that you got a job in the NHS, we will make sure that your new employer will know what kind of a man you are. So, do not go anywhere near any of the National Health hospitals.'

Mr Stewart looked up at the Chief Executive and thought for a minute. Taking everything into consideration, he thought that things could have been much worse. At any rate, he had no choice but to accept.

The Chief executive asked impatiently, 'Well? Do you accept our offer?'

Mr Stewart paused for a few moments and, with a shaky voice, 'Yes, I accept this offer, although I believe that it is very unjust. Very unjust and very unfair indeed.'

Mr Stout shook his head and said, 'I think this offer is very generous and not at all unjust or unfair. So, you better quit while you are ahead before we have second thoughts.'

As Mr Stewart got up to leave, the Chief Executive of the hospital said in a very firm, uncompromising voice, 'I expect your resignation to be on my desk by the end of the day tomorrow, without any ifs or buts. You will have time during the day to seek legal advice and talk to whoever you want to talk to about your situation, but you must put an end to this fiasco which you have created tomorrow; otherwise,

I will start the formal proceedings against you and will also go public.'

Mr Stewart did not respond and just left the room feeling that his whole world had just crumbled and fallen on his head.

The Chief executive and his three colleagues agreed not to take any action, not even to inform Samy about what had happened until they got Mr Stewart's resignation. He was not a man to be trusted, and they needed to proceed carefully.

Chapter 17

The parting shot

Mr Stewart drove home like a zombie, a living dead. In a relatively short meeting, his future and his career were demolished just like that. The more the gravity of what had happened sank in, the worse he felt. It was a miracle that he did not crash his car on his way home because he was unable to concentrate on the traffic around him or even just find his normal way home. He repeatedly went through red traffic lights and nearly ran over some pedestrians more than once.

When he finally arrived at his home, he saw Alison coming out of her car and approaching him. Unsurprisingly, after all the trouble he had that evening, he had forgotten all about his pre-fixed date with her. Alison could see straight away that he was not in a good mood.

He greeted her without smiling. 'Hello, Alison. Good to see you.'

He really meant that because seeing her beautiful face and her tight, short skirt awakened his overactive sexual urges in spite of the mess he found himself in. However, he also knew that after his meeting with the Chief Executive, his affair with Alison would be coming to an end very soon. So, he thought to himself that irrespective of his predicament, he ought to make the most of what could be Alison's last visit to his house.

As they got into the house, Alison said in a cold and indifferent voice, 'You do not look well tonight. Shall I leave you to rest?'

Alison said that more in hope than in expectation, but her hopes of avoiding another sexual encounter with Mr Stewart were quickly dashed because he said firmly, 'On the contrary, I need you tonight more than ever. It has been an exhausting and very stressful day at work, but nothing that will not get better with some passion and a bit of sex with the love of my life.'

Alison looked away and rolled her eyes in disgust. She felt more like a sex slave than 'the love of his life'.

This turned out to be by far the worst night Alison had ever had or was likely to have. Mr Stewart was like a man possessed who treated her just like a lifeless piece of meat. He would make love to her in a vigorous and rough way with all the strength he could muster, following which he would lie next to her, rubbing and squeezing every inch of her body until he was ready to have another erection and ejaculation. Mr Stewart was not making love to Alison; he was taking his revenge on her, on Samy, on Mr Stout and on the hospital's management, or so he felt.

This torture went on for hours until Alison finally could not take any more. She burst into tears and screamed, 'Enough! Enough! What sort of an animal are you?'

Her scream startled him and forced him to snap out of his crazed mood. He collapsed next to her on the bed, looking very flushed and panting heavily. The flood of adrenalin and testosterone, which fuelled the longest and most vigorous session of sexual intercourse that he had ever had in his life, came to a sudden halt. He had made the most of his last encounter with the woman he had obsessed about more than any other woman or anything in his entire life, but he had to admit to himself that this was the end. Alison was definitely going to slip away from his grasp as soon as she knew that Samy was safely out of his predicament. How Mr Stewart wished that she felt for him even just a fraction of what he felt for her, but he knew that if she did not hate him before, she certainly would absolutely hate him after the way he treated her that night.

Mr Stewart remained silent and motionless until Alison's crying calmed down, and she started to get up. He said in a very sorrowful tone of voice, 'I am very sorry if I have hurt you, Alison. That was never my intention. One day, I hope, you will come to realise that whatever you think of me, no one will ever love you as much as I do.'

Alison was wiping her tears as she got dressed, and eventually, she managed to respond contemptuously, 'You do not know what the meaning of love is. You just treat me the same way a rabid dog treats a piece of meat. I did not hate you before, but I never liked you either. Now, what I feel for you is just pure, unadulterated hatred and disgust. You are nothing but a mindless sexual predator.'

This statement from Alison was very upsetting to Mr Stewart at a time when he was looking for her support and sympathy. He said in a resigned and pathetic tone of voice, 'Do not be too harsh on me, Alison. I am not myself today because, as a result of what I have done to save Samy, I have lost my job. So, my career and my reputation were the price I had to pay to save Samy, and I did that willingly because this is what you wanted. Doesn't this show you how much I love you?'

Alison did not respond or react in any way as she slowly got dressed. She had been so traumatized by this session of crazed and violent sex her mind was unable to process what Mr Stewart was saying to her. In addition, she was, by that stage, unable to separate what was true and what was false in anything he said.

Mr Stewart got up and put on his dressing gown. He then followed Alison as she headed for the door to leave the house and said, 'This was our last night together, Alison. Samy will be completely exonerated and returned to work in the next day or two. This has cost me a lot of time and effort, but I made sure that all his problems with that patient are well and truly over. I paid for his exoneration with my career, which is a massive cost to me, but I did this happily just because you asked me to. I hope that this will help you in time to forgive me for any hurt I have caused you and appreciate my feelings for you.'

Alison did not even look at him as she went out and slammed the door behind her. She did not know whether she could believe that Mr Stewart had told her the truth about Samy's situation or not because, at that particular moment, her anger and hatred for him were the dominant feelings that filled her heart and mind. She was also in such pain after enduring this long-crazed sex session she could hardly walk. She just wanted to get out of that hell hole as fast as possible before she could think about what Mr Stewart said at the end. She found it very hard to believe that he managed to end Samy's very complicated problem just like that, having been telling her for so many days that the situation was so difficult to resolve. Even more difficult to believe was his other statement about this being his final session with her and about him losing his career. Could she really believe anything he said? Trustworthy or not, she was determined that she would not have anything more to do with him, whatever the consequences.

Mr Stewart remained standing in the hall, staring at the closed door that Alison slammed shut behind her. This happy time he had spent with Alison was like a brief relief from the utter despair that overwhelmed him after the meeting with the chief executive of the hospital and the others earlier. He rapidly descended again into a bleak mood with absolutely nothing to look forward to in his professional or personal life. He sat up in the dark sitting room with a bottle of whisky, thinking about the events of the previous few days. Gradually, he started to get to grips with what had happened to him and, true to form, his desire for revenge started to dominate his thoughts, pushing to one side his despair and depression. Instead of feeling sorry for himself, his anger and frustration ignited a raging desire for vengeance, which took over his mind totally. He decided that the priority was not for trying to think about what to do to resurrect his utterly ruined personal and professional lives but was for finding ways of taking revenge on those who brought him to this disastrous end, namely Alison and Samy. As Alison had despised and rejected his love and affection, it was time for her to taste his hatred and vengeance.

****

Very early the next morning, Samy heard a faint knock at his door. He was still in his pyjamas when he opened the door to find Mr Stewart standing in front of him with a broad smile. Samy, who was still half-asleep, could not believe his eyes, and he just stood there staring at Mr Stewart without inviting him in.

Mr Stewart said, sounding very friendly, 'Good morning, Samy. I am sorry to disturb you so early in the morning, but I wanted to be the first one to tell you the good news.'

Samy, who still looked dazed, did not respond to his morning greetings and mumbled, 'What good news?'

Mr Stewart smiled warmly and said, 'May I come in?'

Samy was embarrassed at his own discourtesy and quickly stepped aside, ushered Mr Stewart in and said, 'I am very sorry, sir. Please do come in.'

He quickly removed his shirt from the back of the only chair in the room to allow Mr Stewart to sit down. Samy himself remained standing and looking intently at Mr Stewart to see what this was all about.

Mr Stewart was obviously enjoying the suspense and wanted to keep Samy on tenterhooks for a while longer, so he remained silent for a few moments. He then looked at Samy, still smiling warmly and said, 'There is no need to trouble you with the details, but I am very pleased to tell you that you are completely off the hook. The patient has withdrawn her complaint. There is no case for you to answer. It is well and truly over, and you will be able to return to work immediately. All your problems have gone, vanished. Isn't this wonderful?'

Samy did not react at all and just stood there staring blankly at Mr Stewart, who felt that he had to repeat what he had said to make sure that Samy had heard him. 'Samy, I am here to tell you that your suspension is no more. The patient has withdrawn her complaint. You will be able to go back to work straightaway as if nothing has happened.'

On hearing this for the second time, Samy quickly sat down on the bed because he felt that he was going to faint. He never expected this problem to end so quickly, especially as everyone had been telling him that his situation was very complicated and would be difficult to defend. He kept pinching his own thigh to make sure that he was awake and not dreaming. He then held his head between his hands, and his tears flowed. He could not find anything to say in response to Mr Stewart's news.

Mr Stewart sat silently, giving Samy time to calm down. After a few minutes, Samy lifted his head up, wiped his tears and said to Mr Stewart, 'I do not understand how this could have happened. I have read the patient's complaint, which was clearly vindictive, aggressive and very determined, so how could she have changed her mind within such a short space of time?'

'Well, a very persuasive person managed to convince her that complaining about you was not going to get her anywhere.'

Obviously, Mr Stewart meant Samy to understand that he was the one who had saved him by talking the patient out of her complaint.

Samy could not help but jump out of the bed where he was sitting and dived over Mr Stewart, who was still sitting in his chair. He hugged him with all his strength and kept thanking him from the depths of his heart.

'Thank you, Mr Stewart, thank you. You saved my life, and I do not really know what to say. I will be in your debt forever. Thank you, thank you.'

Mr Stewart gently freed himself from Samy's embrace. The latter got up and went back to sit on the bed. The two men stared at each other for a few moments, during which Samy noticed a complete change in Mr Stewart's facial expression. His face gradually got redder and more congested as his warm and friendly smile disappeared without a trace to be replaced by a very hostile and aggressive expression. He clinched his jaw, and a very deep frown dominated his angry and hateful facial features. This unsettled Samy, who thought that he was watching a scene from the movie where Dr Jekyll was changing into Mr Hyde!

Mr Stewart started talking slowly in a menacing and very intimidating voice and said, 'You are such a stupid fucking idiot, Samy. Do you really believe that I would lift a finger to save you when I have been trying all the time to crush you like the bug that you are? But as fate had it, you have won the battle, and the trap that I have laid for you trapped me instead.'

Samy was totally confused and did not know what Mr Stewart was talking about. Mr Stewart, who was trying his best to spoil Samy's joy, felt that he had to explain to him more about what was happening.

'The two of us were engaged in a fierce battle over Alison, who for some unknown reason seemed to favour a nobody like you over me. Since I discovered that Alison has fallen for you, I have been trying my hardest to get you struck off the medical register and even have you jailed, which is no more than you deserve for stealing my girl and breaking my heart. For this reason, I pushed the patient who delivered the breech in the toilet to complain about you and told her what to do and how to say it. However, thanks to the interference of my ex-wife and Mr Stout, my plan was foiled, and instead of you losing your job and your career, I lost mine. My troubles were also aggravated by the Caesarean section case that you saved while I was operating on a private patient in central London. In a flash, I became the villain, and you became the innocent victim and the hero.'

Samy just froze because all these revelations were just too much to take in. Mr Stewart had been condescending and aggressive towards him for a long time, which escalated to a full-on attack with a view to destroying him after the case of the breech in the toilet. Then he changed to be the saviour and adviser who volunteered to help him defend himself, and now he was back to being his arch-enemy who wanted to destroy him. Samy did not really know whether he was coming or going with Mr Stewart.

As there was nothing coming from him in response to Mr Stewart's revelations, the latter was compelled to say more because he was determined to spoil Samy's moment of triumph and glory. Mr Stewart was getting very frustrated because Samy did not seem to react aggressively or angrily to Mr Stewart's admission of his attempts to destroy his career and utterly ruin his life. Why was Samy just sitting there in silence, staring at him without expressing any emotion? Where was his anger, swearing or aggression? Mr Stewart could not find any answers to these questions, so he just had to keep trying to get Samy to react.

Mr Stewart continued, with his aggressive and hateful facial expressions getting more pronounced, 'I am telling you all this because you are going to hear about it soon enough. I am sure that Mr Stout and his mates in the hospital management team will be talking to you later today with all the relevant details. However, I wanted to spoil the joy of your victory over me and show you that I leave this battle with you over Alison with more than my fair share of the prize.'

Samy's continued silence provoked Mr Stewart's anger and frustration more than any amount of hostile behaviour that he could have directed at him.

Mr Stewart had a sarcastic smile as he continued, 'I know that I sometimes behave in a rough and disrespectful way towards some of the staff and the medical students for one reason or another, but in your case, I treated you in this way because of your relationship with Alison. It has always been about Alison and nothing else. If you did not take her away from me, none of this would have happened.'

Finally, a reaction from Samy was forthcoming. He gave Mr Stewart a steely look and started talking back to him, calmly but with a contemptuous tone of voice and a disgusted expression on his face.

'Sir, you talk about a battle between us for Alison. You were in that battle all by yourself, all on your own. I was not fighting you for her or trying to take her away from you as you have imagined. She was not yours to lose or mine to take. She is the most wonderful girl one can ever meet, not just because of her gorgeous looks but also because of her fantastic personality and her brilliant brain. She was the one to decide for herself whom she wanted without the need for any battles to be won or lost.'

Samy then asked sharply, 'If you are so full of hatred and anger towards me, why are you here? Why are you bothering to give me the good news yourself when this was the last thing you wanted to happen? What did you mean by saying that you have taken more than your share of the prize?'

Mr Stewart stared at him, and with a triumphant wide smile, he said, 'The real reason for me being here is to see for myself how you would react to the second half of the story. I am here to show you that you are just as much of a loser as I am. Your triumph over me is not as complete as you might think.'

Samy looked at Mr Stewart coldly and said, 'I do not feel triumphant over you or anyone else. I just feel relieved and happy that I can resume my training and my life. Please believe me when I tell you that in spite of what I now know about your role in this conspiracy against me, I still feel no hatred or anger towards you. On the contrary, I really feel sorry for you. I think that you are a pathetic, sad case, and I pity you.'

Mr Stewart's anger boiled over as he shouted, 'You, bastard! Do you really think that I give a toss about your pity? Let us see how much sympathy and forgiveness you will have when I show you the trump card that I hold, my parting shot, so to speak.'

Samy just looked at him coldly without saying anything, which irritated Mr Stewart further as his attempts to get Samy worried or worked up seemed to have failed thus far. So, he got up and walked towards the door and then turned round and said, 'What I really wanted to tell you today is that I am not leaving Alison empty-handed because, for a good few days, I have been having from her all I wanted time and again and again. I have been fucking her every night for hours on end. Full- blooded, steamy hot, unbridled sex. She came to my house every night, and we were at it like rabbits on Viagra.'

Samy went very pale and was obviously shocked, but he remained silent, which Mr Stewart did not expect. He expected from Samy a violent Middle Eastern reaction to such a revelation, and that was the reason why he went closer to the door before declaring the news of his affair with Alison to him. He thought that he might have to run out of the room in a hurry to escape the physical violence that might come from a much stronger and younger man.

Samy remained motionless and expressionless, staring into space, not looking at Mr Stewart and not reacting in any way.

Mr Stewart was very disappointed to see that Samy did not fall to pieces or explode in an uncontrollable rage, so he tried to add more fuel to the fire: 'Are you deaf or just stupid? I have just told you that I have been enjoying your girl's body every night for so many days, and she has been a willing participant. She enjoyed the sex every bit as much as I did. Oh, how she climaxed time after time after time. I leave her to you as damaged and soiled goods. Enjoy!'

Still no response, so he added, 'If you think that I am lying, I will give you the evidence. She has a small mole on the inside of her right buttock, which I used to tease her about as we were making love. You know what I am talking about. You must have seen that mole when you were sleeping with her yourself. You couldn't miss it.'

Samy still said nothing. He quietly rose up and walked towards Mr Stewart, who recoiled in anticipation of being punched. However, Samy just carried on walking past him to the door, opened it and stood there waiting for Mr Stewart to leave. The latter almost ran out, still expecting some sort of a punch or a kick from Samy as he left the room, but none was forthcoming.

****

As Mr Stewart walked down the corridor in which Samy's room was, he saw Alison coming from the opposite direction, obviously heading for Samy's room. She was both startled and horrified to see him coming towards her because she knew that he could have only been in this part of the hospital to see Samy. As he came closer to Alison, he had a wicked smile on his face and said, 'Good morning, sweetheart. Are you going to see your lover-boy?'

Alison paused for a moment and then asked anxiously, 'What the hell are you doing here?'

Mr Stewart's smile widened as he could see that he had obviously got to her. 'I have been visiting our mutual friend, Samy. I thought that I better give him the good news about the breech case myself. After all, it was me and me alone who managed to get him off. I also made sure that he knew all about our little affair. I even told him that I have enjoyed looking at the mole on your buttock probably as much as he did.'

Alison was stunned and struggled to hold back her tears as she said, 'You bastard! He does not know anything about my mole because we never made love. He is not a mindless sex maniac like you.'

Mr Stewart raised his eyebrows in amazement. 'But I saw you kissing passionately in the car park. How could he not make love to you after that? He must be impotent, gay or both.'

He then burst out in a hysterical sarcastic laugh and said, 'Oh, now I get it. You have been pretending to be this sweet and innocent little virgin, and the stupid idiot bought it. Meanwhile, he has been pretending to be this virile, handsome stud who possesses this fantastic self-control. What a pair! You really suit each other, a perfect match.'

Alison did not have anything to say to him, and she just turned round and went back down the corridor away from Samy's room. She could not face Samy after what Mr Stewart had told him about their affair, not so soon anyway.

Mr Stewart stood there, laughing his head off and feeling very happy that he managed to upset Alison and sow the seeds of destruction of her relationship with Samy. A Middle Eastern man would never forgive a woman who had committed adultery, so he felt confident that he had his revenge on the two of them.

****

Mr Stewart went to his office near the labour ward to gather his personal possessions before leaving the department for good. Afterwards, he stood there for a few moments looking around the room where, for so many years, he spent so much time. This had been his own private space at St Luke's Maternity Hospital for so many years, but not anymore. He mumbled to himself, 'How did it come to this? How could I have lost everything so easily, so fast?'

He left the office for the last time and closed the door quietly. As he walked down the corridor, Mr Stout called him from his office, which was just opposite Mr Stewart's. 'Can I have a word with you, John.'

Mr Stewart went into Mr Stout's office with a grim expression on his face, which clearly illustrated the amount of anger and hatred he held for Mr Stout because of his role in his downfall.

Mr Stout said with a hint of a friendly smile, 'Take a seat, John.'

Mr Stewart ignored his invitation and remained standing near the door. He stared at him and asked sharply, 'What do you want?'

Mr Stout looked disappointed at Mr Stewart's hostile reaction as he said, 'You left the meeting yesterday before we finalized the arrangements for your leaving. You do not need to worry about serving the three months' notice, which is stipulated in your contract. Your salary will be paid in full for the next three months, but we do not want you to come to the hospital anymore. It is best this way for all concerned, especially as I am going to invite Samy today to return to work whenever he feels ready.'

Mr Stewart had a disgusted expression on his face as he got an envelope out of his pocket. He threw the envelope on Mr Stout's desk and said through gritted teeth, 'Do not worry. I have no intention of setting foot in this dump again. I came today to collect my stuff from my office and to leave you my resignation as requested. You turned out to be such a devious and treacherous colleague. After all the years we have worked together and all that I have done for this hospital and its patients, you sold me down the river and for what? For an Egyptian immigrant who has been here for only a few months.'

Mr Stout shook his head in despair and said calmly, 'Far from being treacherous and devious, I have tried my hardest to save you from utter ruin. The other three members of the panel wanted you dismissed from the hospital and struck off from the medical register, but I fought tooth and nail to just have you removed from the hospital with your reputation and medical registration intact so that you could have another start elsewhere. Your work as a consultant and your dealings with your patients have always been impeccable. It is your personal life and your attitude that is the problem, but hopefully, this traumatic episode will help you re-evaluate your behaviour, re-adjust and start again elsewhere away from the NHS.'

Mr Stewart remained standing and staring angrily at Mr Stout. His lips trembled as if he was about to respond, but he remained silent. Mr Stout continued, trying in vain to calm him down. 'There was also a suggestion from some members of staff that you were physically and sexually harassing one of the trainees in front of everybody, Alison. The Chief Executive wanted this added to your list of offences, but I again managed to talk him out of it, especially as Alison has not complained about you formally or informally. Sexual harassment is a very serious accusation, as I am sure you know, and with so many witnesses to the way you touch Alison and talk to her, the charge could have been easily proven. This would certainly put an end to your medical career for good, so as you see, I have worked hard to let you go away with something you can hold on to for the future.'

Mr Stout let him be for a few moments and then said, 'What will you do now?'

Mr Stewart stood silently for a few moments, staring at the floor. He then lifted his head and looked at Mr Stout with his angry facial expression replaced by a resigned sad look. 'I will go to work in the Middle East for a while. An old and close friend of mine runs a chain of private hospitals all across the oil-rich Gulf states. He has been chasing me for a long time to go and work there for five times the salary I make here. I am sure he will employ me right away without asking for a reference.'

Mr Stout nodded approvingly and said, 'This is great. I am pleased for you.'

Suddenly a worried look appeared on Mr Stewart's face because he thought that Mr Stout might try to find out the contact details of this friend in the Middle East and tell him about what had happened in England. Mr Stout realised that Mr Stewart regretted informing him about his plan and moved to reassure him straightaway, 'While I am very pleased and relieved to hear that you have got such an excellent alternative to your job here, I will forget everything you told me about that job and I suggest that you keep these details to yourself because there may be others who may feel differently about what should happen to you after this episode.'

As Mr Stewart turned round to leave, Mr Stout got up and extended his arm towards him to shake his hand. Mr Stewart looked blankly at him, then stared at his extended arm and just walked out without saying anything or shaking his hand. As he walked out of the hospital for the last time, he kept mumbling to himself, 'This is so unjust! This is so unfair!'

Chapter 18

Will things ever be the same again?

Later on that day, Mr Stout phoned Samy and asked him to come to his office right away. When Samy entered the office, Mr Stout greeted him warmly and then said, 'I have wonderful news for you, Samy. You can go back to work right away if you want. The patient has withdrawn her complaint, and you have been totally vindicated.'

Samy had a faint smile on his face as he replied calmly, 'Thank you, sir. I am very pleased.'

Mr Stout was surprised to see Samy's rather muted reaction, without any signs of elation or excitement. It was as if he was not really bothered whether he went back to work or not.

Mr Stout stopped smiling and frowned as he asked, 'Samy, did you hear me? You are totally exonerated, and you can resume your training as if nothing had happened.'

Samy looked impassively and said, 'I had a visit from Mr Stewart earlier today, and he told me about the patient's withdrawal of the complaint.'

Mr Stout's jaw dropped, and he looked shocked, but his shock was quickly replaced with anger as he asked, 'Mr Stewart visited you? In your room?'

Samy nodded affirmatively to both questions, and Mr Stout raised his eyebrows in amazement and asked again, 'What for? What did he say to you?'

'He told me that the patient has withdrawn her complaint and that all my troubles are over.'

Mr Stout did not seem to believe that Mr Stewart had gone to all this trouble just to be helpful and kind to Samy when he was the one who engineered the whole problem that nearly ended Samy's career.

His frown got deeper, and he said, 'This man does not wish you well, Samy. I cannot believe that there wasn't another reason for his visit.'

'Yes, sir, there was something else, but it is rather personal, and I beg you to leave it at that because I really cannot talk about it.'

Mr Stout was very disappointed because Samy would not tell him about what exactly went on between him and Mr Stewart, but he said, 'Of course, it is up to you, and if it is a personal matter, I would not want to pry. You can come back to work tomorrow or have a break for as long as you want and then come back to work well-rested and refreshed. After all that you have been through, we will give you whatever time off you need.'

Samy remained expressionless and silent, which started to frustrate and anger Mr Stout, who shouted, 'Samy, talk to me. I would have thought that you would have been desperately keen to get back to work and put all these problems behind you, but you seem rather indifferent. What exactly do you want to do?'

'I want to find another job elsewhere, sir. I cannot work with Mr Stewart ever again.'

Obviously, Samy did not believe what Mr Stewart had said to him about losing his own job and thought that he was just lying as he had always done.

Mr Stout looked relieved, and with a broad smile, he said, 'Is that all? Well, the other half of the good news is that Mr Stewart has quit his job today. He will not be working at St Luke's as of today, so you do not need to worry about him.'

Samy could not believe his ears, and he asked Mr Stout for more clarification.

'How come? Why has he left?'

'I cannot tell you that, but this is a fact. Mr Stewart is no more. He will not even be working the three months' notice in his contract before leaving, and he will not be having anything to do with this hospital ever again. The details are very confidential, and I cannot tell you anything about them. You are not the only one who has secrets to keep.'

It was Samy's turn to frown as he said, 'No wonder he was so bitter and angry. Did I cause this? I do not see how.'

Mr Stout replied impatiently, 'He brought this on himself. You had nothing to do with it. Mrs Goldberg from medical staffing and sister Morrison on the postnatal ward noticed Mr Stewart's odd behaviour towards you and his very irregular handling of the breech patient's complaint. They both independently got me involved, and it was not difficult to find out quickly that the whole problem you had with this patient was of Mr Stewart's making from start to finish. Added to this, Mr Stewart was doing private work during his on-call, and as a result, a patient nearly died if it wasn't for your intervention that night. There were other problems with Mr Stewart's professional conduct and the whole situation forced him to leave his job in a hurry. As far as you are concerned, Mr Stewart's part in your work and your life is over forever, and you do not need to bother with the details.'

Mr Stout took a deep breath and paused for a few moments to give Samy time to process all this information. He then said cheerfully, 'Now, let us try again to find out what you want to do. Do you want to resume your training here?'

Samy replied without any hesitation this time, 'Absolutely, sir. Tomorrow, if I may. I cannot wait to go back to work.'

Mr Stout's smile widened, and he said, 'Good. This is what I wanted to hear. I think it will be best if you avoid talking about this whole affair or Mr Stewart's involvement in it to any of the staff.'

'Oh, do not worry about that, sir. I am going to put all this behind me and just get on with my life.'

****

Mr Stout informed all the key people in the maternity hospital and the rest of the general hospital about Mr Stewart's departure and Samy's return to work. The news spread like wildfire all around the hospital, with most people feeling delighted that Samy was vindicated, and some were equally delighted with Mr Stewart's departure. The latter had stepped on so many toes with his arrogant and aggressive attitude, and for this reason, no one mourned his departure.

When Samy stepped into the department the next day, he felt like a celebrity. Those who did not give him a hug or a kiss shook his hand warmly; the one exception was sister Smith. When he walked into the labour ward's office and said 'good morning', she did not respond and pretended to be busy looking at some papers. She was sure that Samy knew of her involvement in Mr Stewart's conspiracy and how instrumental she was to his evil plan to destroy him. Her report on the delivery of the breech in the toilet was loaded with statements which suggested that the woman's accusations were true, though not explicitly. She clearly questioned Samy's professional competence and his behaviour during the delivery.

Samy had to make the first move because, after all that he had been through, he certainly did not want a confrontation with sister Smith or anyone else for that matter. As far as he was concerned, there were not going to be any recriminations or postmortem examinations of what happened or who did what. He was just happy to forgive and forget.

'Good morning, sister Smith.' said Samy with the broadest smile he could muster.

Sister responded sheepishly, 'Good morning, Dr Samir.'

Calling him Dr Samir and not by his first name as she had always done previously raised a few eyebrows.

Samy's smile widened as he said, 'It is wonderful to be back. What do you have for me today?'

'There is a lot to do, I am afraid, but the senior house officer for this morning, Alison, is not here yet. Do you want to wait for her?'

'There is no need to wait, especially if there is a lot to do. Let us make a start, and I am sure she will be able to catch up with us when she comes.'

Sister Smith then looked at Mohammad Khan, who was the registrar overnight and said, 'Get on with it then, Mohammad. Tell Dr Samir about the main problem you are leaving behind.'

Everyone, including Samy, noticed that sister Smith continued to call him so formally, which made Samy feel very uncomfortable because he hoped that there would be no hard feelings between them. There were certainly none from his side, and he was going to make every effort to get rid of any awkwardness or unfriendliness that might have crept in between them since this episode of the breech in the toilet.

More important to Samy, though, was Alison's absence. Why had she not turned up for the handover on the labour ward? This was not like her at all as she had always been punctual and if she was going to be late for any reason, she always telephoned to explain. His gut feeling was that he would have a much bigger problem to solve with Alison than with sister Smith, and he knew why. Samy suspected that Mr Stewart would have informed her somehow that Samy knew all about their affair.

Mohammad Khan, who was watching the interaction between Samy and sister Smith with a mixture of amazement and amusement, smiled and, with a sarcastic tone of voice, said to her, 'Of course, your majesty. I will be delighted to inform 'Dr Samir' about the cases that I admitted overnight and the main problem at present so that 'Dr Samir' can sort them out because 'Dr Samir' is such a clever boy.'

Everyone in the room got the point and laughed at the way Mohammad was stressing 'Dr Samir' as he said it.

Everyone except Samy, who looked angry, and sister Smith, who blushed with embarrassment.

It was then time for Mohammad Khan to start talking quickly about the business in hand before sister Smith recovered from her embarrassment and reacted to his unwelcomed sarcasm.

Mohammad listed all the cases that were admitted over night and then added the details of the main problem that Samy will need to sort out first. 'In room 10, there is a 27 years old girl in her first pregnancy with active herpes infection all over her private bits and is in early labour, so she will need delivery by Caesarean section to avoid having the baby infected with the herpes virus as it comes out of the vagina if she was to deliver normally.'

Having completed the handover to Samy, Mohammad Khan was aiming to make a quick escape as he noticed that sister Smith was staring at him like a wild, angry lioness on whose tail he had just stepped. He tried to avoid her gaze as he said to Samy, 'Now, I am dead tired, so can I go home please to have some sleep, although I am sure that my dreadful kids are unlikely to let me have any?'

Samy smiled and said, 'Thank you for the gift you are leaving behind for me to deliver, Mohammad. Go home, and I hope that you manage to have some well-earned rest.'

Mohammad shot out of the room without looking in the direction of sister Smith, got changed as quickly as he could and ran to his car, hoping that by the time he saw sister Smith next, she would have forgotten about his sarcasm.

Samy turned to sister Smith and said with a warm, friendly smile, 'Shall we go round to see the women who need to be seen and then we can see the lady with herpes last as she is only in early labour, so, there is no great hurry?'

Sister Smith did not say anything as she stood up to lead the way. She looked straight ahead and did not talk to Samy or anyone else as she headed out of the office. As they walked in the corridor, Maria, the Greek senior house officer, came running from the other end and said, 'Sorry for being late. Alison has just phoned off sick and asked me to do this labour ward shift for her.'

Samy looked concerned and asked, 'Did she say what was wrong? Is she alright?'

Maria shrugged her shoulders and replied, 'She didn't say, but she did not sound seriously ill, so I am sure it is nothing major.'

As they walked around from room to room, all of Samy's attempts to engage sister Smith in conversation failed, as she remained distant and disinterested. Samy thought to himself that resolving the problems, whatever they were, between him and sister Smith was going to be far more difficult than he had foreseen. He did not know why she looked so angry with him when she was the one who wronged him in the case of the woman who delivered the breech in the toilet. He should have been the one to be cross with her and not the other way round.

Samy finished the ward round and then went into room 10 to see the woman who was in early labour with an active herpes infection.

After the usual introductions, Samy asked the woman if he could have a look 'down below' to see the extent of her herpes infection. The patient looked very embarrassed and reluctantly lifted her gown up and opened her legs. After a very quick glance, Samy covered her up again and said, 'The skin down below is very inflamed, and I can see many of the ulcers and vesicles which are typical of herpes infection. Is this the first time you had this sort of problem?

The patient's face went bright red, and she looked very angry as she replied, 'Absolutely. I have never had anything like this in my life. Is this a venereal disease?'

Samy hesitated for a moment as he noticed that her partner, who was sitting next to her bed, looked very worried. He was shuffling restlessly in his chair and looked more distressed and worried than his wife.

Samy then said, 'Herpes is a group of different viruses that can affect various parts of the body and can be transmitted sexually or otherwise.'

The patient interrupted sharply, looking even more angry. 'I do not want a lot of vague waffling. It is a simple question that I want you to answer: is this a venereal disease or not? Have I got this infection from him?' and she pointed with her finger to her partner, who recoiled in his chair in utter horror.

Samy answered quietly, 'I cannot give a 100% answer to this question. All I can say is that most herpes infections 'down below' are sexually transmitted, but they can also be transmitted occasionally through physical contact with contaminated towels, toilets, bathrooms, etc.'

Suddenly, the woman grabbed the glass of water that was on the small table next to her and threw it at her partner as she screamed at him, 'You, bastard. I could have only got it from you. You are the only partner I have ever had, but this was never the case with you. I know that you have been fooling around time and again, and here is the result.'

The man looked as white as a sheet as he wiped the water off his face and quickly exited the room. The patient continued to curse him until he had left the room, and the door was closed.

The patient and everyone in the room remained silent for a few moments. She then lifted her head up and said to Samy, 'I am very sorry about this outburst, doctor. I just feel betrayed and utterly disappointed. We were childhood sweethearts, and he is the only one I have ever slept with. I suspected for a long time that he had been sleeping around, but I was living in denial.'

No one could think of anything helpful to say, so the silence continued until the patient added, 'What do we do now? Apart from feeling very sore 'down below', would this infection make any difference to my delivery? Is the baby in any danger from this infection?'

Samy said, 'The baby at the moment is safe, but if your water breaks, the virus can get into the baby and cause a very serious inflammation of the brain, called encephalitis. For this reason, Caesarean section is the only safe way to get the baby out without risking him or her contracting this brain infection. In addition, you are so sore and inflamed down below it will be very hard for you to cope with vaginal delivery, especially as it is your first delivery, and you may need stitches in such an inflamed and already sore bottom.'

The woman shook her head in disbelief as she said, 'I will kill him, I really will. Not only has he given me a venereal disease, but he has also deprived me of the natural delivery which is what I have always wanted.' She then burst into tears.

Her midwife sat next to her on the bed, put her arms around her and hugged her until she stopped crying. The patient eventually asked while wiping her tears. 'The baby's safety certainly comes first. When can we do this section?'

Samy replied, 'Right away. You are in early labour, so we must proceed quickly before your water breaks and the virus gets into the baby. We will make the arrangements and deliver you as soon as possible, within the next hour or so.'

Samy then explained to her what is involved in having the section and the process of recovery from the operation.

The patient listened quietly and then said, 'What do you think, doctor? Shall I let my cheating partner come into the operating theatre with me or keep him out? What would you do if you were me?'

Samy was not going to be put on the spot in this way, so he quickly said, 'It is really entirely up to you. No one but you can make this decision. We will certainly follow your wishes, whatever they are. You can have your partner with you in the theatre, or you can choose anyone else, a relative or a friend.'

Samy then moved quickly towards the door to make a hasty exit so that the woman did not have any chance of cornering him further on such an intimate personal matter. He always believed that a doctor's personal feelings and his own views should never influence a patient's ability to decide for herself on relationship matters. He was there to provide a clinical service and not an emotional one. Maria stayed behind to complete the consent form and the rest of the paperwork for the Caesarean section.

As soon as Samy left the room, the patient said to her midwife and Maria, 'Now, girls, I need an honest answer. If you were me, would you let a man like this come with you for the delivery? Please do not chicken out like this registrar who refused to help me make up my mind. We women must stick together, so please tell me what you would have done in this sort of situation?'

Maria and the midwife stared at each other, with each hoping that the other would answer first. Eventually, the patient's midwife said with a very angry tone of voice, 'I will never forgive infidelity, never. I would have told him to get lost and never to come near me again, not just for today but for ever. Once a cheating bastard, always a cheating bastard!'

This situation had obviously touched a raw nerve in this midwife's own personal life.

Maria was busy taking the patient's blood sample, hoping that the patient would let her off the hook after she had heard the midwife's clear-cut opinion, but the patient was determined to hear her views too, so she asked her again, 'What about you, doc? Would you still let him come to your delivery?'

Maria replied hesitantly, 'It all depends on how much in-love I am. True love should give one the ability to forgive, irrespective of the offence. Everyone deserves a second chance if I thought he was worthy of one. So, the real question is: do you love him enough to give him a second chance, especially as now there is a baby involved?'

The patient looked at Maria and sank into deep thoughts. She glanced at the consent form which Maria thrust into her hand and pretended to read it, but in fact, her mind was elsewhere. What the midwife said was clear-cut and easily applied, but was it the right thing to do? Maria's opinion was more thoughtful and more in keeping with her own feelings for her partner, but it was very hard to apply. She was bitter, angry and vengeful. She signed the consent form without reading a word of it as her mind was in turmoil about what to do with her partner.

****

When Samy left room 10 to go to the operating theatre in order to inform the theatre staff and the anaesthetic team about the urgent Caesarean section which was coming their way, he was stopped in the corridor by the herpes patient's partner. He was trembling nervously and said to Samy in a very shaky voice, 'I am very sorry about this dreadful scene, doctor, but I am afraid she is right. I have been unfaithful to her intermittently over the last two years, with several women, but all this stopped as soon as she got pregnant. I will never go back to this sort of behaviour again, never, never, never. I love her very much, and the arrival of my baby will guarantee that I will never step out of line again, of that I am absolutely sure. I have really learnt my lesson.'

Samy looked at him sympathetically, and without the slightest hint of being critical or judgemental, he said, 'You should really be saying this to her and not to anyone else. This is entirely between you and her. The priority now is for her safety and the baby's safety. Everything else will have to wait till after the delivery.'

The man was looking at Samy intently, and before he could ask him about what was to be done for the best, Samy continued, 'I suggest that you get her midwife to ask for her permission for you to go back into the room to talk to her and accompany her to the operating theatre if she agrees. Whatever she says or does, you will have to take it on the chin because this is the least you could do in this situation. It is very important that you do not upset her as she has already got enough on her plate at the moment, so if she refuses to let you back into the room, you must leave it at that and wait for a while after the delivery and try again. If you really love her, you will have to give her the time and space to get over this in her own good time. Do not pressurize her or upset her further. The operative delivery and the herpes are doing enough of that already.'

Samy then added as he got ready to move towards the operating theatre, 'I wish you all the best. Go back and see if she will let you talk to her, but remember that you must accept whatever she decides without any arguments.'

A while later, Maria joined Samy in the operating theatre after she finished preparing the patient for the operation. She had a wide, cheerful big smile on her face as she said, 'There was really a touching scene in room 10. Her partner asked for her permission to come into the room. She was very hesitant but eventually agreed. As soon as he entered the room, they just fell into each other's arms, and both burst into tears. He did not try to deny his infidelity or justify it. He just promised that he would never do it again, not just because of the baby but more importantly because of his love for her, first and foremost. She admitted to him that she had been neglecting him for a long time because of work pressures and physical exhaustion, which she now realises was a contributory factor to their problems, though not an excuse for his adultery. They forgave each other, and he is coming into the operating theatre with her.'

Maria then frowned and said, 'Although they seemed to have resumed their loving relationship, I wonder if, after all this, things can ever be the same again?'

Samy was delighted to hear this and said, 'Yes, they can if they really love each other. Love is the twin brother of forgiveness. If you really love someone, you must always have the ability to forgive, irrespective of the offence. Real love must conquer all.'

And as if he was talking to himself, he mumbled, 'If you really love, you must forgive and forget. If your love is true, then you must forgive and forget.'

When Samy said that to himself, he was thinking about what happened between Mr Stewart and Alison. He certainly would have no difficulty forgiving Alison, but can he really forget that she slept with Mr Stewart time and again? Would things between them ever be the same again after that?

****

The shift on the labour was very busy, but Samy, as usual, coped remarkably well, and everyone seemed to be very happy to have him back in action, except for sister Smith, who did her best to stay out of his way as much as possible. At the end of his shift, Samy handed over the labour ward to Jeremy Bell, the senior registrar, who was in charge of the overnight shift.

As Samy walked back towards his room in the doctors' residence, he wondered if he should phone Alison to see if she was alright. He wondered if Alison was avoiding him because she was too embarrassed about what she had been doing with Mr Stewart. Should he be blaming himself for pushing her into Mr Stewart's arms by being so reluctant to fulfil her passionate desires and physical hunger for him? She made it very clear time and again that she wanted their love to develop into a sexual relationship, and he turned her down every time. Was he wrong? Samy also wondered if he should blame himself for crumbling and falling to pieces when he was suspended and had the threat of losing his career and ending up in prison. This might have made Alison sell herself to Mr Stewart to try to save him because she saw how desperate he was. If he was more calm and able to cope with this problem, she might have felt the need to do what she did. However, part of him thought that she should have never slept with Mr Stewart under any circumstances. Her action could never be justified.

On the one hand, Samy wanted to contact Alison right away, but on the other hand, he thought that he should give her the time and space to decide for herself whether she still wanted him. His mind kept going around in circles, not knowing what to think or what to do for the best. He needn't have worried about the right course of action because Alison had decided that for him. When he reached his room in the doctors' residence, Alison was standing at his door waiting for him.

Samy smiled and said, 'What a lovely surprise. I was worried about you because Maria said that you were off sick. Are you alright?'

Alison did not smile back and just said, 'I will soon find out!'

She was obviously upset and did not look like her normal, glamorous self. She had a crumbled T-shirt on and a pair of worn-out jeans. She looked very tired and had black halos around her eyes, and her lips were dry, indicating that she probably did not have anything to eat or drink for a long time.

As soon as they entered the room, Alison said, 'I want to tell all about this business with Mr Stewart, and I will ask you to just listen to what I have to say without interrupting, and then you can say and do whatever you want. I will accept your verdict in full without any argument or objection. Just hear me first.'

Samy frowned and said, 'Alison, you do not owe me any explanation. You did not have any commitment to me, and I do not have the right to judge you in any shape or form.'

Alison's tears started to flow as she said, 'This is what I dreaded most. You kick me out of your life and end our relationship without even hearing what I have to say.'

Samy shook his head and said, 'You cannot be more wrong. I love you more than you will ever know, and nothing will ever change that. I cannot kick you out of my heart, which you own totally, utterly and absolutely. What happened between you and Mr Stewart is your own private business, and I do not want to know the details because this will be too painful for us both. Whether we still have a relationship or not is more your decision than mine.'

Alison looked at him for a moment through tearful eyes and then said, 'Just do me this favour, Samy, after which I will leave you alone for good if this is what you want. Just listen to my story with Mr Stewart, and then I promise you that I will do exactly what you tell me to do. Just let me get this burden off my chest before it kills me.'

Samy looked at her lovingly and felt like putting his arms around her to comfort her, but he could see clearly that, at this particular moment, she did not want any hugs or cuddles. All she wanted was for him to listen to her, and, reluctant as he was, he could not refuse.

'Alright then, Alison. You can tell me whatever you want, but please remember that I did not ask you to do that.'

Alison looked visibly relieved, and although she was very emotional and stressed, she wanted to tell him all the details as quickly as she could. She took a deep breath and started to tell him the story of her affair with Mr Stewart from the very beginning. She did not try to hide any of the sordid details of what had happened or deny her responsibility for the problems Samy had suffered. She was brutally honest and readily admitted her guilt of upsetting sister Smith and Mr Stewart, which was the root of all the problems Samy had. She did not mince her words or spare Samy the details of her sex sessions with Mr Stewart. She told him everything as it was without omitting any details, irrespective of how embarrassing or disgusting they were. It was as if she was willing him to break off with her by giving him all the ammunition he might have needed to steer himself in that direction.

Samy listened to her in total silence, and Alison was unable to gauge his reactions as his face remained expressionless even when she was talking about her sex sessions with Mr Stewart in the minutest and most disgusting details.

If Samy was shocked or offended by all these revelations, he did not show it. He was looking at her impassively throughout without interrupting her or showing any emotions of any kind.

When she finished telling him everything, she stared at him for a few minutes, waiting for him to say something. When nothing was forthcoming, she said, 'This is everything that happened between me and Mr Stewart. I behaved like a cheap slut and would certainly understand if you tell me to just get lost.'

Samy's impassive expression was quickly replaced with a very angry one as he said, 'Don't ever say this about yourself, ever.'

He then took a deep breath and paused for a moment as if he was searching for the appropriate response. Alison looked at him anxiously, eager to hear what he thought and, more importantly, what he would do as far as their relationship was concerned.

'In one sense, I am in awe of the fact that you saw fit to make this great sacrifice of your body to Mr Stewart to save me. This is just so overwhelming and shows how much you really love me. On the other hand, I am very disappointed because you thought that under any circumstances, I would ever accept such a sacrifice to save my skin. Nothing in the world is worth what you have done, and I would have rather gotten fired and gone to jail than have you fall into the arms of that monster. You should have known that about me and let me decide for myself how I deal with this problem.'

Alison nodded and said, 'I knew that this would be your reaction, but I thought that I must try to save you by the only way I could see, even if this meant that I would lose you forever. I was responsible for getting you into this mess, and I felt obliged to pay for my mistakes, whatever the price was.'

Samy responded sharply, 'Do not blame yourself for what happened to me. It was never your fault. It was all of Mr Stewart's doing from start to finish. No one else was to blame, least of all you.'

She then stood up and, with her tears flowing freely, said, 'Please do not despise me. I am doing enough of that myself. I will do my best to steer clear of you at work, and whenever possible, I will swap my on-calls to avoid being on-call with you, so you do not have to worry about seeing me around.'

As she moved towards the door, Samy said, 'Where do you think you are going? You just do not know me at all, do you?'

Alison turned round and looked at Samy, but she could hardly see him through her tears. He walked towards her, and without saying anything, he threw his arms around her and held her as tight as he could, as if he was trying to prevent her from running away from him. She wrapped her arms around him and held him even tighter. She was not the only one who was crying in that embrace.

Eventually, Alison said, 'Do you forgive me?'

Samy did not respond straight away because he was struggling to control his tears and his emotions. When he calmed himself and was able to speak, he said, 'Only God forgives or not forgive, but for what it is worth, I forgive you absolutely. Real love always forgives, and my love for you is very real.'

They remained in this tight embrace for a long time, with each of them waiting for the other to let go first, but neither of them wanted to. However, in spite of the immense relief and overwhelming happiness they both felt in each other's arms, they were both still wondering in their own minds: would things between them ever be the same again?'

Chapter 19

Revenge is ever so sweet

As the days passed, Samy and Alison regained much of the ground their love had lost because of the events that followed the delivery of the breech in the toilet and Mr Stewart's affair with Alison. They started again going for walks on Hampstead Heath and went out for meals in various restaurants as often as their work schedules allowed. Samy never referred to any of the events that nearly ruined their relationship for good and did his best to put the whole Mr Stewart affair out of his mind as much as it was humanly possible.

However, for Alison, the situation was very different, and she could not help but keep wondering if it was really possible for a man, any man, to forgive and forget his lover's sleeping with his archenemy, whatever the circumstances were.

On one of their evening walks on Hampstead Heath, Alison said out of the blue, 'Samy, I know that you have been avoiding any mention of what happened between me and Mr Stewart, which, of course, is very kind and very sweet of you, but I just want to make sure that this dreadful affair has not fractured our relationship in any way. Are we really back to where we were before all these events?'

Alison could see straight away how Samy's facial expression had changed. It was as if a huge black cloud suddenly descended over him. His relaxed and happy expressions were immediately replaced with that of a mixture of anger and sadness in equal measures. He remained silent for a few minutes as they walked along, and she did not want to rush him, as it was obviously difficult for him to talk about this subject. His reaction confirmed for her what she suspected all along, that he was not really as calm and relaxed about her affair with Mr Stewart as he had tried to appear.

Samy spoke slowly as if he was trying to avoid saying something which he might regret later on. 'As I told you before, Alison, I really want to put this matter behind us as if it had never happened. I have to be honest with you and admit that this is very hard for me, but I love you very much, and although this business with Mr Stewart has certainly broken my heart, it has not damaged or lessened my love for you in any way, of that you can be absolutely sure.'

Samy then paused for a moment and looked away from her as he said, 'What makes it worse for me is the fact that you went through this ordeal for me, which makes me partly responsible for what happened to you at the hands of Mr Stewart. If I had not fallen to pieces when I was suspended and looked so pathetic and helpless, you might not have felt the need to sacrifice yourself to save me. I should have been stronger and more resilient in facing this problem.'

'Samy, to say that you are responsible for what I did with Mr Stewart is utter nonsense. I have not raised this subject again in order to wriggle out of my guilt or deflect the responsibility of what happened to you or anyone else, not even Mr Stewart. All I really want is to make sure that you feel absolutely free to decide where our relationship goes from here. To be honest with you, I know enough about men to make me wonder if any man can really forgive what I have done. This was not a moment of weakness or a casual one-time affair. It was I who went to him and willingly went along with what he wanted to do to me time and again. Irrespective of the circumstances and the reasons for me doing what I did, can you really still love me? Can your love be so forgiving? Does a love like this really exist?'

Samy looked at her with a pained expression on his face, which showed her that he was disappointed because she was doubting the extent of his love and affection for her. After a few moments of hesitation, he replied, 'Of course, a love like this exists. I do not know whether you believe in God as I do or not, but his love for me, which I have experienced throughout my entire life, has always been unlimited and unconditional, irrespective of how good, bad, or indifferent I have behaved towards him. My love for you is but a small reflection of God's love for us. The problem between us at present is not whether I have forgiven you or not. The real issue is that you need to forgive yourself and move on. You should have no worries at all about me and how I feel about you. For me, this has never been in question and will never be.'

Alison listened intently and did her best to force herself to accept that he could really mean what he was saying. She knew that he was a religious man, and he sounded sincere when he talked about love and forgiveness, but this just seemed too good to be true.

Samy realised from the way she was staring at him that she was not totally convinced that he was being honest about his feelings. He stared at the horizon away from her beautiful face and asked, 'I need to ask you the same question you have just asked me, and you must answer me frankly and honestly. Do you really still love me, and do you still believe that our love has a future? Or do you believe that Mr Stewart's affair has fatally wounded our relationship and it is best that we go our separate ways?'

Without any hesitation, Alison replied, 'My love for you is absolute and overwhelming in a way I have never experienced before, and I know that I will never ever experience it again. I have no doubt at all about my feelings for you, and I am sure that I desperately want to tie my life to yours forever and ever. I just want to make sure that I am not abusing your good nature and forcing you to continue with a fatally damaged relationship when you could make a new start with a better partner who really deserves you.'

Samy looked at her and shook his head in disbelief as he said, 'You really talk absolute rubbish sometimes, Alison. After all that I have just said, do you still think that I would want to let you go so that I can start looking for a better offer elsewhere? You are the only one for me. I fell in love with you from the first time I saw you, and ever since, my love for you has just overwhelmed any thoughts of the massive obstacles that should have forced me in normal circumstances to put an end to this very obviously incompatible relationship. Any normal person would have seen from the very start that our relationship is doomed to failure for so many obvious reasons. However, whatever the problems that we are facing, my heart just brushes them aside because it no longer belongs to me but to you. I do not know where we would go from here, but what I know is that I do not want to let go of you.'

Alison had heard enough, so she just jumped on him and hugged him as hard as she could. There was nothing she could say in response to his loving and affectionate statement. She did not have to say anything as her tears of joy said it all.

When they reached the rose garden, they sat on their favourite bench, and Alison rested her head on his chest while Samy wrapped his arms around her. As they have often done on previous occasions, they both remained in a silent embrace for a long time. No words were needed to express how happy they were to be together.

When it was time to leave the Heath, Alison said, 'Before we go, Samy, there is one more question I want to ask you, and I promise you that this will be the last time ever I will mention Mr Stewart to you.'

Samy rolled his eyes in despair and said, 'What is it now? I thought we finished with all that.'

'The last question I will ever ask you about this business is: do you really believe that I slept with Mr Stewart only because I thought that there was no other way to save you and your career?'

Samy replied impatiently, 'Yes, of course I believe that. This was a great sacrifice which you have made on my behalf, a great sacrifice indeed, albeit misguided. Thank God the problem is now over.'

Alison shook her head and said, 'I do not know why you are thanking God. Where was this God of yours when you were about to be ruined for life by Mr Stewart?'

'He was right there. How do you think the whole matter was sorted so quickly? Mr Stewart had no intention whatsoever to help me in any way, in spite of his promises to you. He told me as much himself when he came to my room.'

Alison's eyes widened, and she waited with bated breath for Samy to tell her more as she felt that her understanding of how he was saved from his predicament was about to be radically changed. Up to that point, she had thought that she was the one who saved Samy by getting Mr Stewart to resolve the situation for him in return for her sexual favours, but Samy was about to shatter this illusion.

Samy continued 'I do not know the exact details of how Mr Stewart's conspiracy unravelled, but I understand that sister Morrison, Mr Stewart's ex-wife, who has never had much to do with me, got Mr Stout involved in my problem as soon as he returned from holiday because she suspected from Mr Stewart's behaviour that night that he was involved with the patient in foul play. She talked to the patient's midwife and to the patient herself, which made her realise that Mr Stewart was orchestrating a complex conspiracy to crush me and get the patient a huge financial compensation. In addition, Mrs Goldberg from medical staffing had her own suspicions about Mr Stewart's behaviour in handling the investigations, and she also contacted Mr Stout about this. Mr Stout interviewed the patient, and she admitted everything to him and withdrew the complaint, following which Mr Stewart resigned from his job and left the hospital forever. And just like that, the whole thing vanished into thin air. So, is this a godly miracle or not?'

Alison went very pale and was speechless. Her great sacrifice was not needed after all, which made her feel even worse about her affair with Mr Stewart.

Samy noticed how upset she suddenly looked. He quickly said, 'None of this really matters now. The important thing is that this whole miserable episode is over. Both of us suffered a lot as a result of the acts of Mr Stewart, but he has gone for good, and we do not need to worry about him anymore.'

Alison remained silent with a grim expression on her face that showed how she was feeling at that particular moment. Samy threw his arms around her, kissed her on the cheek and said, 'The only thing you need to remember is that I love you very, very much, and I do not blame you for anything. On the contrary, I feel privileged and appreciative that you were willing to sacrifice yourself in this way to save me.'

Samy then added in an attempt to bring this discussion to a close, 'If you have a Bible at home, read chapter thirteen of St Paul's first Epistle to the Corinthians. This will tell you all you need to know about real love and what it can do. You will see that real love is eternal and limitless. It tolerates everything, is patient with everything, forgives everything and always hopes for the best of everything. So, please let us just enjoy our love for each other and look forward. The past has gone with all its unpleasantness and troubles. Love is the only thing that matters, and we have that in abundance.'

As they walked hand-in-hand towards the exit of the rose garden, Samy said with a very serious tone of voice, 'Now, you have to promise me that you will never ever bring up this subject again in any shape or form; otherwise, there will be no more Chinese meals for you and probably not even fish and chips.'

She laughed and fell again into his arms.

****

The next day, it was during the lunch break that Alison received the phone call that she hoped she would never get. She recognized the phone number of the caller straight away. It was Mr Stewart's.

Fortunately for her, she was on her own in the labour ward's changing room. She hesitated for a moment, wondering if she should just ignore the call, but she thought that it was better to see why he was calling her. She felt confident that he had totally lost his grip on her now that Samy was safe, so what harm could come from this phone call? Her curiosity got the better of her, and she took the call.

'What do you want?'

'Hello, Alison. What sort of response is this?'

'Get straight to the point, or I will cut you off.'

'I am very sorry to see that you are so hostile and angry. However, I am leaving the country the day after tomorrow to work abroad, and I wanted to see you one last time to give you something as a leaving present.'

Alison could not believe her ears. How could he have ever thought that she would want to see him again or take anything from him? She shouted angrily, 'Go to hell. I will never ever want to see your ugly face again and will never take anything from you. Whatever it is, you can just shove it up your …'

Mr Stewart interrupted in the same monotonous calm voice, 'Now, now, Alison. There is no need to be so aggressive and rude. You say that you do not want to take anything from me, but trust me on this one: you would want to take this present from me with both hands.'

Alison's anger went through the roof, and she struggled to find the words that would adequately express her contempt and fury.

Before she could say anything, Mr Stewart said, 'I have been secretly videoing our sex sessions together because I have always known that you will be leaving me at the earliest opportunity, and I wanted something to remind me of the happiest times of my entire life, our times together. I thought that you would be keen to take back these videos.'

He could hear her gasping in utter horror, but he ignored that and continued in the same ice-cold, intimidating tone of voice, 'I never intended to use these tapes to blackmail you or cause you any embarrassment, but as my affair with you has ended up ruining my life and my career in England, I think that I am entitled to use whatever I have at my disposal to get what I have always wanted from you one last time.'

Alison was crying so hard she could not talk, so Mr Stewart, who could hear her sobbing, carried on without bothering about the state she was obviously in. 'I have got everything on one memory stick. There are no other copies. I want to spend one more night with you, following which I promise to give you the memory stick, and you will never hear from me ever again.'

Without waiting for a response, Mr Stewart added, 'I will expect you at my place at 8 O'clock this evening. Make sure that you are wearing your skimpy black underwear, which you know I like best. If you do not come, these films will be all over the internet, and I will be five thousand miles away where no one can get to me.'

He then ended the call without waiting for a response.

****

At exactly 8 O'clock, the doorbell at Mr Stewart's house rang. Mr Stewart smiled to himself and rubbed his hands in anticipation as he got up to open the door. As he walked past the stereo system in the sitting room, he turned it on, and it started playing a quiet romantic collection of music which he had already chosen, especially for the occasion. He also turned down the lights to add to the atmosphere of intimacy and romance, or so he thought.

As soon as he opened the door, his jaw dropped. His overjoyed facial expression was immediately replaced by a look of utter shock and horror. This was not Alison; it was Samy Samir.

Before he could recover from his shock, Samy pushed him in his chest with both hands, and he fell backwards. Samy calmly entered the house and closed the door quietly behind him.

Samy was dressed all in black, with a cap covering his head and a pair of dark glasses masking his eyes, but he was still instantly recognizable by the terrified Mr Stewart. He was wearing leather gloves, and his right hand was holding a gun which he had just taken out of his pocket.

The sight of Samy in this outfit was both frightening and very intimidating. Mr Stewart, like many Westerners, had this biased stereotypical image of people from the Middle East. Aren't they all violent fanatics with pure, unadulterated terrorism running through their veins? Could he have gone too far with Alison this time, trying to blackmail her and get her into his bed one last time? Could Samy be coming to commit 'honour killing' because Mr Stewart had dared to try to force his woman to have sex with him yet again? Samy was certainly dressed for such an act, and the gun in his hand confirmed all Mr Stewart's worst fears.

From his position on the floor, flat on his back, Mr Stewart felt very vulnerable. Even if he ignored the fact that Samy was holding a gun in his hand, Mr Stewart would not have stood any chance in a fistfight against this much younger, stronger and fitter man. He broke into a cold sweat, and his heart was pumping so hard he thought that it was about to jump out of his chest.

He was still lying on the floor with his mind racing in all directions, with his gaze fixed on Samy's right hand with the gun pointed at him, when Samy bent over, grabbed the collar of his shirt with his left hand and pulled him up violently to force him to stand up.

Mr Stewart said in a very shaky voice, 'What the hell do you think you are doing?'

Samy, still holding on to the collar of his shirt, just pulled him in the direction of the sitting room and said through gritted teeth, 'This is exactly what I have come here to ask you. What the hell do you think you are doing? How dare you bother Alison again? I am here to put an end to your evil once and for all.'

Mr Stewart was overwhelmed with sheer terror and could not offer any sort of resistance to being manhandled so violently. He was shaking like a leaf and was struggling for air as he was being dragged by his collar towards the sitting room. His legs were trembling, and he could hardly walk, but Samy was pulling him from his collar so strongly he could not offer any resistance, and he just had to walk along with him.

In the sitting room, Samy just pushed him onto the sofa, where he was planning to make love to Alison as soon as she arrived. He again fell on his back on the sofa with sweat pouring out of his whole body, trying hard not to wet his pants. As Samy pushed him on the sofa, he said, 'You like this sofa, don't you? This sofa witnessed some of your best sex sessions with so many hapless women, hasn't it?'

Samy took his dark glasses off so that Mr Stewart could see his furious, piercing stare. His fierce frown and clenched jaw expressed a terrifying mixture of hatred and contempt. He said quietly but in an intimidating tone of voice, stressing every word to make sure that Mr Stewart understood clearly what he was saying. 'It is payback time, John, but I have difficulty deciding how to give you what you really deserve. It is a toss-up between doing a major operation to re-arrange the anatomy of your genitals or just killing you outright. I must say that I am more inclined towards the latter, so try not to give me any additional reason for wanting to rush to do it.'

Mr Stewart's eyes widened in horror as Samy stood over him with his hand gripping the gun harder and harder to the extent that Mr Stewart was increasingly worried that he might be shot accidentally through Samy losing control of his temper.

'I was prepared to forgive and forget what you have tried to do to me, although you brought me to the very edge of utter ruin, but what you have done to Alison and still trying to do to her is unforgivable. If we were in the Middle East, I would have slit your throat in a public square in front of a cheering crowd, but in England, I have to be more subtle.'

Mr Stewart quickly put his hand in his pocket, took out a memory stick, and screamed, 'Samy, just watch these films to see what was going on between me and Alison. She was the one who came on to me and not the other way around. See how passionate and sensual she was when we made love and how often she climaxed in sheer ecstasy. She is a loose nymphomaniac, and I am not the only one she has been sleeping with while pretending to you to be a shrinking violet, all sweet and innocent.'

Samy looked at him coldly, took the memory stick from his hand and grabbed the collar of his shirt again to lead him, this time to the desktop computer at the corner of the room. He forced Mr Stewart to kneel in the corner next to the computer. The computer was already on. Samy inserted the memory stick into the appropriate port, and it started to play the videos recorded on it. Samy was not interested in seeing any details; he just speeded up the videos to make sure that it was really the memory stick on which Mr Stewart had recorded his sex sessions with Alison. He then deleted all the files on that memory stick, dropped it on the floor and stepped on it with all his strength, which crushed it into smithereens.

Samy then got a memory stick from his own pocket and inserted it into the computer. He pressed a few buttons on the keyboard, and a program from the memory stick was downloaded on the computer. Mr Stewart could not see what Samy was doing on the computer, but he could only assume the worst. Samy was downloading a program, which was actually a scrubbing tool that would permanently wipe out every single file on this computer and write over the deleted files so that they could never be retrieved. This would render the computer completely blank and useless, devoid of any programs, videos, folders or documents.

Samy then grabbed Mr Stewart's shirt and dragged him towards the sofa, where he deposited him on it like a sac of potatoes. Samy pressed the gun against Mr Stewart's temple and said in a harsh and aggressive voice, 'Now, where are the copies, the reserve memory sticks? The CDs and DVDs? I do not believe that you did not make numerous copies of these shameful videos. It will be better for your life span if you just hand them over, believe me.'

Mr Stewart was trembling as he said, 'I swear to you, Samy, there are no copies. I have deleted everything after I loaded all the videos on this memory stick that you have wiped and crushed.'

Samy took the gun away from Mr Stewart's head and slapped him with his free hand on his cheek. 'You are such a cheap liar. I will turn this place upside down, and if I find any copy anywhere, I will kill you, slowly and painfully, with great relish because this is what you deserve. Your only chance of surviving tonight is, to be honest for once in your life and give me the copies right now.'

The way Samy was talking showed clearly that he really meant what he said. His face was contorted with hatred and an overwhelming desire for vengeance. He was waving the gun around while moving towards and then away from Mr Stewart repeatedly like a wild animal that was about to attack his cornered prey. His erratic and restless movements around Mr Stewart suggested that he was struggling to control his urge to do Mr Stewart some serious damage or even kill him. Samy then put the gun to Mr Stewart's temple and pressed it so hard as he got ready to squeeze the trigger.

Mr Stewart rushed to say in a shaky voice, 'Alright, alright. There is another memory stick in one of the drawers of my desk in the study. I will get it for you.'

Samy pressed the gun against Mr Stewart's temple even harder for a few moments, following which he took it away slowly like a man who managed with great difficulty to stop himself from going ahead with the shooting. He then pulled

Mr Stewart up from his shirt and followed him to the study, where Mr Stewart got out from the back of one of the draws of his desk another memory stick and gave it to Samy.

Samy took the memory stick from him and said to Mr Stewart, 'Where is your laptop computer?'

Mr Stewart pointed to a leather case on a table in the middle of the room. Samy ordered him to get it out and set it up so that he could check what was recorded on this second memory stick.

As soon as he confirmed that the memory stick contained the videos of Mr Stewart's sex sessions with Alison, he deleted them and crushed the memory stick on the floor. Further rough handling and threats of serious injury or even death forced Mr Stewart to produce five more memory sticks, which contained copies of Alison's sex tapes, and they were all deleted and then crushed by Samy.

Of course, Samy did not trust that Mr Stewart had given him all the copies of these sex tapes, so he forced Mr Stewart to go with him from room to room, looking in all cupboards, wardrobes, shelves or anywhere where he could have hidden any more memory sticks, CDs or DVDs and they were all deleted and irretrievably damaged. Samy stopped bothering to check what was on these other memory sticks, DVDs or CDs. He just damaged them all, ignoring Mr Stewart's pleas to spare the ones that contained personal files, research projects, and holiday memories.

All laptops, tablets and other computer equipment were also wiped out and then permanently scrubbed with the special program that he had brought with him for this purpose. Samy even slashed mattresses and pillows to ensure that Mr Stewart did not hide anything there. Books, photos and ornaments were all thrown on the floor to make sure that nothing related to Alison was hidden anywhere. All the contents of his wardrobes, cupboards and shelves were thrown on the floor to join everything else that littered every room in the house. By the time Samy finished looking for any more copies of these videos, Mr Stewart's home was totally and utterly trashed.

He then made Mr Stewart carry the desktop computer, the laptop and all the other IT equipment he found to the bathroom, where he put them in the bathtub, which was then filled with hot water to ensure that the computers and all the other equipment were totally damaged so that they can never be reused.

Samy then asked, 'Where is your mobile phone?'

M Stewart pleaded, 'Oh, please, not the mobile phone. I have on it all my contacts, my travel documents, my new job's documents and everything else. You can examine it and see for yourself. There is nothing on it that involves Alison.'

Samy's steely look was enough for Mr Stewart to go to his jacket that was hung on one of the chairs, got the mobile phone out of one of the pockets and handed it over to Samy. Without being asked, he tapped in his password to enable Samy to look through the files, hoping then he might spare it. However, Samy just ignored all his pleas, opened the phone cover, removed the SIM card, cut it into small pieces with a pair of scissors and flushed it down the toilet. He then threw the mobile phone on the floor, crushed it under his feet, and got Mr Stewart to collect the pieces and dump them in the hot water that filled the bathtub with all the other IT equipment.

Samy ordered Mr Stewart back to the sitting room. With the gun pointing straight at his heart, he said, 'Now I think that I can shoot you without having to worry about anything that might harm Alison. However, I do not really want to do that because I have a feeling that you will not be causing her or anyone else any more trouble. Am I right?'

Mr Stewart, with his gaze fixed on the gun, said, 'I am leaving the country the day after tomorrow, and I will never come back, that I promise for real. There is nothing here for me anymore.'

Samy shook his head, and with a fierce disgusted look, he replied, 'I want to believe you, but you are such a slimy liar; only an idiot would believe anything you say. There is only one way to make sure that you will really disappear from our lives forever. Some sort of an insurance policy that will guarantee your good behaviour from now on.'

This 'insurance policy' took Samy an hour to complete, following which he said to Mr Stewart, 'I think we are done here. Now listen to me very carefully. I have struggled really hard to curb my overwhelming desire to cut off your genitals and shove them down your throat before killing you as slowly and painfully as I can because this is what you really deserve. You will do well to remember that this is the last time we meet, and I leave you alive. Next time I see you, I will kill you, and I do not care about the consequences. Any attempt to contact Alison in any shape or form will herald a certain end to your miserable life, wherever you are. Do you understand me?'

A trembling Mr Stewart just nodded to indicate that he had understood. As Samy started to move towards the door, Mr Stewart gathered the last few drops left of his courage and said, 'All this for a girl who chose with her own free will to betray you and sleep with me?'

Samy turned round and gave him a furious stare as he shouted, 'Irrespective of anything she has done or will do in future, I love her, and there is nothing I would not do for her, including cold-blooded murder. A rabid, mindless animal like you would never know or understand what real love is. But never mind that. The one thing that I want you to know is that where I come from, a woman's honour can only be cleansed with the blood of the perpetrator. Remember that.'

Mr Stewart asked hesitantly with a shaky voice. 'Aren't you worried that I would report you to the police?'

'You wouldn't dare. First, because it will be impossible to prove that I was ever here. There is also the 'insurance policy' that we have arranged together, but more importantly, you yourself would not want the police involved in any shape or form; otherwise, all your forgery, deceit and blackmail could come out, and you end up being even more ruined than you already are. By the way, I know where you are going to work in the Middle East, and I must tell you that I have a lot of contacts there, so I will be able to put in a good word for you if there is a need to. I may even come to visit you there to make sure that you have settled in alright.'

This sent shivers down Mr Stewart's spine because he felt that Samy would still be able to get to him in the Middle East or get someone there to harm him over there.

Samy then calmly put the gun in his pocket, put his dark glasses back on and opened the door to leave the house, but he suddenly turned round to face Mr Stewart and said, 'You take care now. Do not forget to send me a postcard.'

Mr Stewart sat on the floor, breathing heavily with his heart pounding and sweat pouring out of his whole body. His whole house had been totally vandalised by Samy, and he had lost all his computers and IT equipment as well as his mobile phone, but still, he had to consider himself lucky to have escaped with his life.

✳✳✳✳✳✳✳✳✳✳✳✳✳✳✳✳✳✳✳

Samy returned to his room at the hospital, where Alison was waiting anxiously to hear from him what went on between him and Mr Stewart. Samy had already removed his cap and dark glasses and put them in his left pocket. The right pocket still had the gun in it.

As soon as he entered the room, he could see that Alison was crying her eyes out while waiting for him. He smiled reassuringly and said calmly as he hugged her gently, 'There is absolutely no need to worry about anything, my darling. It is all sorted out. Well and truly sorted out.'

Alison pulled away from him and stared at him as if she was trying to look inside his mind to see what he meant. How could he sound so reassuring and so confident in this very complex situation, facing a man as evil and devious as Mr Stewart?

Alison said while trembling with a mixture of fear and anxiety, 'I have been worried sick about you going to see that man. I very much regretted telling you about his phone call to me earlier today, but I could not go through this nightmare again on my own, although I was very worried about what you might do to him. You refused to tell me anything about your plan in advance, and I was going mad with worry in case things got out of hand and you ended up back in serious trouble. You have been there for a very long time. Why is that? What have you been doing with him all this time?'

Samy looked at her with a happy smile, winked at her and said nothing. Alison's anxiety was escalating, and she could not control herself. She shouted at him, 'Samy, stop fooling around. What have you done to him?'

Samy had a sinister expression on his face as his smile widened, and he said, 'Don't worry, sweetheart. Mr Stewart will never bother you again.'

He then got the gun out of his pocket and waved it slowly in front of her as he said, 'He sleeps with the fishes.'

Alison almost fell back on the bed as she screamed, 'What? Have you killed him?'

Samy saw straight away that his joke had gone too far, so he quickly said, 'Alison, I was joking. This is a toy gun. Have a look yourself.'

He threw the gun to her, and she picked it up in the air and confirmed that it was indeed just a toy, a replica gun, but a very good one at that.

'A very good imitation, don't you think?' asked Samy.

Alison breathed a sigh of relief but remained very anxious. 'Why did you go to see him with a toy gun? What happened between you and him tonight.'

Samy smiled again, sat down and said, 'Before I tell you everything, what did you think of my imitation of a mafioso from the film 'The Godfather'? 'He sleeps with the fishes' is a Sicilian message, you know.'

Alison lost her temper as she screamed at him, 'I don't know what is wrong with you tonight, Samy. Stop being so flippant and start talking, or I will really go mad.'

Samy responded quickly, 'I am sorry, sweetheart, but I am not myself tonight because I am in a state of euphoria and elation. That is why I am in this jokey playful mood.'

Samy then proceeded to tell her in detail what he did with Mr Stewart blow by blow. The more he told her, the more she wanted to jump up in the air in celebration. However, she tried to control herself so that she did not interrupt Samy's flow of thoughts. The details of Mr Stewart's suffering were music to her ears, and she really wished that she was there to see it for herself.

Finally, when Samy finished telling her all that happened, she asked, 'What was that 'insurance policy' which you said would guarantee his good behaviour forever?'

'Ah, that! You see, because he was so fond of taking videos of his lovemaking, I forced him to do a full striptease while I filmed him on my mobile phone. I made him dance while stripping until he was fully naked. I also forced him to play with himself and do some strange things to himself with a carrot and a cucumber, which I took out of his fridge. He had to do all this while pretending to enjoy it so that anyone who got to see this video would believe that he was really having fun and not dancing naked because there was a gun pointed at him.'

Alison burst out laughing hysterically, and when she finally calmed down enough to be able to talk, she said, 'Come on then, let us have a look at this fantastic video.'

Samy frowned and replied, 'There is no video. I just pretended that I was filming him to give him a taste of his own medicine. I never intended to sink to his level, but just the thought of a video of this kind will be enough to keep him out of our lives forever.'

Samy then laughed and said, 'Moreover, I think that I have succeeded in convincing him that I had acquaintances and friends from the Middle East where he is going, who are unsavoury terrorists and crazy fundamentalists. With a gun in my hand, dressed in black, with my face hidden behind dark glasses and a cap, what else could I be myself but a violent terrorist who is linked to other violent terrorists? He would not want to come across me again, of that I am absolutely sure.'

Alison smiled happily, jumped on his lap and kissed him passionately. 'I am so grateful and so proud of you, my love. You are my hero.'

Samy frowned and said, 'There is nothing to be proud of, Alison. I must tell you that I actually feel ashamed of myself. This violence, anger, deceit and acts of revenge which I committed today are the most unchristian acts I have ever done in my whole life, and I will always feel bad about them. However, my absolute priority was to put an end to this man's evil deeds and ensure that he does not harm you ever again. My feelings for you swept away all my moral scruples about violence and revenge.'

Alison hugged him really hard and said, 'Isn't this what real love sometimes does? For you, I fell into the arms of the evil Mr Stewart against my better judgment and my wishes. For me, you acted in this way tonight against your strict moral and religious convictions. Neither of us will ever repeat these actions in future, whatever the circumstances. As you said to me before, it is time to let bygones be bygones and look only to the future.'

Samy's wide smile returned, and he said, 'I entirely agree. Let us move on and leave all this behind.'

Alison stood up and said, 'Let us go and get something to eat. I am starving.'

'Me too. Let it be chicken curry.'

As they walked to the Indian restaurant across the road from the hospital, Alison had a wicked smile on her face as she said, 'Be honest, Samy, didn't you find that revenge is really sweet?'

Samy sighed and said sheepishly, 'To my shame, yes. Tonight, I found that revenge is ever so sweet indeed.'

373

THE END